A RAGE
AGAINST REASON

E. K. Knef

ISBN-13: 978-1517343682
ISBN-10: 1517343682

CHAPTER ONE

Wyoming, 1874

Reason Cordell could feel their eyes upon him. Animalistic and hungry. And the mere thought made the hair on the back of his neck stand stiffly on end.

The three men were seated at the tree-trunk slab of a battle-scarred table, each eating from a bowlful of mush placed before them that Reason thought tasted like wet adobe clay when, situated centrally between the two on the far end, he shifted uncomfortably in his seat. The throbbing bullet wound clawing at his back wasn't the only thing causing him discomfort inside the tumble-down, rickety old log cabin he now found himself cornered in. These two hulking mountain men seated before him had something raw and unsettling preying on their minds that Reason was sure he wouldn't want to hear uttered out loud.

Finally, when he could stand the strain of silence no longer, he lowered his spoon to the table and lifted his head to meet the sly, knowing eyes of the two burly trappers before him.

"Quit eyeing me up like the main course," he growled softly, his forearms resting on the edge of the crudely chiseled tabletop. His depleted strength made him too weak to eat, and the nagging pain in his lower back made sitting up straight almost too much of an effort to endure.

"More like dessert, if you ask me," the big, bearded man on his left said with a jagged-tooth smile.

"Shut up, Mortie," the one called Buck snarled a harsh warning. Then, disregarding the other man, he turned once again to Reason. "Awful edgy this mawnin'," he rasped in that deep-well voice of

1

his. "Somethin' ailin' you, boy?"

He spoke true enough. Reason's nerves were frayed to the point of exhaustion. From the moment he awoke two days ago to find this pair of hulking giants leaning over his makeshift bed of animal pelts piled four deep on the hard-planked floor near the hearth, and ogling him as if he sported two heads and a tail, his mind hadn't had a moment's peace. His insides were jittery, growing more ill at ease with each passing moment at the thought of sharing these run-down confining quarters with the same pair of dangerous-looking men who had voluntarily saved his life. And he couldn't, for the life of him, remember the last time he'd had a decent night's sleep.

For instead of feeling the relief and security of another human being close by willing to lend a hand with his recovery, he felt, oddly enough, like a war-torn Union soldier locked away in a rat-infested Andersonville prison, full of lonely, bitter, and violent men. Instinct warned him he might have been better off if he had never been found at all. And he wondered why that thought dwelled so prevalent in his mind.

Premonition? Of something worse than death headed his way? More painful than the resulting wound caused by a lead bullet lodged in the small of his back could ever be?

True, he had carried a huge chunk of money on him from the sale of that string of horses both he and Cole had broken to saddle, then sold to auction at Laramie over a week ago. Yet his mind must be slipping. For although he had taken a few necessary precautions, such as steering clear of the main trail and keeping to a lesser-traveled route for one, he never actually expected to be shot from ambush in a botched robbery attempt and left for dead on the way home. The attack had been so sudden and swift, he never once saw the bushwhacker who fired the near-fatal bullet from behind a shelter of trees, and only had time to turn in the saddle for one quick shot in retaliation before he slumped over the saddle and blacked out.

Though how he got turned around on Satan and ended up somewhere high in the Tetons, lost in the wilderness, was beyond him. He must have been feverish from the start, just like he was now, only worse. A shiver ran up his spine at the thought of how close he had come to death, once again, during the course of his harrowing twenty-nine year lifetime, and he forced himself to spoon another mouthful of the sour-tasting gruel between his resentful lips. He needed all his strength, and then some, if he was ever planning on leaving this dead-end shack alive.

Buck was the one who had found him wandering half-conscious and alone, doubled over Satan's muscular neck, groaning in agony with each careful step the horse took. He supposed he should be thankful to the man for hauling him back to the safety of the ramshackle cabin, digging out the bullet lodged in his back with a sharp-edged skinning knife, then patching him up the best way he knew how. Still, Reason didn't feel as if he were out of the woods.

So what if he felt stronger today than yesterday, and could at least rise off that lice-infested bed on the floor to sit at a table to eat. He was still dangerously weak and pitifully vulnerable. No match for any man desiring to cause trouble, least of all the two muscular men facing him.

Although his body thrummed with exhaustion, Reason still retained the razor-keen instincts of a fast gun, and all his senses now warned him of danger. Oddly enough, his very existence seemed more in jeopardy now than when he was shot and left to die alone on the trail.

Once again, his gaze slid upwards to shift between the two pair of dark glistening eyes staring at him. Another portentous chill of doom raced up his spine and his gut tightened with anxiety. Something was going wrong here in the vacant minds of these men. Something dark, violent, and unhealthy.

"What do you think, Buck? Think he's ready?" Mortimer was the first to break the strained silence that had once again settled between the men.

Buck spooned another portion of gruel into his mouth. A small dribble escaped his lips and trickled down his bearded chin. He lifted a beefy forearm and wiped his jaw clean with a soiled flannel sleeve.

"Told ya to wait another day. You don't want to kill him now, do ya?"

Reason's pale blue gaze shifted from one man to the other. Both were sizing him up like a pair of mangy mutts slavering over a juicy T-bone steak. His spine stiffened and his muscles grew tense. Trouble seemed imminent and Reason broke out in a cold sweat. He knew his strength would never support him in an all-out brawl.

Cautiously he laid down his spoon for the last time and braced both hands flat upon the table, preparing to run if need be; yet knowing he wouldn't make it halfway to the door.

"Aw, I'll go easy," Mortimer grinned maliciously. "This bein' his first time and all."

Reason jerked to his feet, kicked the chair out from behind him, and backed up a few painful steps. He had swallowed a bellyful of their sly innuendoes and suggestive actions, and couldn't stand the suspense of being kept in the dark a moment longer. Anything was better than the fear of the unknown, wasn't it?

"Just what the hell are you two hairy apes babbling about! First time for what!" A host of ugly suspicions began forming in his brain, none of which he cared to dwell on for long.

Mortimer rose to his feet, his dark beady eyes never once leaving Reason's face.

"Now simmer down, boy, and you won't get hurt much. Struggle?" He shrugged his burly shoulders. "Now that's another story."

Stealthy as a stalking bear, he began advancing forward as Reason forced his shaky legs to retreat a few steps backwards.

"As for myself, I don't mind a little fight in a man, or woman, as the case may be. But in your instance, you'd be better off givin' in right at the start if you don't want to injure yourself further."

Reason's black-lashed, pale blue eyes grew too large for his face and his heart began tripping violently in his chest as if the thudding organ would leap clear out of his skin of its own free will. His body jerked hard as his spine came up flat against the far wall and he could go no further. A low groan caught in his throat.

My God! This was worse than he thought! What did these animals have in mind? Rape? No, it wasn't called that between two men, was it? It was called.... He sucked in a deep breath. Over his dead body!

"Morty, simmer down some," Buck warned from the table. "You're scarin' the daylights outta him. I told ya we should wait another day."

We? Reason choked. Breathing suddenly became difficult and his vision dimmed. Sidling to his left, he slid along the wall seeking to increase the distance from the man nearest him. The flat of his hands braced against the rough-hewn barrier in a valiant effort to steady himself as his knees turned rapidly to jelly. Bright spots of yellow light danced wickedly before his eyes. A roar of distant thunder filled his ears.

"I ain't waitin' any longer," was the reply. "You said to hold out until the fever went down and he regained consciousness. That was yesterday. You can wait if you want. I'm done with it!"

Like an innocent man about to be lynched by a frenzied mob to the nearest tree, Reason's glance flew around the unkempt shambles of the small cabin, seeking a weapon of some kind with which to defend himself. His gun belt hung on a hook by the door.

Too damn far.

A stack of split wood lay in a busted crate by the stone hearth farther to his right, but even if he could manage to heft one of the sturdy logs, he would never have the strength to swing it with any show of force.

"Stay away from me," he snarled through a throat taut with tension as Mortimer drew closer. "I'm not playing your twisted games. Go find some other poor sucker down on his luck to torment." Cautiously he inched further away from the man before him.

Mortimer's hand strayed to the crotch of his worn baggy pants and he rubbed his dirt-stained trousers suggestively.

"Oh, I think you will, with a little persuasion," he grinned with the confidence of a man who had already won the battle.

Reason's stomach flipped over and the room lost focus for a brief moment. A short stifled groan caught deep in his throat at the thought of what these two savage and uncivilized mountain men could do to him in his weakened state. *Just about any damn thing they well pleased!*

Swallowing down his mind-numbing fear, he stumbled over his own feet sidling further to his left, while Mortimer moved compatibly with him.

"Havin' trouble, Morty?" Buck sneered from the table. "Need any help?"

"Naw, hell. This is like takin' candy from a baby," Mortimer bragged. "Now come on out of that corner, boy. Before I have to drag you out."

Reason, in his haste for distance, had unknowingly backed himself right into a corner. There was nowhere left to run. His body trembled in weariness, pain, and utter disgust at the vile insinuations of the man hovering menacingly before him. The lower portion of his back burned as if a lit torch was pressed hard against his side. His head hurt from lack of sleep coupled with worry and he had to squint just to make out Mortimer's hulking form, for the flickering candle perched on a high shelf against the opposite wall stung his eyes.

An icy chill crept up his spine and he shivered, despite the heat from a roaring fire crackling in the hearth nearby. By all rights, he shouldn't have even gotten out of bed yet. And now he was sorry he had.

"Like hell I will," Reason snarled, flattening himself against the hand-hewn logs at his back as if the staunch wall would afford him any small semblance of protection. If only he could reach his gun....

But that thought died an instant death as Mortimer reached out a burly arm, grabbed Reason by the front of his black silk shirt, and hauled him out of the corner like he would a stray cat.

Reason's futile attempt to twist free was short-lived as a sudden knife-sharp pain in his lower back wrenched an unwitting groan from his throat and almost drove him straight to his knees. The room began to grow dark and only Mortimer's timely intervention kept him upright at all. A sudden paralyzing grip at his right shoulder spun him around and a beefy arm went around Reason's waist yanking him backwards against Mortimer's body with a stunning jolt.

"Oh shit!" Reason's breath left his lungs in a rush. He was trapped. Weak-kneed and weary. In too much pain to summon the strength necessary to break free of the bear-like grip. They had him right where they wanted him. Totally vulnerable and completely at their mercy. And mercy, from what he could see, was not a word consistent with either man's vocabulary.

"Easy now," Buck drawled as he rose from the table and stepped close to Reason with a sly grin. "We don't want to spook ya none. Nor aim to hurt you unnecessarily. We're hopin' to keep you around a good long while. Now be a good boy. Do what we say and you won't get hurt any more'n you should."

"Keep back! Don't come near me." Panic choked him, clawed at his throat with gnarled, bony fingers. He couldn't breathe. His back was a burning torment, threatening his very sanity. The arms holding him were like steel bands across his chest and he could feel the sadistic arousal of the man behind him right through the denim cloth of his trousers.

Then Mortimer lowered his arms and Buck reached up with both beefy hands, grabbing a firm hold of Reason's black shirt. Viciously he yanked the silk cloth wide. Buttons popped and fabric ripped as cool air wafted across the exposed expanse of Reason's overheated chest.

Reason flinched as if struck and jerked his head to the side. In anticipation of further assault Reason struggled anew, but his body was held fast from behind. With a smug smile on his face, Buck slowly reached inside the torn shirt, oblivious to his victim's sudden gasp of alarm. In a subtle, caressing motion, he slid a huge callused palm across and down the muscular hard contours of Reason's bare chest.

"No...!" Reason sucked in a short, painful breath. His gut wrenched in a nauseating way and his nerves almost jumped clear out of his body at the unbearable touch of the man's rough exploring hand pressing insistently against his own hot, feverish skin. "Dammit, no! Don't touch me," he groaned low in his throat. His flesh crawled in silent revulsion and outward rebellion as instinctively he cringed backwards, away from the man looming so large before him.

But Mortimer was like a brick wall against his back, and his futile, desperate last-ditch effort to twist free was thwarted when Buck's left hand jumped up and grasped Reason by the throat in a savage, choking manner, staying all further movement. Reason almost blacked out. Then wished that he had.

"What's the matter, pretty boy," Buck grinned with large yellow teeth, as his right hand strayed down to Reason's belt and fumbled with the ornate silver buckle at his waist. "Don't you wanna have some fun?"

A whimper of revulsion fraught with outright fear caught at Reason's throat. He felt the buttons at the front of his trousers ripped open.

"Jesus! Don't...!" An involuntary trembling began in rubbery legs that instantly gravitated upward. Heart-stopping panic gripped his chest and he felt trapped, unable to breathe, like a helpless rabbit being slowly crushed to death within the steel jaws of a slavering wolf. The tail of his shirt was yanked up, chest-high. Cool air once again wafted across over-heated skin. And Reason began to shake.

"No...please...." When the waistband of his trousers was yanked to his knees, something in his mind snapped. The keen instinctive awareness of his surroundings that Reason had always subconsciously relied upon for simple daily survival slowly began slipping away.

His brain grew foggy, then dim. Time became irrelevant, something to suffer through, and ignore.

For him, life was over, as he knew it.

CHAPTER TWO

Cole Dansing paced the green braided rug in Randall Cordell's study. He ran his work-callused fingers through his dark straight hair, then replace the battered Stetson on his head. *Where the hell could Reason be?* Cole questioned silently to himself for the hundredth time. This simply wasn't like the man to be so damned late.

Jumbled thoughts ran through his frantic brain. Reason had been packing a decent amount of money, five thousand dollars to be exact, after the sale of a herd of handpicked mustangs they had driven into Laramie two weeks ago. Too much money for one man to carry. Many had been shot for a whole lot less. He never should have let Reason ride home without him. What the hell had he been thinking?

So what if he had run into a flirtatious old flame back in Laramie? Then spent some quality time getting reacquainted. He and Sally had just about run their course anyway. Why, his wife probably wouldn't give a hoot or holler even if she heard somehow of his recent, wayward transgression.

Regardless of whether he was caught red-handed or not, to his conscience he was guilty as sin. And no matter what lame-brained excuses he made to himself as to his wife's growing aloofness, or his own negligent loyalty to a worthwhile friend, he knew he had overstepped both boundaries, plain and simple. He had responsibilities after all. And being drunk was no damn excuse.

For now, Reason was missing, and the burden of his welfare fell heavily on Cole's broad shoulders. And rightly so. For weren't they "come hell or high water" partners? By unspoken, mutual consent?

During the past few months, Cole had grown careless in his

vigilance over Reason's safety. Confident in his friend's ability to handle any problems that came his way with a loaded six-gun in his hand, Cole began to think the man was invincible. Yet now he was starting to harbor grave doubts regarding Reason's safety and recalled from past experience that if trouble didn't come looking for Reason, then the man had an uncanny knack of finding it all by himself.

Cole reached the Stirrup C five days later than he should have when he finally rode into the yard that morning and was told by a ranch hand named Curly that Reason never made it back at all. And Cole's guts twisted inside. Just the simple fact of Reason being late spelled trouble with a capital "T." For the man was dedicated to a fault. And if anything happened to Reason, Cole had only himself to blame.

For no matter how tough or lightning fast on the draw Reason was, he was just one man. Why any one of a million things could have happened to him on the trail back home. And five thousand bucks was a lot of money for a single man to carry. Cole should have kept the presence of mind to acknowledge that fact. All right, so the brief sojourn with Sarah Jane had been more than satisfactory. But the short-lived affair was also over and nothing that trivial was worth putting a man's life at risk for.

Cole groaned low in his throat. If Reason was hurt, or worse, because of Cole's sheer neglect, he'd never forgive himself. The money would be hard to lose. That was an undisputable fact. Both men had worked their asses off breaking that string of ornery wild mustangs with kid gloves, until each and every horse was gentle enough that a child could ride.

But money could be replaced. A man like Reason happened along only once in a lifetime.

The heavy scudding of boots on polished wood floors drew Cole's attention like a magnet as Randall Cordell, Reason's older half-brother by seven years, strode into the room.

"Looks like you screwed up again, Cole." Randall threw himself into the swivel oak chair behind the large mahogany desk and leaned far back in his seat with a glower of pure disgust on his face. "I thought by now you'd have sense enough to put business before pleasure."

Randall had good reason for his nasty behavior. He'd been

worried sick about both Reason and Cole's failure to show last week as planned. Had even sent a few of his best ranch hands on the road back to Laramie after the boys. His men hadn't had time to make it there and back to the Stirrup C with a full report when Cole waltzed through the door brazen as all hell this morning, alone and penniless, with a stunning confession sputtering from his lips of spending an extra few days in Laramie, painting the town red.

"How could you let Reason ride out alone with all that cash on him? You made him an easy target for any dry-gulching, hard-up, foot-loose bastard wandering around out there! Are you loco?"

"I was wrong. I purely admit it," Cole agreed, his neck growing hot with shame beneath the dusty sweat-ringed collar of his once butternut-colored shirt. "Go ahead. Fire me. I deserve it."

"You know Goddamn well I can't do that, though the thought is mighty tempting. You own a third of this ranch, same as Reason and myself, and I could no more fire you than I could me. I was counting on that money to see us through the winter. Now I doubt there'll be much left for supplies and wages after the mortgage is paid this month. Some of that choice bottomland on the south forty might have to be sold in order to keep us all afloat for a while. And I hate like hell to have to do that."

Randall swore viciously beneath his breath. "But that's another set of problems I'll deal with later. Right now, my brother's whereabouts concern me more. He knows we need that money, and I'd bet the ranch he wouldn't let anyone stroll right up to him and take it without one hell-of-a-fight on his hands. I'm just hoping against all odds he's still alive."

Cole nodded, in full agreement. He worried about that very same thing. Almost a week overdue was an awful long time to be missing, especially for a man carrying all that dough in his saddlebags.

Although Cole had ridden in less than an hour ago and was trail-dusty and saddle-weary from the long trip home, he said, "I'll round up a fresh horse and see if I can pick up his trail." Then he headed for the door before Randall could utter a negative response.

But his haste was unfounded, for Randall was secretly relieved to see Cole head out after his wayward younger brother. For Randall knew if anyone could find Reason and bring him safely home, Cole would be the man to accomplish it.

"You want to take a few hands with you?" he said to Cole's retreating back. "I'm a little short-handed right now, but if you think you need them...."

"Naw." Cole paused with one foot already out the door and shook his head. "I can make better time on my own. Just see if you can get that ol' cook to rustle me up some grub for the trail. I'm so hungry, Zack could parboil the worn leather soles of his boots and stuff them between two stale crusts of bread, and I swear I wouldn't know the difference between that and a roast beef sandwich."

CHAPTER THREE

Cole had been in the saddle for almost three straight weeks between the trek from Laramie to the Stirrup C, then retracing his route all over again, looking for clues as to Reason's disappearance, and he was more than travel-sore and weary. He was flat-out exhausted. And coming up empty. This time he was following a lesser-known route home, yet still hadn't a clue as to what had delayed Reason's return.

In a fit of pure disgust, he drew the lathered bay to a halt on the crest of a high ridge beneath a lightning split oak tree and scanned the rugged mountainous wilderness beyond with keen cat's eyes the color of amber. Tall pines and stately conifers climbed in a gradual ascent towards the puffy white clouds scudding beneath a clear blue sky, towering over a small grassy meadow scattered with dry leaves and assorted deadfall below. A lone eagle screeched high overhead while his horse blew loudly beneath him but other than that, there was no other form of life to be seen.

Reaching up with a free hand, his fingernails made a raspy sound as he scratched at an itch along his dark bristled jaw. He was sweaty and hot, and his shirt clung damply to his body like a second skin. Although he had bathed in a nearby river twice this past week after making camp for the night, once the sky grew light in the morning he was up and saddled, wasting no time for a simple breakfast, much less a shave. And what did this relentlessly driving, self-sacrificing search reward him with?

Nothing!

He was no closer to finding Reason now than he had been when he first started out. The dead body of a man he discovered only yesterday, killed by a pistol bullet shot clear through the head and although the buzzard-torn, gruesome remains gave him a heart-stopping fright, closer inspection revealed that the unlucky young fellow lying stiff and cold, ravaged by nature, wasn't the same one he sought. This man was shorter by a good four inches, with sandy hair and a pearl-handled pistol, unlike Reason's own mahogany-gripped Colt 44 that he was never found without.

Cole breathed an unconscious sigh of relief. He had been lucky this time. And he worried whether his luck would continue to hold, or had Reason's fate already been signed, sealed, and delivered a few short weeks ago.

There had been no sign of the dead man's killer, nor of his horse. Probably broke loose of its traces and wandered off somewhere, Cole figured. And if he wouldn't take the time for a quick shave, he refused to go chasing after a lost mustang, nor bury what remained of this unfortunate fellow.

Then he found the rifle. Almost tripped over it, in fact, where it lay hidden in the brush when he went back for his horse. After picking up the long-range weapon, he broke open the chamber. One bullet was missing. Cole's gut clenched hard.

Could Reason have ridden this trail on the way home? Taken a different, less-traveled route instead of the well-worn dirt road he normally would have? Could this fellow have attempted to ambush Reason and ultimately died for his efforts? Was Reason even now hurt? Dead?

Cole didn't have an idea in hell. And didn't have a clue as to where to look next. Yet climbing into his saddle, he decided to switch directions and go off-trail. With an impulsive spur of insight guiding him, he headed his mustang west towards the towering shadows of the Tetons. There was water to be found there for a thirsty horse and rider, and protection against the storms that had been plaguing certain parts of Wyoming over the past few weeks.

If Reason had been shot, he might have sought shelter in the mountains when he couldn't make it home. It was a hunch, a slim one at that, but Cole had nothing else to go on, and nothing left to lose. He swiped a dusty sleeve across his sweaty brow. The sun was hot on his face and he itched in more places than he cared to admit. Still he urged his horse on.

He had plenty of time to think as he rode, and he didn't waste a minute. What if his fears were wholly unfounded? Could this be a wild goose chase he was on? Was it possible Reason had never once traveled this out-of-the-way route?

There was no proof to show that he had. The half-decomposed body of the dead man might simply have been the hapless victim of his own bad luck. For all he knew, Reason could even be home by now, Cole surmised. Maybe bad weather, or Satan pulling up lame, or any one of a hundred other excuses had delayed him. Why he could be sitting in an easy chair by a crackling fire in Randall's study with a glass of brandy in his hand right this moment, grinning like a fool, his pale blue wolf's eyes laughing along with his brother at the thought of Cole's trudging, futile quest.

Yet, an empty, hollow feeling deep in his gut made Cole doubt that idea was true. Somehow, he sensed that Reason had already shaken hands with fate, two long weeks ago, and was now either dead, dying, or else up to his ears in ditch-deep trouble.

And Cole wasn't resting until he found out which.

Two days later, Cole found the cabin. He happened on it purely by accident. And if he hadn't smelled the pungent aroma of wood smoke issuing from a chimney nestled deep in the woods, Cole might have passed right by the small clearing beyond the hill and the log-walled hut butted up against the leeward side of a rocky mountain wall, without ever once seeing it.

With his body aching and weary, and his brain in no mood for pleasantries, he rode his dusty bay straight into the front yard and pulled his horse up short. For there, grazing placidly in the knee-high weeds of a lodge pole corral by a rickety old barn just beyond the house was Satan. And Cole knew with certainty that Reason had to be nearby, or buried deep. For no other man could handle the half-broke mustang other than Reason, his wife Rachel, and at times when the stallion was willing, himself.

Cautiously, he gigged his horse to a slow walk. A huge, burly fellow rose out of a chair on the sagging porch with a rifle cradled in his arms at Cole's wary approach. The man squinted at Cole with shrewd, beady eyes that seemed lost in his wide face, then leaned over a broken railing to spit a thick wad of tobacco juice to the ground.

"That's far enough, Mister," he warned. "We don't cotton to strangers around these parts." He shifted the aim of the rifle in Cole's direction. "I suggest you mosey on out of here, while you still can."

Undaunted by the man's words or actions, Cole kept his mount at a deliberate walk until he was within fifteen feet of the porch, then pulled the bay up short. A second man rose out of the shadows from beneath the shabby overhang to Cole's left and stepped into the sunlight. Both men were heavily bearded with long straggly dark hair that needed a good washing. Tall, muscular men that looked as if either one could tangle with a grizzly and come out on top. Thick shaggy fur pelts of various shapes and sizes were tacked to the outer wall of the dilapidated run-down shack like wallpaper, and Cole surmised that hunting game for profit was how these secluded mountain men earned their living.

Born impatient and now trail-weary besides, Cole brazenly rested a forearm across the pommel of his saddle, undaunted by the sheer size and strength of the two men standing before him. For now that he was so close to solving the riddle of Reason's disappearance he could taste it, there was no way in hell he would simply turn around and ride the opposite way.

"I'm lookin' for the owner of that black stallion you got stashed in your corral," Cole said evenly, without showing a trace of the anxiety he actually felt while awaiting the answer. "That man's a friend of mine that's been missin' a few weeks now. The family's mighty worried. So if you just tell me where he is, I'll be more than happy to be on my way."

Both men's eyes shifted slyly towards the sleek black horse with pricked ears, now staring curiously over the makeshift lodge pole fence at the new arrival, then slid back to Cole.

"Don't know about his owner," the tall trapper on Cole's left continued. "We found that horse wandering free a spell back, and we just roped him and took him with us. Right, Mortimer?"

"Uh-huh. That's how it was," the other fellow said. "Don't know nothin' about no rider."

Cole's amber eyes narrowed in anger. These men had, unknowingly just dug their own grave of credibility with their careless answer. Slowly he straightened in the saddle, subtly shifting his right hand nearer his thigh, a scant inch from his holster.

"Much as I hate to call either one of you gents a liar," Cole said with an exaggerated drawl. "But that black spawn of a devil won't be led anywhere he don't want to go, especially by strangers such as you. And you sure as hell didn't rope him, for he'd kill you first. No matter how big you are. And that's a fact. Now if my friend's in there," he jerked his head towards the cabin, "you'd best send him out right now. I'm not known to be a patient man."

The man on Cole's left lifted his rifle a shade higher and cocked the weapon in a menacing way.

"He ain't here, I tell ya. Truth is we buried a young fella about two weeks ago, yonder in the woods. A slim, dark-haired kid. Said his name was Ree...zon somethin' or other, just before he died. That might be the man you're lookin' for. Sorry we didn't tell you earlier. We was only tryin' to save you a heartache."

Cole's face turned a shade paler at the news.

"What?" His horse shifted and stamped nervously beneath him, unsure of his rider's intentions, but a sharp tug on the reins settled him back down. *Reason, dead?* That had been his worst fear right from the start. Cole's insides grew queasy with a guilt-laden sense of remorse, and he was sorely afraid he was going to lean over his saddle and puke his guts up right in front of these two sturdy backwoodsmen.

"Yeah. We found him a few miles south of here," Mortimer ventured, including himself in the rescue. "He must have been dry-gulched somewhere along the trail, because he was shot up good in the lower back right about here." He gestured with his own hand angled behind him, "and bleedin' like a stuck pig. At first we thought he had died on his horse, for he was all curled up over his saddle and barely breathin'."

He recounted what he knew from Buck's own description of the incident to him, while Buck, himself, remained silent. "But we couldn't just leave him there, bein' decent God-fearin' folk like we are. So we hauled him back here and tried to save him. But it was no use. He was too far gone." Mortimer shook his head. "He passed on to his eternal reward nigh on two weeks ago."

Cole was shaken to the core of his soul. His throat closed up with a hard lump of sorrow too painful for words. For a full minute, he just sat there in silence staring at the run-down shack and seeing nothing but a remembrance in his mind of a grinning blue-eyed man lifting a hand in farewell as Reason rode Satan out of Laramie a short lifetime ago. Only to end up stiff and cold in an unmarked grave on some lonely God-forsaken mountain? When his eyes began to sting like blazes and his vision blurred without warning, he ran a rough hand over his face in a concentrated effort to pull himself together.

My God. Was it true? Had his worst fear come to pass? Had Reason been ambushed for the money he carried and left for dead? South of here, they said. That's where he found the picked over remains of that other man. Now he was glad he hadn't taken the time to bury the bones, and left that fellow to rot.

Swallowing his grief, he eyed the two men on the porch with a healthy degree of caution. He didn't trust either one as far as he could throw them. Which was nowhere.

"Why should I believe you two?" he choked through a throat tight with anguish. "You've both lied to me already. What's to stop you from doin' it again?"

"God's honest truth, Mister." The fellow on Cole's left made a shabby sign of the cross spanning his wide flannel-clad chest. "You don't see him around, do ya? Isn't that proof enough?"

Yeah, it was, to Cole's mind. Unless Reason was badly injured and too weak to call out, lost in a coma, knocked unconscious, or gagged and bound, he would have heard Cole's voice by now and come to greet him. And he couldn't help but realize the trapper's story held an unforgivable stark ring of truth. Even the timing was perfect.

He ducked his head to stare down at his own saddle, unwilling to let these strangers witness the full extent of sorrow that grew deep inside and was surely written all over his face. Maybe he should just collect Satan, turn around, and leave without a fuss. After all, even if these strangers led him right to Reason's grave, he wasn't about to dig him up, wrap his remains in an old wool blanket, and cart him home. Just the mere thought made his stomach lurch in horror, and he shifted uneasily in the saddle.

Yet his stubborn arrogant will refused to give up. To his mind, all alternative avenues of mystery regarding Reason's disappearance had not been explored fully enough for his complete and utter satisfaction. And neither his brain, nor his gut, would accept Reason's death without ironclad proof.

Slowly he raised his head. "Then you wouldn't mind if I searched the cabin, would you?"

The pair of burly trappers grew leery at this annoying stranger, their shifty glances darting to each other, then back to Cole.

"Mister, you've already overstayed your welcome. I suggest you move on." The muzzle of Buck's rifle raised until the bore centered a dead bead on Cole's chest. The threat was unmistakable. One wrong move and Cole would be shot right off his horse. Nobody needed to spell it out any clearer than that. A smart man would simply move on while he could. There was no sense in two Stirrup C partners being buried together on this God-forsaken mountain.

Yet something was wrong here. Cole's thoughts grew muddled. Although informative enough about the wounded stranger they supposedly buried, these men didn't act the least bit neighborly — downright hostile if anyone asked. Almost as if they harbored a closely guarded secret. And suddenly Cole wasn't about to "move on" anywhere until he'd exhausted every effort imaginable and seen with his own eyes Reason's grave. Or the body itself.

He leaned slightly forward in the saddle. "I'll give you two boys a little tip, since you've both been so hospitable to me and all," he sneered in his usual insolent way. "I come from a ranch bigger than this mountain you're standin' on, and folks know where I am," he bluffed. "And if I don't return home soon, you're gonna have an army of range-tough cowhands crawling all over this place. There won't be an unturned rock you snakes can crawl under to hide. You fellas want that? Because I ain't leavin' here until I see what's inside your cabin."

The two large mountain men were silent, weighing their odds. They sure as hell didn't want a bunch of outsiders roaming all over their territory if they killed this ornery polecat. And they didn't care to be forced to leave their home because of the young man inside. Game was plentiful here and more than enough to sustain their simple way of life. And they were both afraid that this stubborn man would never leave until his questions were sufficiently answered.

Finally, the man on Cole's left said, "Go get it, Mort. He's not worth sacrificin' our lives for."

Cole wasn't exactly sure just what "it" was that Mort had gone in to get, and he was damn sure these two hombres' could kill him outright with no one the wiser. But they didn't know that. And he wasn't about to inform them of that small fact.

When, moments later, Mortimer dragged the seemingly reluctant, yet unresisting man out the doorway of the shack, Cole was stunned speechless. The badly disheveled fellow, who was held firmly in place by a single hand gripping his left arm near the shoulder, couldn't have been more silent or meekly obedient if he was bound and gagged. Along with a curious mix of elation running through Cole's veins, came a distinct warning bell ringing clearly in his mind that he deliberately chose to ignore.

"Reason...." He breathed a sigh of pure relief. Although the oddly subdued and bedraggled man on the porch never once raised his lowered head in recognition, and only faintly resembled the cool and confident gunfighter Cole knew him to be, there was no mistake. He was the man Cole had set out to find. His partner, his friend. And he was alive! That was all that mattered at the moment.

Cole's face lit up in a spontaneous grin. Without further thought, he swung a leg over the pommel of his saddle, jumped to the ground and bounded up the stairs. Then came to an abrupt, skidding halt.

Not once did Reason move, twitch, or acknowledge Cole's presence in the slightest way, shape, or form. He stood with his head slightly bowed; the pale blue eyes that could cut a man to the quick with one quelling look were now downcast, vacant, and lifeless. His arms hung limply at his sides. Although the dingy white shirt he now wore replaced the satiny black one he had left town in, his clothes were disheveled and stained as if he had rolled down the side of a steep hill a few times, crawled a mile on his knees, then slept in the same outfit for most of the three weeks he'd been gone missing. His dark, slightly wavy hair was tousled and grimy, and the stubby growth of his beard was almost the same length as Cole's. And all this from a man who once had been almost fastidious both in clothes and appearance.

"Reason?" No answer. Nothing. Cole's gut clenched in fear. His mind grew frantic. He had never seen Reason in such a sorry state as this. Shot? Yes, more times than he cared to recall. Beaten? Once. Who wouldn't have lost a scuffle to a yellow-bellied coward that hid a rock in his fist? Even a disturbing loss of memory due to a nasty blow to the head, Reason eventually conquered with time. But this mindless, spiritless, disregard for life in general was beyond Cole's comprehension.

Impatient for a response, he snapped his fingers three times in rapid succession before Reason's face. When there was still no reaction, Cole clapped both hands together in mid-air before him, and was only mildly relieved to see Reason flinch instinctively away from both the motion and the sound. So he wasn't blind, and he wasn't deaf. Then what in hell's name was wrong with him? He acted like a man beaten half to death and barely alive, yet Cole could see no visible bruises on his face, nor knuckles.

With a deadly intent, Cole's gaze shifted to the man on his left. "Are you gonna tell me what's goin' on here? What happened to this man?"

"Don't look at us. This is the way he was when we found him. Right Mort?"

Mort grunted his affirmation.

Cole now had three choices. Somehow, force these proven liars to talk, kill them outright before they knew what hit them, or get Reason the hell out of here as fast as humanly possible.

Since he was already outnumbered, out-armed, and physically unable to best these two mountain men in a brawl, he quickly chose the latter. He'd find out one way or the other what happened in that cabin and one day possibly even the score, but right now, his sole responsibility was to take Reason home.

With a forced show of politeness and between a tightly clenched jaw, Cole said, "I'm obliged to you for carin' for this man. Now if you don't mind watchin' him for a minute while I go saddle his horse, I'd be grateful." Cole's lips twitched in a semblance of a grin, yet if those two dullards would have noted the depth of fury raging in his glinting amber eyes they might have feared for their lives.

Without another word, Cole turned on his heel and headed for the corral, mumbling all the swear words to himself that he'd ever heard uttered and making up a few new ones along the way. Within minutes, he found Reason's tack tucked away in a dark corner of the half-standing barn and had an unusually compliant Satan all rigged out as if the horse was all too willing and eager to leave this place. Unlike his master.

With a sinking heart, Cole led the black stallion to the porch. Reason still stood in the same downcast position as before, never once acknowledging Cole's presence nor acting if he knew, or cared, about a thing that was going on around him. He seemed weary to Cole's well-trained eye, and he wondered whether their story was partially true, that Reason had been ambushed and left for dead as the two mountain men had previously said. Mortimer seemed to be the only thing holding Reason upright, with one beefy hand still gripped tight on his upper arm.

"I'll need his gun belt and revolver, too." Cole had a hard time keeping his temper in check. "And any other personal belongings he had with him, if you don't mind."

Cole's eyes glittered dangerously and if either man so much as gave him a hard time, he knew he'd shoot them on the spot. Or die trying.

But neither did. The one on his left disappeared within the dark confines of the cabin and returned within seconds with Reason's gun belt and revolver still in its holster. He tossed them down to the man on the ground and Cole caught them deftly with his left hand.

"Now let him go," he said with a tight jaw.

"He might fall down if I do," Mortimer answered matter-of-factly.

A muscle bunched in Cole's cheek, but he deliberately checked his automatic response to draw his pistol and fire. Reason was almost home free. He wouldn't jeopardize that fact.

Instead he said with a hard edge to his voice that he couldn't quite control, "Are you gonna fall down, Reason?"

There was an unhealthy silence among the four men in the yard, then, to Cole's surprise, Reason slowly raised his pale blue eyes and stared straight at him. A nerve-shattering chill ran straight up Cole's spine.

No tiny shred of recognition lay in Reason's cold, empty eyes. Cole could have been a complete stranger to the man standing before him for all the lack of emotion he showed. Cole swallowed down a sudden lump of fear in his throat. Was this the same man he'd known for years? A trusted, loyal friend? One to ride the river with? He sensed a threat in Reason that Cole had never noticed before. An unstable danger. Had Reason lost his mind?

Then Reason's eyes dropped back to the planked floor at his feet, and Cole thought he must have imagined it. Shrugging off his fears, he said to Mortimer, "You can let him go now."

"Suit yourself. But I ain't pickin' him up again if he goes down." Mortimer released his huge paw and stepped to the side.

Reason swayed a bit on his feet, then staggered off-balance, but he didn't fall as Mortimer thought he would.

"Come on, Reason." Cole nodded to the horses, even though Reason wasn't looking in his direction. Casually he hooked the black leather gun belt over Satan's saddle. "Let's go home."

Reason acted as if he hadn't heard a word.

Mortimer snickered beside him. "He don't look like he wants to leave."

"Oh, he's leavin' all right!" Cole didn't hesitate. He simply stormed up the steps after him. "You can bet your last dollar on that!" In a fit of impatience, he grabbed hold of Reason's right arm and began to tug him in the direction of the horses. But without warning, Reason balked. With all the stubbornness of a cantankerous old mule, he wrenched himself clear out of Cole's grasp and took a determined step backwards.

Mortimer giggled like a schoolgirl. "I told ya so," he said, while the other man remained studiously silent.

"Shut the hell up!" Cole's patience was nearing a fast end. Just what sort of trick was Reason pulling here anyway?

He tried to talk sense into the man. "Dammit Reason! Don't you want to get shuck of this place?"

There was no response. No acknowledgment of any kind.

"You might have to hog-tie him to get him in the saddle," Mortimer sneered.

This time the other man spoke up. "Do like the man says, Morty, and shut up while you're still able." Was Buck the only man who could see that this man Cole desperately wanted to shoot something? Sometimes Morty didn't have the brains God gave a flea.

Cole saw red, and knew if he didn't get Reason on a horse soon, in one minute he'd be emptying his six-gun into Mortimer's huge hulking body, no matter what the consequences to his own safety might be.

"Reason, if you don't climb onto Satan right now, I'm liable to do just what that damn fool says."

Again Reason ignored him.

"That ties it!" If Cole had to use force to get Reason up on his horse, then that's just what he'd have to do. Once again, he made a grab for Reason's arm. But Reason must have been expecting just such a maneuver, for he jerked backwards a scant second before Cole had a chance to touch him, and slammed himself hard up against the outer wall of the shack. He winced from the impact and Cole heard a muffled groan of protest catch deep in his throat.

So he was hurt. And badly, from the looks of it. Then why wouldn't he leave? He was at a complete loss as to how to proceed next, when Mortimer's insulting laugh made Cole lose all semblance of control. With a snarl of fury curling his lips, he was twisting at the waist, reaching for the pistol glued to his hip, when a sudden iron-fisted grip on his right wrist made all circulation cease in that hand.

"What the hell…?" Cole had always prided himself on his hard-knuckled fists and powerful swing. Fighting hand-to-hand combat was something he had always been proficient at. But this vise-like, numbing grip on his right arm was something he had never experienced before, and hoped never to feel again.

Then the hard round bore of a rifle prodded him in the small of his back. To his utter mortification, he was held fast.

"My friend here never knows when to quit," the trapper behind Cole said. "Now if you'll just back off some, you can take this man and go. We don't want no trouble with you, or the rest of your ranch hands. Unless you push us too far…." He left the rest unsaid, but the message was clear. He held the trump card with his rifle, and had, ever since Cole first rode into the yard. A fact which Cole, in his thirst for vengeance, had forgotten.

Cole didn't wait for him to finish. The punishing grip on his wrist was warning enough, he didn't need the prod of a loaded rifle digging into his spine to convince him he had acted rashly. He might be hotheaded and stubborn, but he was no fool.

"It's a deal," he said hastily, knowing his main goal was to just get Reason safely back home where he belonged.

Then the man released his wrist and as the rifle disappeared from his back, Cole breathed easier. He still eyed Mortimer with a dangerous glare of resentment, yet deliberately held his tongue, as did the other fellow. Once again, he turned to Reason.

"What's it gonna be, Reason? Are you stayin', or goin'? I'll leave the choice to you." *Like hell I will,* Cole thought to himself, *even if I have to sling you over my shoulder like a two-ton sack of grain.* Yet he was curious to see what Reason's reaction to his ultimatum would be. He didn't have long to wait.

Reason never raised his head, but his breathing became labored and difficult as if he were fighting an invisible enemy deep within himself that no one else could see. Reaching blindly behind him, the splayed fingers of his hands pressed his palms flat up against the log wall at his back as if that simple barrier was the only safe and stabilizing force in his world. Then slowly he shook his head from side to side as if in answer to an unspoken question.

"No," he moaned aloud.

Cole's temper grew hot, running rapidly out of control. He was saddle-sore and weary and had taken all the crap in one morning that he could physically stand. Without thought to the consequences he leaned forward, grabbed the front of Reason's half-open shirt in both hands, yanked him forward, then slammed him backwards against the wall with the intent to wake up the man from his disassociation with reality, completely disregarding the fact that he was hurting him.

A gasp of surprise broke from Reason's throat, his teeth gnashing together in pain, as he cringed instinctively against the wall for support. Yet to Cole's utter amazement, Reason never uttered one word of protest, nor lifted so much as a finger in his own defense. And not once did he raise his eyes to Cole.

"Look at me, damn you! Tell me what's wrong!"

Cole knew he was losing it again, only this time his anger was directed solely at Reason. When Reason ignored him a second time, Cole slammed him against the wall once more.

Reason groaned out loud, his body stiffening upon impact, but this time when he caught his breath, his head began to raise by slow inches. Like a wounded animal, he squinted up at Cole with a glassy-eyed stare, then blinked and winced hard in anticipation of a third blow. And Cole almost lost his nerve. Almost, but not quite.

"Don't you know who I am?" Cole shouted inches from his face.

The black-lashed eyes widened at Cole's demand, the pale blue irises becoming unfocused and wildly confused. Then he shook his head ever so slightly. And this time Cole was the one whose gut twisted in remorse witnessing the vast sea of emptiness he now saw in Reason's familiar wolf's eyes.

"It's Cole! Don't you remember? Cole Dansing! Dammit, how the hell could you forget me?"

Yet Reason didn't remember. Cole's answer was painfully apparent in the cold lack of emotion showing on Reason's face.

Slowly Cole's temper cooled and he gently released the ruined shirt.

"I'm not goin' to hurt you. I only want to take you home," he said, wishing he had never chosen the use of force on Reason to begin with. He hadn't realized the extent of the man's misery and only hoped to shock some sense into him. He'd shocked him all right, but not in the way he intended. There was no right way to pound memory back into a man. Only time and gentle handling could do that. And so far he had gone about it all wrong.

"Come on, Reason. Let's go home, shall we?" Playfully Cole slapped him on the shoulder, yet even Cole could see Reason's immediate and senseless withdrawal.

Once again Reason remained standing, head bowed low, eyes downcast, back braced firmly to the wall; only this time Cole wondered if he was hurting too much to move. And he was reluctant to offer a hand to help for fear Reason would only shrug out of his grasp once more and injure himself further.

The trapper behind Cole had no such qualms. He jabbed Reason hard in the side with the unyielding steel bore of his rifle.

"Your friend wants you to git," he said as Reason jerked in alarm. Then all three men watched Reason's vacant stare slowly travel the length of the rifle, up the man's arm, to rest on the bear-like bearded face. "Now since we're through with ya here, I'm guessin' it's a good idea for you to be moseyin' on."

Cole was amazed that the trapper was able to draw Reason's undivided attention without resorting to actual violence. Did Reason need a rifle aimed at his belly in order to comprehend a simple question, or command? And just what had the trapper meant when he said they were "through" with him. What could Reason possibly offer anyone in his present condition that someone would actually want?

Then the trapper shifted the aim of the weapon towards the saddled horses. "Mount up!"

To Cole's further surprise, Reason's deadpan gaze shifted towards the pair of mustangs waiting at the hitching rail. Without a word spoken, he pushed himself away from the wall and, as Cole stepped aside to allow him to pass unhindered, Reason began to advance forward. Yet he moved woodenly, without purpose, and each step he took seemed to draw a huge amount of effort. Cole watched him drag his heels across the porch and down the rickety steps, glancing neither left nor right. Only when he reached the nearest horse did he pause and glance up.

The black stallion tossed his head up high in the air and snorted an alarm. His eyes grew round and wild. And his ears laid flat against his neck. He lunged against the reins tied to the post and his hooves danced nervously in place. Instinctively Reason staggered backwards, out of harm's way.

"Easy, Satan." Cole hurried to the horse's side, snatching at the bridle before the terrified mustang could snap the reins and break free, while running a gentle soothing hand along the sleek, muscular neck. "What's eatin' you, boy?" he crooned to the skittish animal. Why the damn four-legged menace acted as if he didn't even recognize his owner, and from the look of alarm on Reason's face, the feeling was mutual.

Maybe it was the smell that frightened the horse. Reason needed a bath badly. Even Cole found it hard to be near him. He reeked of a mixture of sweat, blood, regurgitated food, among other things Cole couldn't quite identify. As soon as they found the nearest lake, river, or large puddle of water, Cole was going to throw him in. Whether he liked it, or not. Once he was cleaned up and looked halfway decent again, maybe they'd both feel better.

"Ride my horse for now, Reason." Cole pointed towards the dark bay gelding standing patiently at the rail. "He's a mite calmer than this one."

Slowly Reason's gaze slid towards the more docile animal, reminding Cole of a wind-up tin toy that moved mechanically, without thought, feeling, or heart. For a brief second Cole was afraid Reason would balk once again at the simple request, but Reason obeyed without a word of protest and only when he was firmly fixed in the saddle did Cole swing up on Satan's broad back.

Instantly he realized his mistake.

Satan snorted his surprise and executed a neat little side step of displeasure at someone daring to ride him other than his master, while Cole's breath held and his gut tightened. For the horse could surely throw him if he had a mind to and grind him to dust beneath his hooves as he had tried to do years before. And today was no exception to the rule.

With a scream of fury, the black horse reared straight up on hind legs, his front hooves flailing at the air, twisting like a whirlwind, trying to dislodge the annoying man on his back. And the trick was working to the horse's delight. For Cole's seat became compromised and he was starting to slip when a low whistle suddenly rent the air and the horse trembled beneath him. The dangerous hooves paused only a second, then dropped gently to the ground as Cole regained his balance in the saddle. Once again, Satan pranced in place, subdued by the simple sound of his master's signal.

Cole was stunned. In another second he would have fallen beneath Satan and been stomped into the ground once again. And this time he might not have survived.

He glanced at Reason who hadn't once shifted his eyes from the men on the porch to Cole's knowledge.

"Did he just whistle?" Cole said to the two bookends standing on either side of the stairs.

"Don't know," Buck replied. "We was watchin' you. But we heard it clear enough."

And, although Satan fidgeted beneath him, sidestepping restlessly and tossing his feathery black mane around more than usual, he never again attempted to buck Cole off.

CHAPTER FOUR

Cole drew up at a water hole a half-hour later, and to his secret delight Reason hauled up right beside him without so much as a word of complaint. Moments after Cole swung down, however, Reason still remained seated.

Running a weary hand across the back of his sweat-streaked neck, Cole stood there, looking up at the man whose vacuous clear blue eyes stared unseeing over the water at the hills beyond, and wondered which was the best way to handle this man. Reason seemed to come alive only when his life was threatened at gunpoint or else was distinctly ordered to. Cautiously he moved to the dark bay's bridle and grasped a firm hold, just in case Reason decided to bolt and run.

"Get down off that horse." He decided to try a simple command first, rather than meaningless threats with a pistol.

Reason hesitated for the briefest of seconds. Then, to Cole's surprise, he leaned slightly forward to swing a leg over the back of his saddle. A soft grunt escaped his throat as the sole of his boot hit the ground with a jolt, and Cole knew he was hurting. The dark-red bloodstain on the back of Reason's once light-colored shirt was a dead give-away, and Cole wondered if the bandage wrapped around the wound at his waist was as filthy as the rest of him.

"Turn around and face the saddle."

Reason seemed to shrink inside himself. He shook his head slightly from side to side. The word "no" came out as a whispered thought spoken out loud. His breathing became labored once again, and he raised a trembling hand to his horse's flanks in a feeble attempt to steady himself.

But Cole's patience with Reason was already wearing thin.

"Oh, for Christ sakes." Reaching out, he grabbed Reason by

the arm, twisted him around, and flung him face forward into the worn leather saddle. Grabbing a stiff handful of Reason's dried blood-soaked shirt, Cole yanked the material up and out from the waistband of his beltless denim pants.

The bandage was fresher than the rest of his clothes, only a few days old by the looks of it. And Cole was inwardly grateful. For if this wound hadn't been tended to properly in the beginning, Cole would have been dragging home a dead man.

Gently he tugged the shirt back down.

"Looks like those two towering imbeciles managed to save your life after all," Cole grinned. He took a step backward to give Reason some breathing space, then frowned.

Reason's hands were raised and thrown over the back of his horse for support, his shoulders were trembling whether from pain or fatigue, Cole didn't know which, and he was gulping in air as if he were drowning in the middle of the Rio Grande in full flood and had forgotten how to swim. He was still leaning deep into the seat of his saddle and looked like he wasn't about to move until Cole ordered him otherwise.

A wry smile curved the corners of Cole's lips. Six years ago he might have appreciated this newly acquired submissive behavior of Reason's, back when the hotshot young newcomer to the Stirrup C gave him nothing but trouble. But now the unnatural meekness of the man simply irked him. He wondered what rare form of miracle would manifest itself in order to restore Reason to his true self.

"What do you say to us peelin' off these vermin-crawlin' duds and coolin' off in the lake?"

That did it. Reason jerked around as if shot from behind. He'd moved so fast he had to reach out a hand to his saddle once more to prevent himself from falling.

"No," he said once again. Only this time he was glancing straight at Cole when he said it. Fear glazed his eyes with a pale blue sheen. His breathing remained irregular. And he appeared ready to run at the slightest provocation.

"Now take it easy," Cole drawled deliberately slow, trying to calm the man's nerves. "I just want to wash some of this trail dust off and, no offense Reason, but you could use a good scrubbin' yourself."

Reason acted as if he hadn't heard a word Cole uttered.

When Cole took a step towards him, preparing to drag him all the way to the water's edge if necessary, Reason sidled further away. And when Cole reached out a hand to restrain him, Reason jerked around and took off running straight across the sunburnt prairie grass like the devil, himself, was chasing him.

Cole swore a blue streak and charged after him. Reason was fast, but Cole was faster. And pain slowed down Reason's reflexes considerably. It didn't take more than a minute to tackle him about the hips and fling him to the ground like he would throw a half-grown steer.

But even though Cole tried to cushion his fall, by twisting in mid-air, landing first and letting Reason roll effortlessly over him, Reason still landed hard on his back, groaning upon impact.

"Sorry fella," he said, rising to his feet, "but you need a bath even worse than me and I'm not takin' no for an answer. Now are you gonna strip down to your birthday suit and jump in on your own, or do I have to do it all for you."

For an answer, Reason flung an arm up over his eyes and flinched on the ground as if to avoid a blow.

"Oh...shit!" he breathed softly.

"Aw hell, I ain't partial to them myself," Cole chuckled good-naturedly, mistaking Reason's reluctance to wash. "But the women tend to favor them some, and once a week on Saturday never killed a man, I reckon." He reached down, grabbed Reason's left arm near the elbow, and yanked him to his feet. Too weary to resist, Reason stumbled, staggered, then swayed to a halt.

"You okay?" Cole queried. He wasn't afraid of Reason high tailing it again. In fact, the man didn't look like he had the strength to make it back to the horses.

Reason steadied himself, then ignored him, as usual.

"Get goin' then," Cole snapped, knowing the harsh tone of voice he carefully adopted was the best way to keep Reason's fuzzy attention.

A full ten minutes passed before they finally neared the water's edge.

"Hold up," Cole commanded, when he thought Reason was going to stroll right in with his boots on. And, as Reason jerked to a shaky halt, he said, "Now shuck those filthy rags you're wearin' and jump in!"

Cole proceeded to do just that. First went his hat, gun belt, shirt, and then hopping on first one foot and then the other, threw each boot to the ground. He slipped off his socks, then the tan leather belt from the waist of his faded blue jeans and was reaching for the buttons of his pants when he glanced over at Reason.

Reason hadn't moved one inch. He was still dressed in the same foul-smelling clothes as before, staring vacantly out over the water as if waiting for a damn ship to come sailing in.

Cole fumed. Dammit, did he have to do everything for the man? Carelessly he stepped over his own shirt lying in a crumpled heap on the ground, came up on Reason's right side, and gave his shoulder a hard shove.

"Wake up!"

Reason stumbled sideways, then instantly righted himself.

"You heard me. I know you did. Last one in's a rotten egg," When Reason still didn't move, he snarled, "Strip, dammit! Or I'll rip those rags right off you myself!"

Slowly Reason's hands lifted to the one brass button still clinging by a slim thread to the half-open shirt at his chest. Cole watched in amazement as the thin deft fingers trembled uncontrollably. For Reason's nerves of steel had always been a fact Cole secretly admired. And now look at him. If he hadn't seen this lack of composure in the man with his own eyes, he'd never have believed it. And at the rate Reason was fumbling with his shirt, another hour would go by before he ever got the damn thing off.

With a curse on his lips and his mind teetering with impatience, Cole moved behind him. He raised one hand and, grabbing the neck of the soiled shirt in one brief violent motion, ripped the whole thing clear off Reason's upper body.

A harsh, choking groan of denial caught in Reason's throat and his head ducked low as if expecting a crushing blow from behind to knock him straight to the ground. The corded muscles across his back bunched tightly, and his shoulders shook as if he were caught in a wild blue norther in mid-January without the protection of a sheepskin jacket.

And Cole swore out loud. For ugly masses of bruised flesh stained nearly every square inch of Reason's back. Various shades of pink, purple, yellow, and black blurred together across his shoulders, down his back and beneath his arms that Cole hadn't seen before. And when he stepped around Reason to face him, more abrasions than he could count were splayed across his chest and arms, stopping only at the stark-white bandage wrapped tight around his waist and the scabbed over rope burns showing through the ragged cuffs still buttoned at his wrists.

Cole looked ready to kill. His gaze slid menacingly up to Reason's face. "Why didn't you tell me you were tied up and beaten senseless," he said with a tight jaw and raspy voice.

There was no obvious response. Cole wasn't sure if Reason had even heard him. Furiously he flung the shirt that he had torn off Reason's back to the ground, then with both hands gave Reason's shoulders a hard shove.

"Answer me, damn you, or I'm liable to give you more of the same."

Cole was bluffing through his hat. He wouldn't touch Reason again with a ten-foot pole. But Reason didn't know that. He staggered backwards, lost his footing, and fell. Then with the grace of a mountain cat, rolled halfway to his feet. He froze in a crouch, his chilling wolf-like eyes staring right through Cole as if he were made of transparent window glass, preparing to run again if Cole so much as took a single step towards him.

Cole ran trembling fingers through his own hair. Then drew in a deep, stabilizing breath. Damn his hot temper. He'd almost lost it again. He realized too late the utmost importance of remaining cool and confident around this man if he ever intended to help him.

"Take off your boots and jump in," he snapped churlishly, unable to shake off the gut-clenching nausea that the sight of Reason's badly bruised torso aroused. "I'll throw you a bar of soap."

Turning his back on Reason, he headed for his saddlebags. He was taking a big chance, ignoring Reason like that. There would be no stopping the man if he decided to leap on Satan's fleet-footed back and head out for parts unknown.

And if he decided to run this time? Cole wasn't sure he'd have the heart to chase him down.

Yet when he returned, much to his surprise, Reason had his boots off and in socked feet was slowly wading into the lake.

"Here, catch!"

Instantly Reason swiveled around and with his left hand, deftly caught the small bar of lye soap that Cole tossed high in the air. Then he stood there, with water skimming just above his trousered ankles as if awaiting further orders, and Cole smiled. So far his reflexes hadn't been hampered by his injuries. That was a start in the right direction.

Cole waded into the cold, spring-fed water until he was knee-deep.

"Start washin'," he ordered sternly. "And don't worry about keeping that bandage dry. I have fresh ones in my saddlebags." Then, taking a deep breath, he dove headfirst into the lake.

CHAPTER FIVE

Cole set his own sweet pace all the way home. He was in no immediate rush to face Randall's wrath by bringing home a brother that was a whole lot less than perfect both in body and mind. And Reason appeared to sag in the saddle after occasional stretches of hard riding. Even though he never voiced a word of complaint, Cole would catch him nodding off at times, and for once Cole had nothing to say.

If the truth were known, Cole didn't trust himself to speak. The idea that Reason had been bound and beaten still rankled like a badly infected splinter to Cole's brain, and he was afraid if the subject came up again, Cole might just light into him once more. If only Reason had mentioned something, anything, when Cole found him, about the senseless brutality he'd endured over the last few weeks, Cole would have shot those two backwoodsmen before they knew what hit them. But Reason had remained stoically silent, and now Cole thought he knew why.

He had been afraid! As simple as that.

Just the mere thought seemed incredulous to Cole's mind. The Reason Cordell he knew feared neither man nor beast. He was an island unto himself, requiring nothing from no one, yet somehow possessing the uncanny ability to earn the undying respect of nearly every man he met.

But now? Now he reminded Cole of one of the wild horses roaming the vast Wyoming territory, unlucky enough to get roped by an impatient, merciless cowboy who used cruel spurs and a braided rawhide whip to break his spirit in two.

Cole grew uneasy at the thought. Wasn't Reason made of tougher stuff than that? Or did every man have a set limit as to just how much hardship and suffering he could endure and still remain a man.

Although the weather was cooperative and made for easy riding, they made frequent rest stops along the way. Cole saw that they rose late in the morning and made an early camp towards sunset. Besides, he was hoping that by the time they reached home Reason would have some semblance of memory back.

But four days later as they hit the Stirrup C boundary in the form of barbed-wire fencing and a passel of stocky white-faced cattle replacing the scrawny long-horns of years ago dotting the grassy valley beyond, Reason was no better off now than when they first started over a week ago. He hadn't uttered a word since the afternoon at the lake, and even though he cleaned up good and was now wearing the blue chambray shirt Cole had stuffed in his saddlebags as a spare, the glazed, vacant look was still in his eyes and his short-lived attention span hadn't improved any. Randall was sure to give him holy hell when he set eyes on his brother. And Rachel didn't even bear thinking about.

Ranch hands hollered and waved gaily from the cluster of nearby corrals as Cole and Reason cantered slowly into the yard. Well, someone was glad to see him at least. If only he could say the same for….

He was unprepared when Reason hauled hard on his reins and drew the bay up short. The big black cantered unconcernedly past him before Cole had sense enough to rein Satan around. The look of sheer panic on Reason's face was warning enough. Cole reached out and grabbed the nearest strap of leather before Reason could even think of running.

"Easy, Reason," he crooned as if speaking to a recalcitrant Satan. "We're home now. There's no cause for alarm."

The bay horse danced sideways as Reason shifted a wary glance towards the men at the fence. Was Cole the only one who noticed Reason slide the palm of his right hand along his denim-clad thigh, automatically searching for the pistol normally found there which was now safely tucked away in Satan's saddlebags?

"They're your friends," Cole explained, watching Reason swallow down his senseless fear as his gun hand came up empty. "And they're just tickled to see you're all right."

But was he, really? Reason seemed to have more problems than Cole could count and he began wondering if this happy homecoming was going to prove downright worse than he first thought. Softly he clucked to the horses and began to lead the bay gelding at a walk towards the main house, breathing a deep sigh of relief when Reason gave him no further trouble.

"Wait here," Cole said as he swung down and tied both sets of reins securely to the rail. "I'll only be a minute."

His intention was to find Randall first and give him a short recap of Reason's situation before the man even laid eyes on his brother. But such an idea was not to take place.

The screen door swung open with a bang and an enthusiastic "Reason" split the air before Cole could turn around.

The man on the horse hadn't once moved. He was still staring down at the bay's pricked ears as if he hadn't heard a thing out of the ordinary.

Slowly Cole turned to face Randall.

Randall's face went pale beneath his normally sunburnt tan and he paused halfway across the porch. He was staring wide-eyed at his brother as if a ghost had suddenly appeared in his path.

"Is he deaf?" he asked Cole when there was no response from the man on the horse, and his worried mind searched for a plausible explanation as to his brother's odd behavior.

"No such luck," Cole scoffed. But after seeing Randall's stark confusion turn instantly into a troubled frown, he sobered quickly enough. "He's just been worked over real bad. It's gonna take some time gettin' used to...."

Cole hesitated. Even he didn't know if Reason would ever come to his senses again, or was this becoming a way of life for him? Sure, Reason had been shot before. A man who lived by the gun was destined to pack lead occasionally. And many of those wounds had been life threatening. But beating a man that was already down and hurting, and then tying his hands so he couldn't fight back, still rubbed Cole the wrong way. For Reason would have been no threat to those trappers. Although he could hold his own in an all-out brawl, he was no match for Cole. He was a gunfighter by trade and rarely ever felt the need to back up his words with fists, so long as his mahogany-handled colt revolver was strapped to his thigh.

A mental vision of the two burly mountain men flashed before Cole's mind. All right, so they roughed him up some. Even Cole wouldn't have stood a chance in their clutches. He recalled the firm grip on his wrist and an involuntary shudder of revulsion crept up his spine. Yet, as far as he knew, Reason had no broken bones to speak of. No lasting injuries that wouldn't heal in a few days. And Reason did have a stubborn streak a mile wide running straight up his backbone. He could be tough to handle at times, as Cole knew from first-hand experience. Even with someone who was only looking out for his own good. Something else must have happened along the way to cause Reason's mind to snap like a dry twig.

"Then what the hell's wrong with him?" Randall argued from the porch. "And did he have the money on him, or not?"

Cole hadn't once thought of the five thousand missing dollars in his haste to bring Reason home. He turned to the man on the horse.

"Get down," he ordered curtly, and as Reason slowly obeyed, he added, "Stand over there by the rail."

Cole knew he didn't carry the money on him, not after the bath in the lake. But he didn't trust Reason to sit tight for long around a brother he obviously thought of as a stranger while Cole was otherwise occupied.

He moved over to Satan's side and unbuckled one of the saddlebags, rummaged around inside for a minute with a free hand, then moved to the other.

Just as he thought. Nothing! There was no sign of the plain brown parcel that Cole knew held the five grand.

Slowly he shook his head.

Randall ran an exasperated hand through his dark wavy hair. "Dammit, I was hoping…." Then his brown eyes shifted to his brother as he addressed Cole. "What do you mean, worked over?"

"Look, I don't know the whole story. Maybe I never will," Cole attempted to explain. "All's I know is he's got a bullet wound in the small of his back that's slow to heal, and he's sportin' more bruises than there are stars on the Fourth of July flag. I found him in a Godforsaken cabin somewhere high in the Tetons, cared for by a pair of thick-skulled mountain men, one named Mortimer, and…. Well, I never got the name of the other."

What Cole deliberately neglected to mention was the bedraggled condition he found Reason in, nor the trouble and lies he encountered trying to drag him out of there.

"Doesn't he talk?" Randall queried, squinting at the silent man staring at the ground beneath his feet, yet still standing obediently where Cole had left him. "And why isn't he riding his own horse?"

"Doesn't seem to recall him. Nor me either." Cole added matter-of-factly, knowing this was as much of a shock to Randall as it had been to himself when he had stumbled upon the cabin a week ago. His gaze slid sadly to Reason. "And no, he doesn't talk much at all."

Randall swore beneath his breath then, after a moment's hesitation, veered around and headed for the screen door.

"Well come on in then, and I'll have Rosa rustle you up something to eat. I'm sure you're both damn near starved. We'll chat more inside."

Cole smiled. Randall was taking this better than he thought. At least he wasn't blaming him again for all the hard luck that had followed Reason home.

"I'm so hungry I could eat a grizzly raw while still wearin' his winter coat," Cole laughed as he sauntered towards the house. "C'mon, Reason. Supper's waitin'."

He was halfway up the steps before he realized once again that Reason hadn't moved an inch. Damn, he had hoped that in more familiar surroundings Reason would start to act like his old self. Guess he was wrong. What would Rachel say when she saw him, Cole wondered. She was probably already out of her head with worry when Reason didn't show up as scheduled. Then Cole dismissed the worrisome thought. Maybe they could put off telling her anything until Reason was better, both in body and spirit. After all, this wasn't the house both they and their families lived in. This was Randall's home, the place where they were supposed to meet after the sale of the herd, to divide the cash between the two neighboring ranches. Their own spread the Stirrup C Bar, was still another twenty odd miles northwest of here. The distance separating the two households might give Reason the time he needed to get back on his feet. But first things first.

He backed down the stairs.

"Reason, I see you act like you don't hear me. But I know you do. So listen up! We're both goin' inside now, to eat whatever Rosa can scrape together in the way of chow. Now let's go, okay?"

Cole wondered why he was wasting so much breath. "Move, dammit!"

Slowly Reason's eyes shifted towards the house, then dropped back to the ground. To Cole's dismay, he backed up a step.

"Okay, I get it. So you're not all that hungry. Well, you should be. We both ate the same amount of food all last week, and my stomach is about caving in on itself right now. And don't think I'm leavin' you out here alone."

That's all he needed was for Reason to fork a horse and high tail it back to the high country. And Cole was determined to satisfy the rumbling complaints of an empty stomach before he was forced to chase after Reason once more.

"Let's go!"

When he reached out to grab Reason's arm and lead him into the house, Reason twisted away.

"What's he doing?" Randall said, returning to the porch. For when the two men didn't immediately follow him, Randall retraced his footsteps to find the cause of delay.

"I don't reckon he's all that hungry right now," Cole snapped in annoyance. Yet even he sensed that Reason wanted to avoid the house at all cost. "Let's not go through this again, Reason," he growled low, so Randall wouldn't hear.

Once more he took a step forward and, again, Reason backed further away. If this kept on they'd be out by the lower forty in no time. If orders didn't work anymore....

Cole pulled his gun. Reason's spine stiffened in response. And Cole grinned in a smug way. He finally had the man's full attention.

"Now, let's go." He gestured with the pistol for Reason to walk ahead of him towards the house.

And, after a moment's hesitation, Reason obeyed.

CHAPTER SIX

The three men sat at the large oak table in the warm and cozy kitchen. Cole was wolfing down the meat and potato leftovers that Rosa, Maria's eldest daughter, had been asked to heat up for them, while Reason picked disinterestedly at his food and seemed to consume only enough to keep him alive.

Finally, Randall's impatience got the better of him. Scraping back his chair along the hardwood floor, he rose abruptly to his feet.

"Cole, I'd like to...." Scarcely had he opened his mouth to speak, when Reason suddenly lunged up and backwards out of his seat only to pause in mid-flight like a startled deer about to bolt for the safety of the trees. Randall hesitated, struck speechless with surprise.

"Easy Reason," Cole warned low as he swallowed the last bite of his dinner. Then, swiping at his mouth with a napkin, he glanced up.

The man was more skittish than an unbroken mustang, Cole mused silently to himself as brother stood facing brother; one afraid to move for fear of startling the other, the other unable to move because of heart-stopping fear. Cole shook his head in a state of utter hopelessness. This obvious example of mental instability was more Reason's department than his. He was the one with experience in gentling the wild ones. And Cole had never prided himself on being a patient man.

"Cole, I just wanted to speak to you privately," Randall said when he finally found his tongue. "I figured we could leave him alone for a few minutes while we went in the study to talk. Guess I was plumb wrong."

"Like a big ol' stick of dynamite lyin' too close to the

campfire," Cole sneered. "There's no tellin' what he'll do next. Especially in unfamiliar surroundings such as this. What was it you wanted to say?"

Randall, ever so cautiously, regained his seat. The abrupt move had frightened his brother for some unknown reason, and Randall wasn't about to make the same mistake twice.

"I just wanted your opinion on what the hell we should do with him. Do you think he needs a doctor?"

"Wouldn't get within five yards," Cole laughed. Then at Randall's dark frown, he hastily explained. "The bullet wound is healing, slow but sure. I know because I changed the bandage twice on the way here. And that was no small feat, let me tell you."

Randall ignored the sarcasm. "What about the bruises?" Randall had to peer up at his brother now, for Reason still hadn't regained his chair, and Cole didn't seem to consider Reason's wary stance an important enough issue to enforce.

"Nothin's broken. The rest will heal with time."

"What about…?" Randall was reluctant to voice his brother's limited mental capacities right in front of the man.

"Don't know if a sawbones can fix that." Cole guessed what Randall was driving at.

"Then what do we do with him?"

Cole shrugged and fiddled with his fork. "Hope he comes to his senses before all hell breaks loose?"

Randall threw Cole a sharp look. "What do you mean by that?"

"Aw, nothin'." Cole began to fidget uneasily in his chair. "I don't know why I even said that. If anythin' he's more afraid of us, than we are of him."

"Funny," Randal stated calmly. "I've never known my brother to be afraid of much in this world." He hesitated. "Just what are we supposed to tell Rachel?"

Cole ran a hand over his jaw. He was worried about the very same thing.

"Nothin'," he finally said. "What she don't know won't hurt her. Let's give him time to get his act together. I don't think even Rachel could handle him in the condition he's in right now."

CHAPTER SEVEN

Sunlight cast dappled shadows through the leaves. Tall sturdy trunks of ponderosa pine surrounded the small clearing in which he stood, far more intimidating than the staunch iron bars of a locked prison cell. A jaw squawked raucously from above, warning danger, and there were soft scuffling sounds of a small rodent burrowing to safety beneath the dead leaves scattered haphazardly beneath his feet.

Reason held his breath and stood his ground.

Something was stalking him. And there was no place to hide, nowhere to run. He was trapped! Like a small fur-bearing animal locked in a wooden cage, awaiting execution.

A dead branch snapped loudly nearby as if a heavy weight had broken the limb in two. And Reason's nerves jumped almost clear out of his skin. He jerked halfway around, his eyes searching the dense wood and brush beyond for some form of life-threatening danger to show itself.

There was no one there.

The hair on the nape of his neck stood stiffly on end. His flesh crawled.

Someone was watching him. He could feel the keen eyes of a predator zeroing in on the small of his back.

He turned full circle. Heavy breathing rasped in his ears. Close, too close. Maybe it was his own.

Panic seized his chest, grabbed a tight-fisted hand around his throat. Where the hell was his horse? His gun? How did he get out here in the middle of the woods without them? And just where the hell was he? He remembered nothing beyond this minute in time. Then he heard it again.

A large animal shuffling through the forest. And it was

coming nearer.

Reason froze. He was afraid to move so much as a finger for fear he'd be seen. His heart thudded in his chest like a damned frightened rabbit. The thrashing, crashing sounds were growing closer by the minute. The thing was almost upon him. And his boots felt weighted with quicksand.

Then it sprung. A powerful, muscular force landed hard on his back and knocked the wind right out of his lungs. He staggered as the thing grabbed him tight about the waist, pinning his arms to his sides, the huge paws wrapping themselves around his belly, hurting him, as he struggled desperately to keep his feet. With every last ounce of his being, he tried to twist free of the suffocating grip and shake the bear-like thing off, but the animal was too strong, too powerful. Fear clawed at his throat. He couldn't breathe. There was a pain in his back that stabbed like a Bowie knife. The weight of the beast dragged him to his knees. And he hurt. God, how he hurt. He moaned softly, yet he couldn't seem to break away.

And then there were two of them. And they weren't bears at all.

They were men!

"Reason! Wake up!"

Cole had been sleeping soundly in the next room when muffled groans of distress coming through the wall behind his head pierced his subconscious brain and jolted him into full and utter awareness. "What the hell…?"

He stumbled to his feet in the middle of the night, slipped on his pants, then fumbled his way to Reason's room in the dark. He groped blindly for the matches that he knew lay on the table beside Reason's bed and, raising the glass globe, touched the flame to the kerosene soaked wick. A soft glow lit the interior of the room.

Reason was lying on his back, thrashing in his sleep. He was still fully dressed, down to his dusty boots. His frantic movements made a wrinkled shambles of the tan coverlet beneath him. Both arms were thrown over his eyes in a vain attempt to blind himself from the images he was seeing in his mind, and his body was writhing as if trapped in the throes of a nightmare too powerful to ignore. Another soft groan issued from his throat, and Cole had seen enough.

"Wake up, dammit! You're havin' a bad dream." Dropping to one knee he balanced himself on the edge of the mattress, yanked Reason's arms away from his face, and then shook him hard. "Wake up, I said! Are you listenin' to me?" he hollered out loud.

Reason gave a sharp gasp of alarm and his eyes flew open wide. Cole could see the stark, mind-numbing terror in the pale blue gaze staring frantically up at him.

"No!" Reason yelled softly as if in answer to his own nightmarish dreams. Then, with a sudden violent wrench, he tore himself free of Cole's grasp to roll off the opposite side of the bed. His boots hit the floor with a thud and, in one fluid motion, he threw himself backwards against the large mahogany chifferobe along the far wall, as if that simple piece of furniture at his back would protect him from all harm.

Cole had seen him do that once before, at the woodsmen's shack and he was as shocked then as he was now. Why Reason acted as if every man alive was out to do him some sort of bodily harm. In his deranged state of mind, was he instinctively trying to protect his back against the threat of another sniper's bullet? Didn't he feel safe? Even in his old bedroom?

Okay, so Reason couldn't remember anything at the moment. But didn't his keen sixth sense tell him Cole was no threat?

"What are you afraid of, Reason?" Cole had to ask, even though he knew no answer would be forthcoming. "You know I won't hurt ya."

If Cole had said, *I'm going to stick a knife between your ribs now,* the same look of horror on Reason's face would have remained. Slowly Cole backed off the bed. He didn't want to spook Reason any more than he needed to.

"Easy now." Cole began sidling towards the door, palms open wide at his sides in a silent gesture of surrender. "I'll leave you alone, if that's what you want." Maybe if he left, Reason would calm down.

One could only pray.

Five full minutes passed before Reason could tear his gaze away from the closed door to his room. His brain was a jumbled mass of threatening images. His body trembled in outright fear.

Sweat clung to his clothes like a second skin. He ran shaky fingers through his dark hair, feeling bereft of time and place. Where was he? Who was he? Why did everyone keep calling him Reason? And who the hell was Cole?

His glazed pale-eyed glance swept over the small unfamiliar room. He remembered being led here by someone, probably that Cole fella. Then being left alone.

"Rest," the man had said as the door closed shut behind him. He recalled standing in the middle of the sun-lit room until his legs ached. And he was tired, so damn tired. He thought he had lain down only a minute. But now a lamp was burning low on the bedside table, and the rest of the room lay deep in shadows. When had night fallen?

Slowly he ran an unsteady hand across the back of his head. His skull throbbed annoyingly as if there was too much information stuffed inside his foggy brain that he couldn't rightly recall and felt ready to explode from the sheer pressure of it all. The lamplight hurt his eyes. Had someone slugged him when he wasn't looking? He couldn't for the life of him remember.

All he knew was that he wasn't safe here. He'd be trapped, once again, if he stayed within these four confining walls much longer. He had no choice but to run before they caught him again. And this time the punishment would be more than his body could stand.

He didn't stop to wonder who "they" were. It didn't matter anyway. He couldn't differentiate between friend and foe. Every man was his enemy. And he couldn't even remember what the word "friend" stood for in the first place.

His glazed eyes slid to the one window in the room. A bright moon lit up the ground two stories below the ranch house he found himself in. A large barn stood in the near distance, with half a dozen split rail corrals filled with the slowly moving shadows of multi-colored mustangs. Smaller wooden outbuildings dotted the eerie landscape beyond.

Hesitantly, Reason moved closer to the window and peered straight down. The distance was too far to jump. He'd end up breaking his damn neck. His eyes drifted back to the door. Too risky. They might be waiting for him outside, like they were the last time.

The nearby walls began closing in on him and panic squeezed his insides in a giant fist. His heart thudded madly in his chest. In a few short minutes the small room would collapse right on top of him and he would die, pinned helplessly beneath the rubble. His breathing became erratic. He was suffocating by slow degrees in the confining atmosphere of the steadily advancing walls. He had to get out of here, and fast!

Before another incoherent thought could flash unbidden to his mind, he reared back his arm and sent his right fist straight through the clear pane of glass with the shattering force of a battering ram. There was a loud crash and tinkle of falling debris hitting the ground below, but as he pulled his arm back through the ragged sharp-edged hole, he found the opening still wasn't large enough for a man to crawl through and escape. Again and again, he smashed his fist through the remnants of cut glass that remained framed in the window, until a force stronger than himself pulled him backwards by the shoulders and flung him hard against the nearby wall.

"What in hell's name do ya think you're doin'?" Cole shouted, as searing pain shot through Reason's back like a bullet upon impact against the wall. He winced hard, groaned softly, then buckled at the knees to slowly slide down to the floor. And there he stayed.

Cole glanced once at the blood-streaked, broken remains of the shattered window, then over towards the still and silent man now huddled on the floor. Reason sat with his back braced against the wall. His eyes were squeezed tightly shut and his teeth were clenched so hard a muscle bulged in his cheek. Yet he sat there without one sound of protest, cradling his torn and bleeding right arm snug against his belly.

He must be loco, Cole thought with alarm. Why else would he smash at a window with his bare fist, his favored gun-hand no less, instead of just lifting the sash and opening it easily if he wanted some air?

Cautiously, he dropped to one knee before the injured man. "Let me see that hand," he said softly.

No answer. When would he ever learn?

Reaching out, he gently tugged on Reason's right wrist in an effort to free the ruined hand and inspect the damage, but the grip held firm and reluctantly Cole released him.

"Reason?"

Cole was at his wit's end. This was all going too far. There would be no quick fix for Reason, Cole knew with sudden clarity. Whatever happened to him out there was buried deep in his soul. And just maybe he'd never again be the grinning, cocky, and confident man he once was.

"Let me help you," Cole said low, as if speaking to a small child. "You've hurt your hand and it needs tending to. There might be a whole pile of glass still stuck in there."

But still there was no response.

Then Reason drew in a deep shattered breath, as if it would be his last. He began struggling, gasping for air as if he were having an attack of some kind. Cole swore in fear and frustration. This was beyond his range of understanding. Reason obviously needed more help than Cole could give.

He was rising to his feet, all set to go to the door and yell for Randall, when Reason's shoulders shuddered violently beneath him. His ragged breathing turned into huge, gulping sobs. Cole hesitated, dropping back to his haunches.

For although Reason's head was bowed low and his eyes were still shut, Cole could clearly see the telltale wetness of tears trickle down his clean-shaven cheeks.

Sweet Jesus! Reason was crying!

CHAPTER EIGHT

Reason was never left alone from that moment on. Rather than tie him up, which both Randall and Cole were reluctant to do, each man took turns sitting with him both day and night. And when that grew too tiresome to handle, they alternated shifts with a few trusted hands from the bunkhouse. Although Reason never tried to harm himself again, Randall wasn't taking any chances. Better to be safe, than sorry, he said.

The window had been boarded up and the room lay mainly in darkness now, except for the small lamp that was kept constantly burning at the bedside table. To Cole the room looked more like a prison cell than an actual place of comfort. But Reason didn't seem to mind. In fact, he was calmer of late, not leaping wildly to his feet the minute the shift changed and a new man entered to see to his care. He had grown resigned to his fate, if anything. And Cole wasn't sure which was worse.

At least when his nerves were on edge, Reason appeared to be dimly aware of the goings-on around him. But lately he just lounged in an easy chair in the far corner, staring at the floor for hours on end, seemingly content. He ignored the rotating shifts of men, no matter how they talked and joked with him to pass the time, and only barely acknowledged the orders Cole was forced to give. For it was Cole who saw that he washed, shaved, dressed and ate what was put in front of him. Cole who took him for short walks outside, when even he couldn't stand the hot, stifling confines of the small room any longer.

He didn't know how Reason could stand being cooped up for so long. The man he used to know would have gone stark raving mad in a short amount of time. But Reason was already half out of his mind and didn't seem to care about anything anymore.

Randall found them one warm and sunny afternoon in mid-August taking advantage of the shade beneath the overhang of the back porch.

"Thought I'd find you two out here," he said to the broad-shouldered, slim-hipped man leaning his back against an upright post, for Randall had ceased talking to Reason long ago.

"Rachel's here. She came over in the wagon to see if we had any news of...." He jerked his head in Reason's direction. "You know who. She's waiting in the front parlor. What do you think I should tell her?"

Ever since both men had returned to the Stirrup C, Randall had deferred all matters pertaining to Reason's welfare to Cole, who had automatically assumed the role of caretaker without once asking why. For Cole was the only man on the ranch capable of handling him, the one man Reason grudgingly tolerated to step within five feet of. All questions regarding Reason had to first be presented to Cole for approval, and Randall found himself to be no exception to his own rule.

Cole peered over his shoulder at the man lounging on a wicker chair staring blankly across the yard at the fringe of green-leafed woods beyond. There was no sign that Reason heard a thing Randall had said. Not even the mention of Rachel's name brought about any outward sign of recognition. And Cole was not a bit surprised.

"Can you stall her?"

"She looks like hell, Cole," Randall said low. "And we've lied to her long enough. She's frantic with worry. I'm afraid she'll take off after him one of these days, alone, if we don't tell her the truth soon. You know how headstrong she is."

Cole shrugged in a hopeless way, then turned back to Randall. "Well, there's your answer then. Do you want to send her out here? Or should we come on in?"

"Give me ten minutes, then meet us inside. I'll try to prepare her the best way I can." Then Randall ran an exasperated hand through his clean-cut dark hair and to Cole's surprise, uttered a profane oath beneath his breath. Without another word, he veered around and stormed back into the house.

Rachel was seated at a chair in the parlor with a damp handkerchief in her hands, wiping the last vestiges of tears from the corners of her red-rimmed eyes, when Reason strolled into the room fifteen minutes later, with Cole right behind him.

"That's far enough," Cole said, grabbing his arm near the shoulder to stop him when Reason began heading for the stairs and the relative safety of the small room above.

Although Reason flinched from the unwanted contact on his arm, he didn't panic, or try to lunge out of Cole's grasp, as he would have a week ago. Instead, he came to an abrupt halt.

His eyes were downcast, and his manner subdued, but Cole wasn't fooled for a minute. Reason's inner clock was ticking like a time bomb with mere seconds to spare and the whole thing could blow up in their faces at any given moment once again. Only this time Cole was both mentally and physically prepared if such an event were to happen.

Slowly Rachel rose off her chair and stepped closer to Reason. Her heart was in her eyes as she devoured her husband's familiar lean-muscled frame with longing, her face showing obvious, joyous relief that he was safe. She wanted to run to him, enfold him in her arms. She wanted to kiss him and love away his fears. Yet Randall had cautioned her to remain calm so as not to spook him unnecessarily. No sudden moves, he'd said. She was just so thankful he was alive; she'd do anything that was asked of her.

"Reason? It's Rachel, sweetheart," she said softly, peering up at him with the moist sea green eyes that Reason had fallen head over heels in love with five long years ago. "I'm so glad you're finally home. I've been so worried...."

She didn't know what she expected. Some sort of recognition? A light in his eyes meant only for her, no matter how slight? But there was no response. Nothing! She could have been talking to the air, for all the good it did.

A stifled sob caught at the base of Rachel's throat. She was beside herself in misery. How could he not remember her, after all they'd meant to each other? Randall's warning rang in her ears, and she peered over her shoulder at Reason's older brother. He had already spoken at length to her, preparing her for Reason's insufferable reaction to anything and any one. Or lack of it. But still, witnessing his deliberate withdrawal from the entire world, first-hand was hard for her to stomach. When Randall gave her an encouraging nod, she bravely squared her small shoulders, swallowed her pride, and tried again.

"Reason? Can you look at me?"

When there was no answer, she raised both hands and, tucking the tips of her fingers lightly beneath his jaw, gently guided his head upwards just high enough so she could meet his direct gaze. For a split-second she had his undivided attention. Once again, she peered into her husband's familiar black-lashed, pale blue "wolf's" eyes she had once laughingly called them, before he jerked his head away from her touch to stare at the far wall behind her. But he wasn't fast enough to avoid her seeing the bottomless depths of despair contained within the unfocused, haunted eyes of a stranger. A man whose deep-seated emotions were now kept walled-up tight, imprisoned under lock and key, by his own uniquely elaborate design.

"Reason, I love you," she stated simply. "I always have. And I always will."

Cole shifted his stance, hating to watch Rachel's ravaged heart being slowly torn in two, and feeling about as necessary as a fifth wheel on a broken-down abandoned old wagon. Yet he was uneasy about leaving Reason alone with Rachel, even for a minute, and refused to let go of his arm. If anything, his grip had tightened in a silent warning to the man beside him to act carefully, far within the bounds of common decency. For there was no telling what Reason would do when emotions ran high, and neither he nor Randall wanted to place Rachel in jeopardy.

So he stayed put. But damn, if she didn't knock Reason off his hinges, he doubted anything would. For Rachel was a beautiful woman with long wavy auburn hair that seemed to outshine the most vibrant sunset. The cute little pixie face. And if Reason didn't come to his senses after looking straight into her crying eyes, Cole was afraid nothing ever would.

But Reason wasn't seeing any of this. He was lost in his own solitary world where every man, woman, child, and even a few select four-legged critters were something to be feared and avoided at all cost. So he stood there, sullen and silent, inwardly cringing from the tightening grip on his arm, staring beyond the woman at a painting nailed to the wall of a lone stallion standing high on a hill with the wind in his face. Because he knew if he didn't, he'd be beaten within an inch of his life once again.

"It's not gonna work, Rachel," Cole finally said. "He's been like this for over a month now. And his memory hasn't improved all that much."

"Can't I at least take him home? Maybe there he'd have a chance...?" A glimmer of hope shone in her wide green eyes, while her lips trembled with fear of rejection, and Cole glanced over her head at Randall. He simply could not bring himself to utter the words that he knew would bring fresh tears to Rachel's eyes.

But Reason's brother had no such qualms.

"No!" Randall's booming voice thundered throughout the room as he rose to his feet from a chair behind her. "Not the way he is now. I have to agree with Cole. To him, we're all strangers, not to be trusted. Besides, he can be a bit unpredictable at times, to put it mildly." Randall shrugged, then his voice softened. "If he starts showing signs of progress farther down the road? Maybe then."

He had neglected to tell Rachel of Reason's recent battle with the window, and despite a wide strip of heavy gauze wrapped around his right palm as protection from further injury to his hand, Rachel didn't seem overly concerned with it. Randall was reluctant to inform her of the full extent of Reason's sometimes violent behavior.

"You have Jocelyn to consider, Rachel. Besides yourself."

Rachel swiveled to face her brother-in-law. "Reason would never hurt me, or the baby," she stated, her indignant green eyes flashing sparks at him. "Never in a million years."

"You don't know the man he is now." Randall wasn't backing down. "None of us do. We're all learning as we go. Maybe in a few weeks...?" He hesitated, because even he didn't think Reason's condition would improve that much in so short a time that he would entrust him to his three-year old niece's care.

But Rachel refused to give up. "What if I sit with him?" She glanced back to Cole for help, for Reason stood stiff and silent as a statue cast out of solid granite. "Could I see him alone? For a few minutes? Surely there's no harm...."

Cole was shaking his head before she even finished her

sentence. "That's not possible. Listen to Randall. He knows what he's sayin'."

Helpless tears once again flooded Rachel's eyes, as Cole glanced sheepishly away. This was exactly what he had been afraid of. He ground his teeth together in frustration. There simply had to be a way to make Rachel understand there was no getting through to the man in his current mental state. No matter what!

Then Rachel did something she would later regret. On impulse, she stood on tiptoe and gently brushed her lips against Reason's mouth in a quick intimate kiss. She only wanted to be close to him. She needed the warm physical contact, a simple reassurance that only he could give, that would show her he was still the gentle and caring man she had married.

But Reason jumped as if he'd been stung by a bee. In a hasty reflexive action, born of man's natural instinct for survival, he wrenched himself backwards so fast he would have tripped over his own feet and fallen if Cole hadn't had a sure grip on his arm. Then when he realized he was still bound to Cole's side like an anchor to a ship at port, his gaze flew about the room as if seeking the closest avenue of escape. His breathing became rapid in his chest and Cole knew the warning signs. He needed to get Reason away from Rachel, and fast! To take him back to his darkened room where he felt safe once more before Reason put thought into action and bolted for the door or nearest window, regardless whether it was left wide open or locked shut. Before Cole had to physically restrain Reason in whatever way was deemed necessary from doing himself, or anyone else that stood in his path, harm.

But Rachel didn't understand any of this. She gasped in shock, fear, and outright indignation. "What in the world? What does he mean?" Rachel was so flabbergasted at the thought of the man she loved shying so violently away from her embrace, she found it hard to put two coherent words together. She turned to Cole for an explanation. "Why he acts like...."

"Yeah. I know." Cole's voice was laden with deep regret as he began guiding the panic-stricken man towards the stairs. And rightly so, for weren't all Reason's problems due to his own neglect? If he had never let his partner leave Laramie alone carrying all that cash, Reason would have been home long ago where he belonged, enjoying his wife and family. Instead of being restrained here now, fighting for his very sanity, the muscles in his corded arm trembling beneath Cole's hand from the simple velvet touch of the same woman he had once fought valiantly for, and almost lost his life to possess.

What a cryin' shame! And still Cole hadn't a clue in damnation as to what tragic moment in time had broken Reason's wild, untamed spirit and made himself think he was less of a man.

Reason stumbled after Cole in a muddled haze of confusion. He was lost in his own private hell once more and couldn't seem to get a clear bearing on his surroundings. All he knew at the moment was that someone had dared to breach the stone wall of indifference he'd built so snugly around himself, threatening his fragile existence, his very sanity. And he wanted out of that room in the worst possible way. The walls were closing in on him again, and breathing became a chore he found increasingly difficult to perform.

"Don't take it personal, Rachel," Cole was saying as he coaxed and practically dragged a reluctant Reason up the first three steps before the man gained solid footing. "Just give him time. He'll come around."

But not this time. For, without warning, Reason lunged backwards against the restraining grip on his arm as if Cole was attempting to haul him straight into the depths of hell, instead of towards the safety of the small room above. Cole was jerked hard and almost lost his balance, when Reason twisted around and came to an abrupt halt, his back braced against the interior wall of the stairs as if for protection against an unseen assault from behind. His chest began heaving from both exertion and fear and the unbridled madness glinting in his pale blue eyes was disquieting for Cole to see.

"Steady there, Reason. Easy, man," Cole soothed, backing down a step to ease the tension on the inwardly quivering arm. "There's no cause to get yourself all worked up now."

Although Cole's grip still held firm, the treacherous rise of the stairs put Cole at a distinct disadvantage and gave Reason a much-needed edge if push came to shove. Cole knew it was only a matter of time before a struggle ensued and Reason wrenched himself free. And then more drastic measures would have to be called for.

As if Reason could read Cole's mind, he broke away from the

wall in a desperate bid for freedom and tried to bolt past the man beside him. But Cole had anticipated just such a reaction and a hard shove to his chest slammed Reason backwards before he could build up steam. Then Cole stepped in front of him, blocking his retreat.

"Sorry pal," he said with all sincerity, and as Reason glanced up in surprise, Cole reared back his right fist and swung. His bunched fist connected solidly with a weak spot he knew from experience lay along the lower left side of Reason's chiseled jaw.

A sickening thud of bone meeting bone filled the air as Reason's head snapped sideways. The force of the blow flung him hard against the wall once more, and he winced upon impact. Then a soft groan caught in his throat as he started to topple forward. Cole caught him in his arms, before he had a chance to fall.

Yeah, he'll come around all right, Cole swore to himself as he shifted his limp and unwieldy burden over one shoulder, then started up the staircase, ignoring Rachel's startled cry of outrage below.

Or die trying.

CHAPTER NINE

Weeks turned into months. The winter was a tough and grueling one for the Stirrup C, with snowdrifts reaching all the way up to the second floor of the house at times. Reason could have walked right out his bedroom window, more often than not, if the damn thing still hadn't been boarded up tight. And if he so chose.

Days were short and nights were long. The house rattled and shook from the prevailing squalls that constantly blew out of the north. Wind whistled eerily through the rafters of the barn. Cattle starved and many died from the extreme cold. The Stirrup C suffered, isolated from all neighboring ranches, lost in a vast sea of white.

Rachel's weekly visits drifted down to two, then one, a month. Finally, she stopped coming altogether. She was busy now, more than ever before. For she had taken over the sole running of the Stirrup C Bar, along with a few choice hands. The same ranch that Reason and Cole had worked their tails off over these past four years to maintain. And along with Jocelyn's daily care, she didn't have the time, energy, or desire to brave the storms and travel through a snow-white world for twenty odd miles, just to speak to a man that didn't even know she was there.

And Reason remained the same.

Spring brought welcome relief from the harsh, cold, terrible weather of the past few months. And somehow they all managed to squeak through the winter without experiencing the cruel financial setback that Randall had previously anticipated.

So it was natural that during one mild spring day in early April, Cole grew restless. He was bone-weary tired of playing nursemaid to a man that couldn't look him directly in the eyes without blinking in mindless confusion based on all-consuming fear. Nor even speak his name out loud. Cole's patience had finally come to an end.

Early that morning he sent a man into town to order a new pane for the broken window, then decided to check the newborn calves on the upper forty, figuring both he and Reason could stand a welcome taste of freedom, no matter how brief. After all, hadn't they both earned a day off?

Throughout the long, hard-won winter, Reason had remained stoically silent and subdued, mechanically obeying the orders Cole was still forced to give. That single panic-stricken incident on the stairs last year had seemed to be the last, and hope flared anew in Cole's chest. Maybe a brisk canter would clear the remaining cobwebs from his brain, Cole mused, as he saddled the two horses in the barn. Couldn't hurt. Could it?

Reason still wouldn't set foot within half a yard of Satan, and Cole now had the sole responsibility of the temperamental stallion's care. Although Cole hadn't ridden the black since the day he'd brought Reason home last summer, in fact, no one had since no other man on the ranch would stray within six feet of him, he knew Reason in his right mind could handle the horse with ridiculous ease. And Cole figured even Satan would benefit from a good hard run.

Reason was standing on the porch where he had been instructed to wait alongside his brother, staring blankly beyond the yard towards the distant tree-lined horizon, when Cole led the two horses up to the hitching rail.

"All set." Cole grinned up at the two men.

"You sure this is wise?" Randall was the only one on the porch who acknowledged Cole's presence and both men knew his fears were well grounded. "He's never strolled farther than the barn since you've been back," Randall argued. "Maybe you should wait a few weeks longer. At least until he shows some sign of...." He shrugged. "Normalcy?"

"It's been almost a year." Cole's grin vanished in an instant. "Somethin's gotta give, sooner or later." A silent challenge blazed like wildfire within his hard amber eyes. "I'd rather it be sooner." He jerked his head at the waiting animals. "Mount up, Reason. Your horse is waitin'."

Reason's impassive pale gaze slid toward the black stallion.

He hesitated, and without a word spoken, Cole could sense his inner withdrawal. It was nothing a stranger would notice, just a slight lowering of his head beneath the dark brim of his newly purchased black Stetson, a ragged in-drawn breath, a subtle sinking shift of weight to his boot heels. If someone had shouted "Boo" to him at the moment, Cole wasn't sure which the man would do; take off running for parts unknown, or throw himself backwards against the shiplap boards of the house in fear. Regardless of what he'd just said to Randall, Cole didn't want to push Reason beyond his endurance.

"Aw hell." Without another word, Cole turned towards Satan and swung into the saddle, forgetting for the moment the horse's intolerance of man in general.

Big mistake!

Satan hadn't carried a man on his back for over nine months. And the one that dared to sit his saddle now was not the man that had painstakingly trained him, nor earned his undying trust throughout the years they had known one another. Although the stallion had carried this man once at his master's command, that fact had no bearing on this instance. And as Cole's left foot found the stirrup and his body settled in the saddle, the horse's ears flattened against his neck. His lips pulled back in a snarl and every muscle in the powerful body bunched beneath him. Before Cole realized his error and could leap off to safety, Satan threw up his head and reared with a trumpeting squeal of outrage.

Cole swore as the horse went up, his thighs automatically tightening against the animal's sides. He leaned forward, trying to maintain his balance as the horse's menacing hooves pawed at the sky, battling an unseen enemy. Then the horse leaped into the air as if he'd sprouted wings.

Air rushed between Cole and the saddle as the black's head disappeared from immediate view, and his powerful body came back to earth with a spine-snapping jolt on all four iron-shod hooves. Cole's jaw clenched upon impact, his neck almost snapping clear off his shoulders. The horse's nose barely missed the ground, his head tucking between his forelegs as he gave one short hop and his back end raised to the sky.

Choking dust flew up around them. Cole's body was thrown backwards, his head banging against Satan's muscular haunches as if his spine had turned into jelly. Gritting his teeth, he hauled uselessly on the reins as the stallion came down hard, the sleek back humping with rage, his satiny sides heaving, glistening with sweat. The horse then whirled in a circle, executing a few short neck-breaking, crow-hopping jumps that almost bucked Cole right out of the saddle.

Before he had a chance to catch his wind and regain his seat, the black's head went up again. This time Satan's upper body twisted in mid-air. He screamed his fury, dancing backwards on hind legs, trying to rid himself, in every possible way, of the annoying man on his back.

Cole's heart leaped to his throat. Fearing disaster he grabbed for the horn, afraid they were both going over backwards. The ground rushed up in a dizzy wall before him. The stallion's labored breathing rasped in his ears. He knew with all certainty he was going to die beneath this wild, locoed horse. This wasn't just a simple battle of wits and will between horse and rider. This stallion was battling to the death.

Snatching at the mane blinding his eyes with a free hand, Cole set his teeth, preparing for the worst, when the shrill, piercing, ear-splitting whistle shattered the dust-filled air. He felt the enraged stallion's body shudder between his knees while still poised precarious in mid-air. And time crawled to a halt as Cole knew it.

Then as if in a whiskey-induced dream, the horse dropped gracefully back to earth. He shook his feathery mane once, pranced sideways with a few mincing steps and blew hard before coming to a complete standstill. He pawed at the ground churned beneath his hooves in a silent form of rebellion, then all aggressive motion ceased as if the death-defying frenzied battle for supremacy between man and beast had never been.

"Son-of-a-bitch!" Air left Cole's lungs in a rush. His entire body trembled. It had all happened so fast, he didn't have time to think. Or breathe! The hand that clutched the saddle horn, along with the fingers that were twisted in Satan's mane, shook from fright. His taut knees quivered like dry leaves in a stiff wind against the broad sides of the sedated horse. Sweat streaked his face, dampened the shirt on his back. He had forgotten in his haste, his unhealthy fear of the animal beneath him and the dangerous, fickle temperament of the horse itself.

He raised a shaky arm to wipe the beads of perspiration dotting his upper lip and trickling down his clean-shaven cheeks. That had been too damn close. If this horse had gone over backwards to rid himself of the unlucky rider, Cole's chest would have been crushed to death by the saddle horn along with the animal's powerful weight in a lightning instant. There would have been no time to escape. He would have died, plain and simple. It was the whistle that stopped him.

Cole lifted his gaze to the two men standing on the porch. Reason hadn't moved one inch in any direction to Cole's eyes. In fact, he was still peering at the horse from under the low brim of his hat. Yet Randall had swiveled halfway around and was eyeballing his brother in surprise.

"Was that him?" Cole's voice was shaky and weak. For only Reason in his right mind, or not, could draw such a prompt and carefully executed response from that black whirling nightmare just as he had nine months ago.

Randall's face seemed paler than before, yet he nodded just once, in awe of his brother's subtle, yet timely, interference. Then glanced over at Cole, his brown eyes wide with surprise.

"It sure as hell wasn't me."

The black shifted beneath Cole and began chewing at the bit between his teeth. He pawed restlessly at the ground. The stallion was ready to leave. This time he was giving the man on his back due warning, and Cole didn't care to antagonize the animal a minute longer than necessary.

"Let's go, Reason." Somehow those words didn't come out with the force Cole intended, and not one breath of air stirred between the two men standing on the porch. He cleared his throat in an attempt to sound more decisive.

"Mount up!"

And this time as if he'd been expecting such a command, Reason stepped down off the porch. With the grace of a mountain cat, he moved up to the bay gelding, grabbed onto the pommel with both hands and, without using the stirrup, leaped into the saddle. Then he picked up the reins and glanced over at Cole as if awaiting further orders.

As Cole reined Satan around and cantered towards the meadow, Reason sent his horse after him.

The ride out to the open range was a strained and silent one. Cole's frazzled nerves had finally abated and he was wondering whether the shrill whistle that had resulted in saving his life was geared to protect the raging horse beneath him, or the unsuspecting rider on its back. Maybe both? Maybe neither. Had it been a purely automatic response to a life-threatening situation? One that had overruled caution along with mind-numbing fear? Or a deliberately calculated one.

Reason wasn't talking and Cole wondered if he even remembered how. He was so used to Reason's silences he'd probably fall out of the saddle right now if the man uttered a simple sound. That's why the whistle had thrown him and Randall for such a loop. Cole shook his head in disgust. It must have been an instinctive gut reaction. Just like the last time at the cabin in the mountains. There was no other excuse for it.

Both men drew up their mounts on a low ridge overlooking a wide grassy stretch of undulating prairie. The black snorted beneath him, reared up slightly, then came back down as if he suddenly remembered he'd be chastised for bad behavior once again if he didn't toe the line. In a fit of frustration, the stallion shook his feathery mane then danced in place, wanting to run so badly Cole could taste it.

"Race you to the tree yonder?" Cole grinned playfully as he peered over at Reason. Then he shook his head in despair. When would he ever learn? Reason's pale blue gaze was blank, empty. He was lost in his own private world once again, oblivious of the man riding beside him.

Reaching upwards with a free hand, he whipped off his black Stetson and, leaning sideways in the saddle, whacked Reason's horse hard on the rump. The bay bolted forward, but only when he was halfway down the hill, did Cole loosen the reins and nudge Satan with the worn-down heels of his boots.

Satan leaped as if shot out of a cannon. He practically slid down the hill on his haunches before finally settling into a smooth striding gallop at the bottom that easily overtook the other horse and passed him by like a whirlwind.

Cole gave Satan his head. He was enjoying himself to no end. After being cooped up all winter long, caring for a man that existed only in body rather than spirit, the mild spring breeze felt like a long-lost lover's silky caress on his face. A chuckle of pure joy sounded from his throat. This brief burst of freedom was an elusive, tricky thing meant to be savored to the fullest. Even the horse knew it.

The stallion's powerful muscles rolled smoothly, effortlessly, like a well-oiled machine beneath him; thunderous hooves beat a pounding rhythmic melody against the hard valley floor. Harsh rasping sounds caused by rapidly pumping lungs filled his ears. The long black feathery mane stung Cole's face like a whip as he leaned slightly forward over the thick muscular neck, then glanced over his shoulder at the dark-clad rider far behind. Satan was running for all he was worth, while Reason's leggy bay was following at a slower, more controlled pace.

Cole grinned, reveling in the tightly bunched power between his legs; the wind beating against his face, tugging at the rolled brim of his hat. He was thinking that for once in his life he was going to beat Reason at a horserace when, without warning the black stallion stumbled, completely disappearing from beneath him. The next thing Cole knew he was catapulting through the air, executing a perfect heels-over-head somersault any daredevil would have been proud of. But what goes up, must come down.

All too soon the ground rushed up to meet him without mercy, and he landed hard on his back in the dirt with a stunning jolt to his spine. Every bone and nerve ending in his body trembled upon impact. His jaw clenched and his teeth rattled as his head bounced cruelly against the ground. A harsh grunt of surprise flew from his throat as he slid in the dust a few more inches. And then all was still.

For a brief moment, Cole laid there, stunned into silence, gasping for breath, the wind knocked completely out of his lungs and wondering if he'd broken every bone in his body. Eventually his heart slowed to a calmer, normal rhythm and the rapidly whirling sky overhead came into focus once again. With a great deal of caution, he rolled slowly to his belly and, gathering his knees beneath him, climbed stiffly to his feet. A grimace of pain creased his face as he gently brushed the dust off his clothes with both hands, then bent to pick up his hat from the ground and jam it securely on his head. His back ached maddeningly from the fall, but as he flexed his shoulders and straightened his spine, he found that no major harm had been done except for a few scattered bruises and a badly crushed ego. However when his eyes shifted towards the black horse, he was surprised to see Reason in a crouch before the now docile animal, carefully probing the stallion's left foreleg with gentle, knowing hands.

"How is he?" Cole asked in an unthinking, automatic query as he limped cautiously near the troublesome pair.

Reason's hands abruptly left the horse. He rested his elbows on bent knees as if actually considering an answer. Then finally rose to his full five-foot ten-inch height, his gaze never leaving the black stallion standing before him.

"You could have lamed him for life," he growled low in his throat.

Cole stared at him, stunned, for a full speechless minute. This was the first time Reason had put more than two coherent words together to make one complete sentence since Cole had brought him home last year. Was he finally starting to come around?

"Would you care if I had?"

Reason's pale blue eyes gradually shifted to face Cole, and what he saw chilled him to the bone. He had all he could do just to stand there, resisting the impulse to flinch backwards to relative safety, away from the bottomless blue well of hate Cole saw aimed at him. Then, as if a shutter slammed shut on all feelings, Reason blinked twice and the blank, uncaring stare was back as if it had never left at all.

But Cole was shaken to the core of his soul. He kept forgetting that Reason's mind was a tenuous thing that could snap at any given moment, and instead of handling him like the demented man that he was, Cole had been guilty of treating him as an equal. A simple act of kindness could prove to be a fatal mistake one day if Reason happened to grab a weapon of some kind and turn on him like a rabid dog, biting the hand that fed him. He'd have to remember to be more careful around the man in the future. There was no telling how Reason would react outside the limited confines of the small, square room he was used to.

Swallowing his anxiety, Cole bent down and carefully examined the stallion's foreleg. The pastern was swollen and the horse flinched when he touched it, but nothing was broken or permanently damaged to Cole's mind. Nevertheless, the animal couldn't be ridden for a while.

Cole would have to walk back.

And if he had to walk, Reason would too.

CHAPTER TEN

About three miles out, Cole called a halt. He was hot, winded, dusty, and foot-sore as Satan. Too weary to walk further, he plunked himself down to the ground, placed his hat carefully on a flat rock, then stretched his lean, broad-shouldered body flat-out against the newly-greening prairie grass that grew thick as a carpet beneath his back and blew a heavy sigh of relief.

"These legs ain't made for walkin' ten miles at a clip," he grumbled out loud, mainly for his own benefit, for no one else was listening.

Reason just stood there, staring off into space, until Cole squinted up at him.

"Sit, dammit! We're not goin' to be here all day. Might as well take advantage of a little rest when we can."

Reason hunkered down, but he didn't sit. And he didn't appear a bit winded either. Maybe he didn't have sense enough to feel tired.

The hell with him. Cole stretched his arms up over his head, yawned widely, and gradually closed his eyes. He figured he'd rest for a minute. The warmth of the sun felt good on his face after being cooped up in the house half the winter. Why if he didn't watch out he could fall asleep as easy as….

A slight tug at his holster brought him instantly awake. He blinked twice, blinded by the sun, his brain dulled and muddled by sleep. Automatically he raised a hand to shield his eyes, then started to rise to his feet.

"Don't move!" a chilling voice above him said.

Cole froze. Afraid his worst nightmare had come true, that Reason finally found a gun and turned on him with the calculated intent to kill, he casually lowered his arm and summoned the courage to glance up.

Just as he feared. Reason's cold, menacing form stood close to his side with the black bore of a pistol aimed straight at his chest. Cole let his shoulders drop back to the ground.

"Easy, Reason," he whispered, barely recognizing his own fear-choked voice. Then swallowed hard. One slight squeeze of that trigger and Cole was a dead man. Mentally he cursed himself six times a fool. Knowing the man's deadly prowess with a six-gun, he had stupidly fallen asleep when his very existence depended on staying awake. And this time he might have to pay the price for his negligence with his life.

Not willing to rile the unstable man further at the moment, Cole forced a shaky grin. "You don't want to shoot me, do ya?"

"Take it off."

"What...?"

Reason gestured impatiently with the pistol as if he was through talking and Cole's throat closed up in dread, unsure of exactly what article of clothing he was expected to shed. To make sure he got it right, he figured he'd shuck every damn thing he owned. With due haste, his fingers started fumbling with the wooden buttons on his shirt.

"Not that. The gun belt." That ice-blue murderous look was in Reason's eyes once again.

Both his hands dropped lower to unbuckle the metal clasp secured about his waist, then Cole bent a knee so he could reach the rawhide thong tied around his thigh without having to rise any farther off the ground than he had to. When the gun belt was free, he lowered his shoulders back to the grass and rested his hands, palms up, against the ground, afraid to move an inch further without explicit orders to do so. For he was still lying half over the holster. And the cold bore of the pistol was still centered dead on his chest.

"Go easy with that thing, will ya?" Cole's throat was tight as he spoke. For Reason had a clenched fist wrapped around the butt of the gun, and Cole was afraid that with just a tiny bit more pressure the revolver would explode right in his face.

"Get up and move over there." Once again, Reason made a quick, jerky gesture with the revolver.

Cole did as he was bid.

Cautiously, Reason bent down, picked up the holster, and slung the heavy belt over his left shoulder. Then he just stood there as if he had all the time in the world, the pistol still aimed dead center at Cole's chest.

Cole swallowed hard. One wrong move on his part and it would be all over. Is that what Reason was waiting for? For Cole to jump him, forgetting for the moment of the loaded six-gun gripped in his hand? If so, then he'd have a long wait coming. There was no way any man would be that stupid.

Slowly he raised his hands in the air, palms out.

"I'm unarmed, Reason. I'm no threat to you."

Reason squinted at Cole as if seeing him for the first time.

"Just who the hell are you," he demanded harshly.

Cole sucked in a deep breath. Was he kidding? From the look on his face, he was dead serious.

"You know me, Reason. I'm Cole…Dansing. We rode together for years. We're buddies. Remember?"

Reason determinedly shook his head. "You're wrong. I don't know you." The pale blue eyes that peered from beneath the low brim of his black Stetson hat were cold as a frosty morning in February; his normally husky voice, flat as a wooden board.

Cole forced a small grin. "Sure you do. You were best man at my wedding, four years ago. Don't tell me you don't.…"

"Shut up!"

Cole's breath held. Reason was going to kill him now, Cole was sure of it. Cole could read death in the pale blue eyes staring right through him clear as the bold black print on the pages of an open book. And with no weapon at hand, he didn't stand a chance in hell to come out of this mess alive. If only Reason would give him a chance to explain.

Slowly he began to lower his arms to his sides.

"Reason, you have to let me.…"

"Don't move!" The command was short and crisp.

Cole froze in position once again. "I only want.…"

Reason thumbed back the hammer with practiced ease.

"You don't listen worth a damn."

Cole went rigid with fear. His heart thudded wildly in his ears. This was it then. Just one bullet in the right place was all it would take.…

Then he heard it.

The deadly hiss of a coiled rattler ready to strike sounded loud in his ears. Close. Too damn close to be healthy.

Without moving his head more than a fraction of an inch, his eyes slowly shifted towards the direction of the gut-wrenching sound. And there in the tall grass, not two feet from the run-down heel of his left boot, sat the snake.

Cole broke out in a cold sweat. He swallowed hard and glanced back at the man standing still and silent before him. What was he waiting for? Why didn't he just shoot the damn thing?

Then Reason smiled, if you could call it that.

"Scared?"

Cole couldn't move a muscle for fear the snake would strike out in defense of its own territory and sink its poisonous fangs deep into the corded muscles of his left leg. And although he opened his mouth to speak, with the intent to plead his case and beg for mercy, his throat refused to form words for that very same reason.

"Good." Reason finally said, yet still made no move to help him.

The sun beat down unmercifully on the two men that stood facing each other squarely in the grassy meadow. Sweat dripped down the sides of Cole's face from beneath the rolled brim of his Stetson. His mouth grew dry as the hot desert sands of New Mexico. The beat of his own heart pulsed loudly in his ears. His hands started to grow numb from the effort of keeping them raised for so long a time. And still the deadly hiss of the rattler sang loudly in his ears.

He didn't know which was worse. Have Reason shoot him here and now? Or let the deadly rattler take a bite out of him for a noonday snack.

Neither man moved so much as an inch. Agonizing minutes ticked slowly by until panic settled a firm hold in Cole's chest and the thought of turning tail and running became the ideal solution to his mind. Yet before he could act on his decision, the menacing rattle gradually dissipated, and then ceased altogether. Slowly the snake uncoiled its long, mottled body and continued on its winding path until the deadly triangular head came flush up against the sole of Cole's left boot. There it hesitated, the forked tongue darting in and out of its mouth with all due haste.

Cole held his breath. Running was now out of the question. Any minute now the snake would attack. Or else Reason would put a bullet through his chest. Or maybe both. Either way he couldn't win to save his life.

Reason's eyes glittered like pale shards of chipped ice. The hand that held the gun was steady as a rock, while Cole's insides were steadily turning to mush. He let his breath out slowly, afraid he was going to turn blue and pass clear out. Slowly he inhaled, as the snake decided to continue on its merry way. It slithered over one trail-dusty boot then, without pause, crawled right over the other. Within seconds the rattler had disappeared into the tall thick grass on Cole's right.

Cole breathed a heavy sigh of relief. That tense, nerve-wracking moment had been the closest he'd ever come to getting snake bit in his entire life. Without thinking, his hands dropped low to his sides.

"I didn't say to move yet!"

Cole's eyes snapped up to Reason's stern and unforgiving face. His nerves were already stretched taut from the incident with the rattler and he was in no mood to be subtle.

"Shoot and be damned, if you want to see me dead that bad," Cole shouted, without an ounce of caution. "Just do it and be quick about it."

The sudden blast of the pistol made Cole jerk hard. Instinctively he threw an arm up over his face, the other across his chest for protection against an unseen bullet, then gasped aloud in shock and fear. My God, when would he ever learn to keep his mouth shut, he chastised himself. Who knew Reason was actually crazy enough to shoot!

But when minutes passed, the smoke cleared and no further shots were fired, Cole gradually lowered his arms and straightened in surprise. He felt no pain, saw no blood staining his clothes red, and discovered a lead bullet hadn't found him after all. Yet Reason still had the barrel of the gun aimed straight at him.

Cole's eyes grew round in confusion and he didn't understand at first when Reason said in that same deadly voice, "There were two of them."

"Two...what?" he said, thoroughly shaken. Then he

remembered the snake. When he jerked his head to the left, he saw what was left of the second rattler that never had time to strike.

"I...I didn't know," he stammered, secretly pleased that Reason had acted in a coldly deliberate, though annoying way, simply to save him from harm. Maybe there was hope for him yet! But it was still too soon to tell, for Cole knew he was still neck deep in trouble as long as Reason still had his revolver trained point-blank on his chest.

"I just want to know one thing," Reason said in that same flat, deadly voice as before.

Cole's head bobbed in a brief, eager-to-please nod.

"Sure, shoot!" Bad choice of words, Cole thought to himself. Reason might take him literally. "I mean, go on," he corrected himself.

"You already told me who you are. Now just who the hell am I?"

CHAPTER ELEVEN

So Cole told him all he knew. From the moment he first laid eyes on Reason, an angry young man with a chip on his shoulder caught in the act of rustling his half-brother Randall's cattle six long years ago, all the way to the present. Where despite much animosity among the ranch hands at the start, he gradually rose in the ranks of the Stirrup C hierarchy to become a respected and valuable addition to the Ranch. Of his close-knit relationship with his brother, and finally himself. He deliberately left out the part about his wife, Rachel, and daughter Jocelyn, for he was afraid too much information at this time might be more than his mind could handle.

"And that's the story, Reason. Any questions?"

Cole was hunkered down in the dirt as he spoke, while Reason remained standing, yet the bore of the pistol hadn't once shifted away from Cole's chest. It was just tilted at a sharper angle now.

"You're lying."

Cole's heart skipped a beat. He wondered if Reason heard half of what had just taken him close to thirty minutes to relate. His credibility, or lack of it, could very well mean his life.

"Why do you say that? What the hell reason would I have to lie?"

"Maybe so I don't kill you, here and now?"

Soft-spoken words, yet menacing in their context. Unconsciously, Cole sucked in a deep breath, then let the air out slowly. Steady there, he warned himself sternly. Don't panic just yet. Some tiny thread of past history had to have pierced through the fog of Reason's brain, even though the man refused to acknowledge a single thing. He couldn't be that dense. Could he?

"Are you going to shoot me, Reason?"

Reason grinned without mirth.

"Maybe."

The distant thudding sound of rapidly approaching hooves drumming rhythmically on hard-packed soil, made Cole slowly rise to his feet and glance over Reason's right shoulder. Three horsemen were heading their way at a hell-bent clip. Stirrup C wranglers. In a moment they'd be right on top of them, while Reason seemed not to hear them at all.

"Don't do it, Reason. I'm not worth hangin' for."

"Says you."

The three horsemen pulled their lathered, heaving mounts up short, directly behind Reason. Two men grabbed for their rifles secured on their saddles, while a third reached for the revolver at his hip.

In an effort to avoid gunplay, Cole held up both hands, palms out.

"Go easy, boys. No sense gettin' riled now. This can't be as bad as it looks."

Reason never once turned, or acknowledged the deadly line of armed riders behind him in any way, shape, or form. One would think upon looking at him, that he was stone-cold deaf.

"You got a problem here, Cole?" The red-headed fellow named Curly said, sizing up the tense situation as he shifted the bore of his revolver to aim high at Reason's right shoulder. Within the blink of an eye, the other wranglers followed suit. For no man there stood a chance in hell if Reason suddenly decided to turn around and make a fair fight of it. They were cow-hands, not gunslingers, and they were all too consciously aware of that fact.

"No...," Cole started to say. But Reason's spine had gone rigid as a tent pole at the sound of another man's voice echoing so close behind him. His pale blue eyes glazed over with remembered pain and the gun hand that was rock steady only seconds before, now started to tremble. Cole knew he had lost his friend to a haunting memory from the past once again.

"Now lookit here, Reason," Curly broke in, planning on talking some sense into the man before he was forced to fire, and perhaps kill, the boss's younger brother. "The boys and me know you're not quite right in the head. And we sure as hell don't want to shoot you if we don't have to. So what do you say? Suppose you just toss that pistol you have in your hand to the dirt and we can all ride home together, safe and sound."

Reason didn't move. He seemed frozen in a distant time and place. Then ever so slowly, his slightly unfocused, pale blue wolf's eyes sought out Cole. He seemed to be waiting for something. For what? A word? A gesture? Then Cole knew.

"Drop the gun, Reason!" Cole pointed straight to the ground. "Drop it now!"

As if the revolver had bit him in the hand, Reason's fingers let loose their fierce grip. The revolver dropped harmlessly to the ground with a dull thud while his right arm fell limp to his side. And there he stood, tame as a housecat with eyes dull as dishwater, acting as if he'd been placed in front of a heavily armed squad of men with the order to "fire" ringing loudly in his ears.

Cole breathed a grateful sigh of relief. If Randall's men hadn't shown up when they did, who knew what locoed action Reason might have taken.

With a good degree of caution, Cole stepped up to the unnaturally subdued man. Slowly he bent to pick up the fallen revolver then straightening, casually slipped the gun belt off Reason's unresisting shoulder.

Only when he had the belt buckled around his own waist, with the pistol lodged firmly in the holster, did Cole glance at Reason and force a grim smile.

"Let's go home, shall we?"

CHAPTER TWELVE

Rachel rode over the next day, but she didn't stay long. It was hard for her, she said, seeing Reason so cold and distant. And now she limited her visits to the Stirrup C to once a month by choice, rather than necessity.

Cole studied Reason from the top porch step. He was lounging in a chair in the corner, his favorite resting spot of late, staring at the same line of trees that he did every day. There was still no shred of recognition in the man for anyone, or anything, that dared to exist around him. Yet he had protected Cole from harm when he whistled the stallion down yesterday and then, hours later, shot the rattlesnake. He'd seemed concerned when Satan slipped on a rock and went down.

The horse was doing fine, but Reason still wasn't. And Cole didn't fool himself for a minute. Reason could have killed him easily out on the range yesterday, without blinking an eye. And he very well might have in his present state of mind if Curly and the boys hadn't ridden up when they did.

Reason had killed men before. Had even made a living from it by hiring out his gun shortly after the War Between the States to ranchers bombarded by rustlers and outlaws, or small spreads trying to make a stand against the larger ones that wanted to swallow them whole.

Cole knew his life story even if he hadn't known the man at the time. He knew Reason could kill at the drop of a hat. Knew he could put the eye out of a rabbit on the run at fifty yards. Had seen him in action, triumphing with practiced ease over worthy rivals more times than he cared to count. And had felt his own share of Reason's punishing bullets when the two men disagreed over some monumental difference of opinion.

But now Reason didn't seem to know Cole from a hole in the ground. Any more than he knew himself.

Once again Cole wondered what on God's green earth could have happened to him that would have shattered his defenses so drastically and destroyed all sense of trust and common decency in his fellow man. Reason had been his carefree, confident self when Cole had last seen him in Laramie, riding out of town eager to get home to his ranch and family. And now look at him. He was a mere shell of a man, a cringing shadow of his former self. And a dangerous one at that.

His memory drifted back to the day he found Reason at the trapper's run-down shack. Broken and beaten. A complete role reversal of the brazen, fearless man he once had been. What tragic chain of events could possibly have happened to make him so?

A picture of the two burly mountain men flashed through Cole's mind and his gut clenched in mindless hate mixed with pure disgust. They'd lied to him right from the start. *Never seen him,* they'd said. *He'd died and we buried him out yonder.* Only when Cole threatened to unleash an army of ranch hands with the express purpose of combing the mountain searching relentlessly for Reason until he was found, did they finally drag him out of the hovel.

Why, they hadn't planned on letting him go at all. What on earth were they keeping him around for? He was no good to anyone, even himself. He couldn't haul wood, shoot game, even tend to his own welfare in the state of mind Cole found him in. What did you do with a man like that?

Sport? The thought came unbidden to Cole's mind. Two lonely mountain men with only themselves as company? Ugly suspicions began forming in Cole's brain. Had they made Reason a plaything? A toy? With a bullet wound in his back, he would have been putty in their hands. Had Reason been manhandled? Sexually assaulted? Had Reason's mind simply shut down because he couldn't handle the thought, or the deed?

He recalled Reason's sudden fear of strangers. How he cringed whenever someone laid a hand on him, no matter how gently. The raw ugly bruises mottling his body in various shades of purple, pink, and yellow. Had he been beaten repeatedly when he'd tried to fight them off?

A scene flashed in Cole's mind of that day at the lake when he was determined Reason would bathe and he forced him to strip. How Reason swore in despair after Cole tackled him to the ground, and flung an arm up over his eyes as if in shame.

Cole choked down the bile that suddenly rose to his throat. Dear God! He prayed he was wrong.

Slowly Cole rose off the porch step. "Let's go for a walk," he said to the silent, staring man in the corner.

Reason's pale wolf's eyes slid his way. A sudden chill ran up Cole's spine. Every man he saw as a potential threat to his own well-being. Reason's mind had snapped long ago and this madness was his only way of protecting himself from further harm.

Cole was only beginning to scratch the surface of the bitter resentment and fear that coursed through the man. He knew he still had a long way to go with Reason, but time was on his side. And he hoped that one day Reason would feel comfortable enough with him to fill in the missing blanks.

With his old cat-like grace, Reason rose from the corner and as Cole left the porch, followed him down the stairs. Without breaking stride, Cole strolled a few feet ahead, leading him across the yard, through the trees, then down a slight incline towards a swift-running brook where on better days they used to take a day off from work and go trout fishing.

The bank of the river was a picturesque spot away from the harsh grind and daily routine of the backbreaking dusty chores of branding cattle and taming unruly mustangs fresh off the range. The water ran clear and had a soothing rushing sound to it. Sunlight filtered through the leaves of the cottonwood trees and left long shadows from the tall pines. A slight breeze shuffled the carpet of last year's autumn leaves and brown needles at their feet. Cole pointed towards a flat rock that Reason had often lounged against. It was time to break that impregnable wall of silence that Reason surrounded himself with and start anew.

"Sit!"

Reason obeyed without question. He sauntered towards the designated stone and cautiously sat down. Bracing the heel of his right boot against the boulder, he rested an elbow on his bent knee. But he sat stiffly, without the apparent ease of earlier times.

"Now talk!"

Reason's unsettling stare slid Cole's way. Then a slight sneer tugged at the corners of his lips and he slowly glanced back over the rippling water.

"Nice weather we're having."

"That's not what I want to hear."

As Reason glanced once more at Cole, the smug smile gradually died on his face, and abruptly his eyes shifted back to the river.

"We'll stay here all day if we have to," Cole warned. "And on into the next, and so on. We won't eat, we won't sleep…. You get the picture?"

There was no response. But Cole expected that and he wasn't giving up. This time he'd be more explicit.

"I want to know what the hell happened to you from the time you left Laramie until the day I found you in that trapper's shack."

There was a long silence. Then Reason cleared his throat and slowly said, "I don't remember."

"Now who's the one who's lyin'?"

A muscle bunched in Reason's jaw as if he were trying to keep a tight rein on an anger that was threatening to destroy his inherent self-control. Then slowly, Reason rose to his feet with the stealthy, menacing grace of a mountain cat and turned to face Cole.

"I told you I don't know."

Cole scoffed insolently, deliberately. He was undaunted by the subtle, dangerous challenge in Reason's loose-limbed demeanor. Besides, Reason was unarmed. And that made all the difference in the world.

"Oh yes you do! And we're not leavin' here until I know the whole story. Now spill it!"

Reason blinked in the face of Cole's determination. Gone was the man that handled him with kid gloves. The gloves were off. And Reason knew Cole could wring the truth out of him with his bare hands whether he was agreeable or not. His pale blue eyes widened in fear and his gaze became slightly unfocused.

"No!" He shook his head and began slowly backing up.

"Stay put!" Cole shouted. And Reason halted like a trained seal in a circus sideshow.

"Now you're gonna tell me exactly what happened," Cole demanded. "I know you took the long way home…."

"I...I figured it was safer."

"Someone tried to rob you."

"I never saw him."

"I did. What was left of him anyway, after the buzzards ate their fill. His horse had high-tailed it before I got there. He must have been the one carrying all the money."

"What money?"

"The five thousand dollars you left town with."

Reason remained silent. He didn't recall any cash on him at the time.

"You were shot in the back. Do you remember that?"

Reason winced in remembrance, then slowly nodded.

"What happened then?"

"I turned in the saddle and fired back."

Cole nodded. That would explain the dead man.

"Then what!"

"I don't know."

"Do you remember those two mountain men finding you?"

Reason squinted at him as if he were having trouble seeing. Then he finally said, "No, only one."

"One what?"

"Buck found me. I don't know when...." His voice trailed off soundlessly.

"So Buck found you and brought you back to the cabin?"

Reason swallowed hard and slowly nodded.

"Then what."

Reason's chest started heaving. He was having difficulty breathing.

"Nothing," he finally said. He shook his head twice and began backing up once more. "Nothing."

"Reason, stop!"

He halted dead in his tracks, but his breathing was erratic and harsh. His head lifted and he peered at Cole with eyes that were glazed with remembered pain.

"They took the bullet out, right?"

Reason nodded frantically. "Yeah, that's right."

"Were you conscious at the time?"

"No."

So far Cole hadn't come across anything that was useful in his assessment of Reason's tormented mind.

"Then what did they do to you?"

Reason was silent, but Cole was afraid that if he kept breathing like that Reason was going to pass out before he ever got his answers.

"You had tons of bruises covering your body. Did they hit you?"

Reason slowly nodded.

"With what."

"Fists. And whatever else they could find."

Cole winced at the thought. He hated putting Reason through this hell again in his mind. But he needed to find the cause of the man's despair before he could find an answer that would help Reason regain his former self.

"What about the rope burns on your wrists. Did they tie you up?" Cole knew they did, but he wanted to hear Reason admit the fact out loud.

Reason raised his hands and glanced down at the cuffs on his dark blue shirt as if he could still see the red welts on his skin. Then dropped them back to his sides.

"Yeah," he finally said.

"Why?"

There was no response.

"Answer me, Reason. Why did they rope your hands together?"

"So I couldn't fight back."

Cole was beginning to get a mental picture that was making him sick to his stomach.

"Then what did they do, Reason?" he said softly.

Reason's shoulders shivered of their own accord. He began backing up once more. His face was ashen and his eyes loomed large in his face. He appeared to be reenacting a terrible scene in his mind.

"Reason! Stay where you are!"

But this time Reason wasn't listening. He kept moving backwards until Cole lunged at him. Reason was in such a state of near panic that he didn't move fast enough and Cole caught him easily. He grabbed him firmly by both shoulders, so he wouldn't slip away. Then shook him until he had his undivided attention.

"Now talk! Tell me, dammit! Did they touch you wrong? Is that what this is all about?"

Reason choked. Blindly he reached out his hands to brush Cole off, but he couldn't budge the strong arms holding him. A violent shudder wracked his frame. Cole could feel his shoulders quaking beneath his hands. Then he moaned deep in his throat and ducked his head to his chest as if he would be struck.

"God no! Please don't. Please...."

Cole released him as if he suddenly caught fire, and Reason dropped straight to his knees in the dirt. As if he were protecting himself from attack, he bent at the waist and curled his upper body in a tight ball at Cole's feet.

"No, don't..." he groaned softly. "Not again. Please... dammit... please."

Cole turned away, and this time Cole was the one staring across the water with unseeing eyes. His stomach flipped over with nausea as if he had chowed down on spoiled meat and he was afraid he was going to vomit. Then, when he couldn't stand Reason's pleas for mercy any longer, he dropped to his knees at the water's rippling edge and threw up his breakfast.

"Reason! Reason! Look up! It's Cole!" Reason was still hunched over his knees in the dirt. Though his body continued to shake, his gut-wrenching cries for mercy had long ceased. His breathing was still ragged and shallow, but he seemed to be coming out of it.

Inch by slow inch the rolled brim of his black Stetson lifted high enough for Reason to meet Cole, braced on one knee, at eye level.

"Who?" he asked.

Cole almost broke down.

Reason's keen wolf's eyes were glazed with pain and suffering. A thin trail of wetness trickled down both cheeks. His right-hand trembled as he reached up to swipe at his stinging red-rimmed eyes.

"Cole. Your partner. Your buddy. Your friend!"

Reason ducked his head low once again.

"I don't have any friends." He spoke as if Cole was lying to him. Could those two mountain men once have insinuated the very same thing to him?

He tried again. "Nobody's gonna hurt you anymore, Reason. I swear. Look at me."

When Reason refused, he repeated the command.

"Look at me!"

Slowly Reason lifted his head once more. Suspicion was now foremost in his pale blue gaze, but at least he was thinking again.

"Do you believe me?"

Reason's lips curled in the familiar sneer that he'd been wearing lately whenever he was spoken to.

"Like hell I do."

Cole rose to his feet. It was hard having a conversation with a man on your knees.

"Get up!"

Reason blinked in surprise. As if he was wondering what the hell he was doing kneeling on the hard cold ground anyway. Slowly he rose to his full five-foot ten-inch height.

The stream gurgled peacefully beside them. A gray squirrel chattered from a low branch above. A slight breeze billowed the sleeves of Reason's dark blue chambray shirt and rustled the leaves at his feet.

"Do you recall what just happened here?" Cole voiced his fears out loud. A change had taken place in Reason's mind once again when Cole wasn't looking. And he wasn't sure just what Reason remembered of it all.

"Should I?"

Cole drew in a deep breath. This was worse than he thought. Reason had purposely locked away all memory deep inside his brain and thrown away the key. Only when he was forced to remember, did all the misery and suffering he received at the trapper's hands come to the surface. And, although Cole knew Reason would never be the man he once was unless he came to terms with it, Cole was reluctant to force his hand once more.

"No," Cole finally said. "It wasn't all that important."

CHAPTER THIRTEEN

The days grew warmer. Randall was having trouble meeting the mortgage once again and needed the sale of cattle bound for market desperately. And he needed every available hand working the remaining herd while a large group of men took the yearlings and castrated steers east to the stockyards in Abilene.

Cole was glad to oblige and managed to drag Reason along on every backbreaking chore he was elected by Randall to perform, for he was reluctant to leave him in another man's care for long. He could see the fear leap to the pale blue eyes, the wariness and distrust tensing his spine, whenever another fellow unwittingly ventured too close. And now that he suspected the true nature of Reason's distress, Cole could well understand his abhorrent reaction to the rest of the world in general.

Yet, despite a few minor setbacks, Reason did well around the cattle. Instinct and routine replaced fear in Reason's vacant mind and hard work seemed a healing refuge. Cole never had to ask twice when he assigned Reason an unpleasant task, or difficult maneuver, and Reason was quick to collect the calves in the brakes when ordered to do so.

Although the two men worked side by side during the long daylight hours, there was no shred of the familiar camaraderie they once shared. No laughter, no neighborly slap on the back for a job well done. And very little conversation sallied back and forth between either men.

Cole gave the orders. And Reason obeyed. It was as simple as that.

Until the afternoon the yearling got bogged down in the mud-hole.

The rain started around noon, and by two o'clock the downpour was so heavy you could barely see the man riding next to you. Cole was ready to call a halt for the day when he heard the bawling, frantic sound of a cow in distress. Breasting the crest of a narrow ravine he peered down at a young steer buried hip-deep in a mud-slick river, all the way at the bottom.

"Reason!"

Reason's head snapped to attention and at Cole's wave, he turned the sorrel gelding in his direction. As Reason drew up beside the dark bay, Cole pointed downhill.

"Go down there and get that steer out of that slick, and then we'll head on home." Cole had to shout to be heard over the storm.

Reason glanced once down the slope and then over at Cole.

"Why me? Why don't you do it?" Reason hollered back. This was the first time Reason had deliberately bucked an order and he couldn't have picked a worse moment.

Rain poured down in torrents around them. Their hat brims were natural sluices and every time they glanced down, a deluge of rainwater poured forcefully into their laps. Neither man wore a slicker and their clothes were drenched to the skin. Reason's face was streaked with brown mud running in rivulets down his cheeks and his hands were slippery on the reins. Only his clear blue eyes shone bright in his work-grimed face.

"Because I told you to," Cole roared. All he really wanted to do at the moment was find someplace dry and out of the rain. "Now get goin'!"

"Go to hell! I don't care about no damn cow!"

Cole swore. He was getting nowhere fast.

"Aw, damn it all. You probably couldn't rope it anyway," he grumbled in a voice that couldn't be heard above the rain. Then hastily urged the horse forward.

The dark bay daintily picked up his feet traveling down the mud-slick slope yet, regardless of his care, he couldn't seem to stop himself from slipping and sliding sideways, slinging mud all the way to the bottom. By the time they reached level ground, Cole looked filthier than Reason. He reached for his rope and shook out a long loop, then swung it twice in the air. With a spark of impatience, he watched the noose settle neatly over the half-grown steer's head. Then he began to back his pony up the hill.

The horse slipped. He slid. And he skittered sideways. Then he went down. Cole went rolling in the wet muddy hillside. When he scrambled to his feet, his boots skidded in the mud, he lost purchase and fell face-forward again. By the time he finally regained his feet, there wasn't a clean spot on him.

With a muffled curse, he gathered his horse beneath him once more. But every time the gelding jerked, Cole slid right out of the saddle and into the mud once more. Finally, he gave up the horse and began to haul on the taut rope with his bare hands. But his boot heels kept skidding out from beneath him, and his muddy hands lost their grip and kept slipping through the rope.

In a fit of disgust, he went trudging through the roiling water towards the yearling's head, grabbed him by the horns, and tugged hard. The ornery steer braced his forelegs in the mud and resisted all humanly efforts to save him. And Cole didn't have the strength to pull the obnoxious beast clear of the river all by himself.

He gave up that end and instead splashed through water thigh deep to brace a shoulder against the animal's hindquarters and began to push from behind. When the cow kicked out a dislodged hoof and painfully connected with Cole's ribcage, he grunted in surprise, lost his balance, and fell backwards into the river.

This time he was slow in rising and when he tried to get behind the cow one last time, found he couldn't move. His boots were stuck fast in the mud-sucking muck at the bottom.

The rain was coming down so fast and hard Cole could barely see straight. He had lost his hat somewhere when his horse had fallen and a torrent of rain was pelting his unprotected face and head like hailstones. But worst of all, the mud-slick river he had fallen into was starting to rise. The mud was only at his ankles, but the water was creeping up to his waist. If he didn't get out of here soon, he'd drown. Plain and simple. Once again, he tried to pick his feet up and move, but it was useless. He was trapped, right along with the damned cow. And the water was rising higher.

With hope born of fear, he glanced up the hill. Reason was still sitting his horse in the pouring rain, right where Cole had left him, staring off into space as if he had all the time in the world.

"Reason!" Cole shouted as loud as he could, but the pounding rain, along with the frantic bawling of the steer drowned out his voice. And Cole knew Reason wouldn't move unless he was commanded to do so. And sometimes not even at that.

Cole swore anew as the water began to rise clear up to his chest. In a fit of desperation, he tried to twist his body free of the mud-sucking river, but a knife-sharp pain suddenly thrust deeply into his side.

"Oh shit." He gasped out loud, fearing a rib was broken. Then he groaned deep in his throat as all hope of survival suddenly drained right out of him. He couldn't move a muscle and the water kept rising. If the rain didn't stop soon, Cole was a dead man.

Reason sat his horse at the top of the hill. He'd watched Cole slip and slide down the muddy incline. Saw him rope the steer and watched his horse go down. And him with it. Then watched him try again and again, until he became bored with it all. The rain came down in buckets, like a dam in the sky had burst and was flooding the world.

He threw a glance over his shoulder at the rest of the herd. They were all hunkered together with their tails to the wind. Whoever said they were dumb animals? Reason swiped at his wet dripping face with the sleeve of his shirt. That didn't do a hell of a lot of good. His shirt was drenched like the rest of him. A warm fire and a hot bowl of mush sounded good to him at the moment.

Then his insides turned to ice and he shivered uncontrollably as a memory of another banked fire and sour-tasting gruel crept into his mind. Two large men sitting at a table were eyeing him up like a cooked goose at a Christmas dinner. The fire was warm on his back, yet he jumped to his feet in alarm. One of the men was heading towards him, fiddling with the buttons at his crotch. The rough wall of the cabin slammed him hard in the back. There was no escape. And the man kept coming.

"Reason...!" The shout came from somewhere far below and jolted him out of his reverie. Had he imagined it? Or had he heard a cry for help? Hesitantly he peered down against the gloom of the storm. Rain poured off the brim of his hat into his lap once again and he jerked his head in annoyance. But he didn't see Cole.

He saw the horse, though. Saw the damned steer who had somehow managed to break loose of the muck and head for dry land. But no sign of the man.

Reason wasn't alarmed. Nothing much shook him lately anyway. He'd just wait for Cole to get back and when he did, they'd both go back to the house and dry out.

Cole was panicking. The water was up to his shoulders now and still rising. In another few minutes it would be over his head. He struggled to free his legs until another sharp pain in his side made him cry out loud. Then he just gave up. He was done for. What was the sense in hurting himself further? He couldn't move, the water was rising too fast and the damn incessant rain wasn't letting up a minute. His frantic eyes strayed towards the crest of the hill, but there was no dark outline of a horse and rider in sight.

Cole swore. Reason must have, calm as you pleased, rode off and left him to drown. Well, what did he expect? That Reason would try to save a man he had nothing but scorn for? Cole would have broken down and cried out of sheer helplessness if he thought that might have helped. The rain pelted his bare head so hard his scalp hurt. And the swollen river rolled menacingly beneath his chin, tugging at his sore ribs.

With an icy fist of fear clenched tight around his heart Cole began to pray for a quick and merciful death, for God was the only one who could hear him now, when something slapped the water beside him. In sheer, mindless terror, he opened his eyes to find a lasso widely circling his head and bobbing wildly upon the river's roiling surface. Without hesitation he raised his hands up and tucked the rope beneath his arms. Then as the rough prickly hemp began to tighten around his chest, his eyes searched through the pouring rain towards the water's rippling edge.

Reason had the opposite end of the rope wrapped snug around the pommel of his saddle and he was backing the sorrel gelding gently up the mud-slick slope. Cole felt the pull as the noose grew taut beneath his shoulders, felt the strain against his unyielding body as his ribs screamed in silent protest. Regardless of the agony, he set his teeth and grabbed onto the slippery rope for dear life.

Gradually his legs broke free of the muck, but Cole wasn't on safe ground yet. Besides almost passing out from the pain of the rope tugging at him, plus the turbulent water pummeling against his injured side, Cole almost drowned in the process of being towed to shore as the swift-racing current swept over his head time and time again. When he was finally hauled clear of the water and dragged on his belly across the bare, muddy incline to safety, Cole was gasping for breath and could barely find the strength to lift his head. His right side blazed like fire and every breath he took only fueled the flames higher.

"Are you ready to go yet?"

Cole heard Reason's flat emotionless tone as if from a huge distance, and suddenly he thought the situation was shockingly funny. A chuckle built in his throat that he couldn't control. Here he was, sacked out on a muddy hillside in the pouring rain, face down in the cold, wet muck with a cracked rib or two and a man that couldn't even remember his own name had just saved him from drowning to death in a river that should never have been there in the first place. He must be going loony as Reason, laughing about it all with the rain beating at his back, when he should be trying to rise up from the cold, slimy ground and find a warm dry place to hole up in.

"Are you all right?"

Reason had dismounted and was now standing by his side, frowning down at him.

Carefully Cole rolled to his back and grinned into the rain.

CHAPTER FOURTEEN

The line shack was just a scrap pile of logs nailed together with a sod roof, but it was shelter out of the storm, and it was dryer than anything else they would find within a half-mile span. Reason had been ordered to take the horses around back where there was a wide overhang with a high pile of hay stored in the loft for overnight guests, while Cole grabbed his saddlebags and went through the front door that was barely hanging by one hinge. There was an old stone fireplace against the far wall and a stack of dry kindling nearby. Cole grinned once again. What more could a man ask for?

He was in the process of lighting a fire with a dry match that he found in an old tin box above the mantel a few minutes later when Reason stepped through the door.

"I should have us warm and dry in no time flat." Cole breathed a welcome sigh of relief when a few crumpled pages of an old Montgomery Ward catalog burst into flame and rapidly began to ignite the smaller, thinner pieces of kindling.

"There, what'd I tell ya," he said with a note of triumph in his voice. Cole twisted around with eyebrows raised, expecting an answer of some kind. But he was unprepared for the sight of Reason standing flush in the open doorway, dripping wet, with rain pouring in both behind him and over him, staring blankly at the fire as if he had never seen one before in his life.

"Either go back out, or come on in," Cole yelled. *For Christ sakes, the fool didn't have sense enough to come in out of the rain.* "Just close the damn door. You're gonna flood us out in a second. And I've just about swallowed all the water I can handle."

He meant what he said, but when Reason took two steps backwards, Cole rose stiffly to his feet. Impulsively he reached out a hand, palm up, in a humble gesture of compassion.

"Look, I was only kidding." His voice dramatically softened. "Come in and shut the door. You're soaked to the skin."

Reason blinked once, then glanced over at Cole. When there were no further orders, his eyes swept over the small one-room shack. As if he were choosing the lesser of two evils, he finally turned and closed the door behind him.

"That's better." Cole ran his fingers as a comb through the dark hair plastered damply to his scalp, then shook his head furiously like a longhaired dog that just had a bath. Large droplets of water sprayed every which way and a few made sizzling, hissing sounds as they hit the fire. Then, with the palms of both hands, he slicked his short wet hair back behind his ears. A sudden shiver wracked his body from the chill of wet clothes lying against cold, clammy skin, and he began to yank at the mud-encrusted buttons of his ruined denim shirt.

"What are you doing?"

Reason's voice sounded deep and unsteady in the close confines of the cabin. Cole glanced over his left shoulder, a frown of annoyance creasing his chiseled features.

"What's it look like? You expect me to catch pneumonia? I'm getting out of these filthy, river-soaked duds just as fast as I can."

In his haste to peel the grimy shirt from his back he was a trifle too careless with his movements and a sharp, breathless, stabbing pain ripped through his injured side. Cole buckled and gasped, his left hand cradling his badly aching ribs, while his right forearm leaned against the stone wall for support.

"Damn, I forgot about that," he swore with a tight jaw.

"What's wrong?" Reason spoke mechanically, without one ounce of feeling, from his position by the door.

"Think I busted some ribs back there when that damn ungrateful four-legged Delmonico on a hoof kicked me."

"I didn't see that."

Cole glanced over at him. "How could you? Up on that hill, in all that rain and everything."

Reason looked pale through all the grime on his face. His voice was unusually flat and lifeless and he was speaking in short stilted sentences once again. His clear blue eyes were slightly glassy and contained a touch of panic.

Cole's eyes swept the shabby, unkempt interior of the cabin, searching for something that might have alarmed the man. All that the measly hovel contained was a straw-filled bunk on each opposing wall and a high shelf where a few canned goods and other necessities were stored in case of an emergency layover by any of the cowhands caught out in a torrential storm like this one.

There was nothing within these four shabby walls that should put that trapped, frantic look back in Reason's eyes. Unless...?" Unless he was remembering another cabin high in the Tetons.

Cole swore. What a damn fool he was. Of course, that was it! Reason was remembering. Slowly, but surely. And without a necessary show of force.

That had to be a good sign. Hadn't it?

Cole shrugged the wet muddy shirt back up over his shoulders. It would either dry on him, or else stay wet. Suddenly he didn't care which.

"Are you okay?"

Reason swallowed hard, then shifted his gaze towards the fire. Cole could see the dancing orange flames reflecting back at him through Reason's pale eyes. Rainwater still dripped off the curled brim of his black Stetson. He was soaking wet, drenched to the skin the same as Cole, and he shivered as he stood there. Yet the man remained silent and staring.

"Hey. It's Cole. Remember?" He grinned. Then at Reason's lack of response, he sobered. "You don't have to fear me, Reason. For cryin' out loud. You just saved my life!"

But words weren't working.

Reason backed up a step towards the door.

Cole swore beneath his breath.

"Look." He held out both hands, palms up. "Come on over by the fire where it's warm." He began sidling towards the farthest bunk. "I'll stay over here by the west wall. I won't bother ya. I promise."

Reason didn't move a muscle. Then suddenly he squeezed his eyes shut and his face twisted into a tight grimace of pain. He ducked his head and brought the backs of both hands up to his eyes. Cole wasn't sure if he was trying to ward off a blow to the head in his mind, or hide his face from a disturbing memory.

Then Reason groaned low in his throat and dropped to his

knees on the damp wood floor.

"No. No, don't...." He bent slightly forward at the waist and huge, gulping sobs shook his shoulders that had nothing to do with the chill of the wet clothes on his back.

Oh, shit! Reason was reenacting the same scene over and over again in his mind. Just how long was it going to take him to get over this? After all, it had only been a one-shot deal. Hadn't it?

Cole raised an unsteady hand to rub against his bristly jaw. Hadn't it?

Suddenly Cole wasn't so sure. Cole's memory raced back in time. How long had he been missing? Two weeks? No, more than that. Three? Cole's gut became queasy once again.

No, he had to be way off base. No man would....

Then a clear picture of the two burly trappers came to mind. They had been isolated from all forms of humanity for long stretches of time. They could do anything they damn well pleased, with no one the wiser. And if Cole hadn't shown up when he did? A muscle twitched in Cole's jaw. One week later and the only merciful thing left to do would have been to shoot a clean bullet straight through Reason's brain.

Cole's first instinct was to go to Reason. Tell him everything was all right. But he squashed that idea as fast as he would a bug crawling beneath the sole of his boot. The last thing Reason needed or wanted at the moment, was a stranger stepping up to him. And Cole had no illusions to friendship with this man, even though Reason had just saved his life. The act had been a purely automatic response. Nothing more, nothing less. And if Reason had thought about it for any length of time, he probably wouldn't have done it at all.

"Reason! Get up!"

Slowly Reason's shoulders ceased shaking and he gradually lifted his head.

"What...?"

"Get up off your knees."

Again, Reason glanced around in surprise, just as he had done at the river where they had once gone fishing. He climbed to his feet, then stared at Cole as if seeing him for the first time.

Raising his left hand to the rough-hewn mantle built into the stone wall behind him, Cole grabbed the rolled-up gun belt that he had carelessly tossed there upon entering the shack. The pistol had been kept dry in his saddlebags during the worst part of the storm and Cole had salvaged the belt before Reason walked the horses around back. Now he threw the whole works in Reason's direction.

Once again, Reason caught the flying missile deftly in his left hand just as he had done with the soap last year.

"Strap it on! And that's an order!"

After a brief awkward moment, Reason glanced down at the weapon in his hand, then slowly wrapped and clasped the loaded belt comfortably around his hips.

"Now get over there by the fire and stay put until you dry out."

Cole was hoping the pistol's weight, anchored securely to Reason's thigh, would balance the scales more in his mind and might cause him to lose the senseless confusion and stark-raving fear showing in the pale blue eyes.

Reason hesitated. His right hand slid sensuously across the brown leather cartridge belt worn low on his hips, not unlike a lover's tender caress, then lightly dropped downward to touch the worn contoured holster in a disturbingly familiar yet deadly way.

Cole swallowed hard. Had he just made a huge mistake? The last time Reason held a pistol in his hand, he was intending to empty the bullet-filled chambers right into Cole's chest.

"You're unarmed," Reason said in that flat way of his.

An uneasy grin tugged at the corners of Cole's lips.

"Don't need it right now. Figured you could hold it for me while I dry out."

Deliberately he turned his back on Reason, sauntered towards the cot against the far wall, and gingerly sat on the straw-filled mattress's soft edge. His side was beginning to complain a bit and Cole knew he had to tape himself up soon with whatever rags were handy, or he'd never be able to make it back home in one piece.

A subtle movement near the door made Cole glance up, and what he saw made his breath catch in his throat. For Cole's pistol now sat tightly gripped in Reason's hand — the cold, deadly bore aiming directly at his heart. Once again, Reason was in full control of a weapon, and this time there would be no hard-riding ranch hands coming to the rescue.

Cole swallowed his fear and mentally listed his options. He

had none. If Reason wanted to kill him, there was not one damn thing he could do about it. He was seated obscurely in the shadows, too far on the opposite side of the room to defend himself, for he had moved out of the firelight to give Reason some much-needed space. And now he was sorry he had.

"What're you doin', Reason?" he said as calmly as he was able.

In answer, Reason's dripping, dark-clad form sidestepped with sinewy grace towards the fire, never once taking his eyes, or his aim, off Cole.

"You wanted me to dry off, didn't you?" He spoke with a mocking sneer.

Reason's eyes glinted with a maniacal gleam and the hand that held the gun was steady as a rock. He halted inches from the fire.

"Get up," he said simply.

Cole's stomach dropped to his knees. Reason was going to shoot him. Of that he was certain. And it was his own damn fault. Cautiously he rose to his feet.

"You know who I am, don't you?"

"My friend Cole." Reason spoke in that same flat, frightening way. And the words itself held a new and sinister meaning.

But Cole chose to misunderstand.

"That's right, Reason. I'm your pal. Don't forget that. You saved my life, remember?"

Reason squinted as if he were having trouble seeing clearly.

"Move out into the light."

At least he wasn't firing yet. Cole wondered if he dared try to tackle the pistol away from him and mentally cursed himself for handing it over in the first place. But as Cole took one carless step forward, banging his left shin on a jutting log from the woodpile, he knew he wasn't fit to tackle anyone. He buckled slightly, winced hard, then raised a protective hand to cradle his injured side.

"Complaining already? I haven't even shot you yet."

Cole glanced up in alarm. Reason was dead serious.

"Reason, I'm hurt. Can't you see? That steer down in the mud-hole kicked me in the side. Remember?"

"What mud-hole?"

"The one you just pulled me out of and saved my life!" Cole's voice raised in exasperation. "Dammit! Don't you remember anything?"

Reason stared at the wet and muddy clothes of the man standing before him for a full minute. Then he said, "Guess not."

Cole's side was aching badly. Every time he drew a simple breath, the pain grew sharper than before. And all the yelling just made it worse.

"I need help. I think somethin's broken inside."

"Is that a fact."

"Damn you! Put down that gun and go find somethin' to tape me up with!"

Cole had spoken impulsively, in an act born of pain and frustration, before his brain had time to worry about the lethal consequences of such a remark. Cursing a man's soul to hell was the perfect excuse to instigate a notable gunslinger to squeeze the trigger. Especially an unstable one, like Reason. He should have bitten off his own tongue first.

Yet, to his utter amazement, Reason jerked as if slapped. He blinked twice in rapid succession, then stared hard at the man facing him as if he had just noticed Cole standing there. Ever so slowly his hand lowered to his side. Cole breathed a whole lot easier when the pistol slid effortlessly into its holster.

Determined to silence this time, Cole watched as Reason's blue-eyed gaze scanned all four corners of the room with heated interest, as if searching for a long-lost item of dire necessity. Then, as if finding the object of his search, he strode in a beeline towards the cot behind him and yanked a moth-eaten blanket off the top of a bare mattress. From there he proceeded to tear the coverlet into thin strips. After tying the ends together to make a lengthy bandage, he held it up to the firelight for Cole to comment on.

"Is this long enough do you think?"

A wry, self-satisfied smile split Cole's lips.

"It's a beginning."

CHAPTER FIFTEEN

The rain lasted throughout the evening but by mid-morning, the sun was shining through the worn chinks in the wood walls, and meadowlarks were singing high in the surrounding pines. The night, itself, had been a harrowing event to Cole's mind in the sense that he was surprised to find himself still alive with the dawn. Truth was he hadn't slept a wink, although he hadn't let on that small fact to Reason. If anyone happened to glance his way, they would have thought he lay in a deep coma.

For Reason had been fidgety as all hell. Every five minutes or so, he rose off the far cot and paced the small planked floor of the cabin. Back and forth, back and forth. Worn leather soles scudding abrasively on battle-scarred wood. Until Cole thought he would go nuts.

Yet every time Cole's patience would reach its breaking point and he decided to risk his life by hollering out "Stop!" Reason would plunk himself down on his makeshift bed to stare fixedly up at the crude sod ceiling above. It was those times that Cole didn't know which was worse. The frenzied pacing or the deathly silence.

This was the first time Reason was armed for any length of time and stuck in a situation he wasn't entire comfortable with. Cole wasn't sure what to expect next.

But when dawn finally broke over the horizon, Reason had finally worn himself out to the point of exhaustion and, with one booted foot still on the floor and an arm flung haphazardly over his head, he was fast asleep. And the thought of waking him never entered Cole's mind.

By the time they cantered up to the main house of the Stirrup

C late that afternoon, Randall was already waiting on the front porch.

"Where the hell you been?" Randall shouted before Cole even touched ground. "I sent five men out looking for you this morning."

"Got caught in the storm. Spent the night in a line shack up in the hills."

Randall's eyes instantly shifted to his brother. Neither man looked the worse for wear. A bit muddy and travel-stained around the edges, but no major harm was done. Yet he didn't fail to note Cole's gun belt buckled around Reason's waist.

He waited until Cole reached the porch, then he grabbed the man's arm as he began to saunter past him.

"Do you think that's a good idea?" he said low, jerking his head in Reason's direction. "The gun belt and all?"

Cole paused, glancing once over his shoulder at the man climbing the porch steps behind him.

"Do you want him back, Randall? The way he used to be?"

"Of course. But...."

"Then let it ride for now. I'll be responsible if anything should happen because of it."

"You'll be dead, you mean."

Cole laughed in an insolent way. "Yeah."

As Reason cleared the stairs, Cole broke free from Randall's grip and continued on into the house. Reason followed close behind, never once acknowledging his brother's keen scrutiny.

After the two men had scraped and scoured the mud off their bodies, changed into clean clothes and had a quick bite to eat, Cole led Reason into Randall's study and closed the door behind them. He sauntered over towards a large cabinet against the far wall, swung open the door, and retrieved a black leather, hand-tooled gun belt from an inner shelf. Then he moved back to Reason and held out his hand.

"Does this look familiar to you?"

Reason's gaze dropped to the object Cole was holding. He seemed to study the well-oiled holster with the mahogany handled revolver sticking out the top a bit longer than Cole deemed necessary. But then Reason's right hand moved to his own waist in that caressing gesture Cole had seen him perform only yesterday. His glance shifted lower to the brown leather gun belt he wore buckled at his hips, then raised his eyes to Cole and nodded.

"Then take that one off and put this on. It's yours, you know."

"Is this a trick?"

The man was leery as a twelve-point buck standing in front of a hunter's rifle.

"Nope. I'd just like my pistol back. Figured you'd be more comfortable wearin' your own." Reason stared at him for a long minute, then slowly began to unbuckle Cole's belt.

"And after this we're gonna take a stroll over to the barn. There's somethin' else down there that's yours and needs lookin' after."

Satan was in high mettle. He'd had about enough of this small confining stall as he was capable of standing. He stamped, he blew, and he swung his black feathery mane around wildly. He couldn't understand why no one came to ride him anymore, or why the man that usually tended him had abandoned him to another's care and lately seemed more like a stranger than a trusted companion.

Then Cole sauntered into the barn with Reason right behind.

"Go saddle him up." Cole nodded his head to the suddenly stock-still horse. The black's head was high, his ears pricked in curiosity at the two men who had just entered the barn.

"Me?" Reason exclaimed in disbelief. "That horse is a killer!"

"No more'n some men," Cole snapped back, annoyed at Reason's obvious reluctance to saddle a horse he had once gentled by his own hand. "Go on. He won't bite ya."

Reason gave Cole an uncertain look, then grabbed the nearest saddle and gear off a half wall which just happened to be his own, slung it over his shoulder and proceeded to the stallion's stall. He hesitated at the entrance to the stallion's quarters and glanced over his shoulder at Cole who was lounging against a thick wooden post.

"Aren't you going to give me a hand?"

"Nope." *Not unless you get into trouble*, Cole added in his mind.

Disgusted, Reason turned from him and swung open the stall door. The black stallion backed himself into the far corner.

"Easy boy." Reason could sense the stallion's distrust in him. "Steady there," Reason crooned as he moved to the horse's sleek side and slapped the blanket on.

So far, so good. But just as he was about to swing the heavy saddle over the stallion's broad back, Satan lunged for the open gate. The blanket fell to the straw-strewn floor and before anyone could stop him, the horse raced down the middle of the barn with mane and tail flying, and tore out the open door into the empty corral at the opposite end.

Reason swore, while Cole chuckled beneath his breath. He had expected something of the sort and wasn't much disappointed.

"What's so funny?" Reason snarled as he stormed out of the stall. And Cole sobered up fast.

"Not a damn thing. It's just that you're gonna have to catch him to saddle him now."

Reason threw the saddle he was still holding to the floor.

"Like hell I am!"

Cole was silent. Reason was well armed and dangerous, growing more belligerent by the day. He would have to tread lightly around this man.

"You could whistle...?"

"You whistle!"

Cole attempted a smile, but it fell flat. "I could sure as hell try. But it's not the same unless it comes from you."

Reason squinted at him. "I don't understand."

"He's trained to come at a whistle. Not just anyone's. Only yours. I've tried once or twice before, but it takes me a few times to get it right."

Suddenly Reason's revolver was in his hand.

"Do it now." He said coldly. "And get it right!"

Cole paled. When was he ever going to learn not to grow too comfortable around this man? He never knew when Reason might snap.

Slowly Cole straightened but he could see no easy way out. He was no match for Reason with a gun in his hand, no man would be. So he pursed his lips, but only a thin, reedy, useless sound broke the stillness of the barn. It was hard for a man to whistle when a loaded six-gun was aimed your way.

Cole's breath held. Would Reason give him another chance before he fired?

"Again!"

Cole swallowed hard. "It'd be a whole lot easier if you'd do it, Reason."

"Seeing as I don't know how, I figure you're elected," he replied woodenly.

Cole was becoming resigned to Reason's erratic lapses in memory. He recalled the piercing shrill sound when Satan had almost thrown him a week ago, and he tried his damnedest to imitate it. This time an ear-splitting shriek filled the barn and it caught the ears of the fiery stallion galloping around the split-rail enclosure.

The horse came to an abrupt halt and stared curiously at the open doors of the barn. Then curiously, he began ambling towards it. He halted just shy of the entrance and stuck his head inside to eye up the odd pair of stiff and silent men at the far end. The sound had been almost identical to the one his owner used to make. Almost, but not quite. And the horse wasn't exactly sure what was expected of him. And he would move no further until he did.

Cole shrugged helplessly. "Sorry. That's the best I can do."

Slowly Reason's eyes slid towards the black stallion peering through the open doorway on his left. Now would be a good time to jump him, Cole thought, if he had the guts to attempt such a feat. Which he didn't. And if his ribs weren't still aching from the battle with the steer yesterday. Which they were. For if he was unsuccessful in his attempt to overpower Reason, the impulsive act would probably cost him his life.

Then suddenly a low well-tuned whistle pierced the air, and the stallion snorted, threw his head in the air, and with short, mincing steps, waltzed daintily into the barn. He didn't pause until he was standing directly beside Reason. Then he reached out a tentative nose and snuffled the front of Reason's black shirt.

Cole watched in amazement as Reason reached out a hand to gently rub the stallion's sleek head. When the hell had he holstered his revolver? Cole had been so startled at Reason's soft whistle and the temperamental horse entering the barn meek as a kitten, he had lost track of all movements of the man.

Without another word, Reason reached behind him for the bridle and slipped the bit between the stallion's teeth. He picked the blanket up off the ground with one hand, then the heavy saddle with the other and slung them both easily, one at a time, over the stallion's broad back. The horse didn't move a muscle except for a slight swish of his tail and a contented snort. He just stood there patiently awaiting the next command.

An unconscious whistle of amazement blew softly from between Cole's lips, and Reason jerked his head around in the act of tightening the cinch. The icy clear blue eyes bored a hole through Cole with a detached and menacing intensity. Slowly he straightened.

"Was there something you wanted to say?"

Cole leaned his back against the wooden post behind him.

"Nope. Not one damn thing."

CHAPTER SIXTEEN

Days turned into weeks. The heat soared into the nineties. The two men still worked the herd, yet Cole maintained a discreet distance between Reason and the other cowhands. He wanted no trouble between the men that Cole couldn't simply squash with a single word or a heavy fist. For when it came down to gunplay Cole was well aware of his limitations. There was no way he could go up against Reason in a gunfight and expect to come out unscathed. In fact, there wasn't a man on God's green earth that could, to Cole's way of thinking. Except for maybe one other that he knew of.

Reason had a reputation of being not only fast, but deadly accurate. And Cole had seen him in action more times than he cared to count and knew his prowess with a six-gun wasn't pure rumor. It was a hard well-known fact. And that's why he kept Reason separate from the other men. They were short-handed enough as it was, without Reason taking out a man or two if one happened to glance at him the wrong way.

But, although Reason wasn't growing any worse, he didn't seem to be getting better either. And Cole was becoming tired of Reason following him around like an unweaned mongrel pup. He decided the time had come for a true test. To see if Reason could follow orders on his own, without a man watching his every move every second he was awake. He was curious whether Reason would bolt and run, or whether he'd continue to follow orders as directed.

Early the next morning Cole led Reason into Randall's study. Cole sat down behind the heavy mahogany desk, grabbed a clean sheet of yellow lined paper, and scribbled a few words at the top. Then he folded the paper in quarters, rose from the desk, stepped up to Reason, and stuffed the note into the high breast pocket of his black denim shirt.

Reason flinched from the abrupt, unwanted contact and drew in a sharp, bated breath. His pale eyes grew distant through conscious intent, but he didn't jerk backwards in fear, nor cringe at the simple touch as he would have a few short weeks ago. And that, to Cole, was a good sign.

"I want you to ride over to the Stirrup C Bar and deliver that note to a woman named Rachel. Do you remember where it is?"

Reason slowly shook his head no.

"Come on over here. I'll show ya."

Cole moved back towards the desk and drew out a large folded map from the drawer. He leaned over the precisely detailed, pencil-drawn design and pointed to a circled dot on the paper.

"Here's where we are." Then his finger traced a line further north. "And here's where you're goin'." He straightened up. "Any questions?"

"Can't think of any."

"Good." Cole slapped him companionably, deliberately, on the shoulder. He noticed the sudden tightness of Reason's strongly chiseled jaw and a distinct wary look creep into the pale blue eyes, but one again the man didn't try to move out of the way. Cole smiled. Baby steps.

"Take your time. There's no hurry back. But I do expect a hand-written answer to that note. Understand?"

Reason nodded just once.

"Okay." The conversation was over, yet Reason still stood there as if awaiting further orders. "You can leave now," Cole added.

Reason blinked, his pale blue eyes growing round in confusion.

"What about you?" he finally said.

"I have work to do around here, and this job don't warrant two people to handle it. Try to be back before dark, or some of the men around here might start to worry."

The black stallion seemed to know exactly where he was going. And that was good, because Reason had plumb forgot the way.

He knew the man called Cole had pointed the directions out to him on a map, had instructed him on what to do with the note when he arrived. But for the life of him, he couldn't seem to remember the simple drawing tracing the route on paper.

Reason knew his memory was hazy. Sensed there were violent images going on in the back of his mind that he was scared to death to recall. Yet he wished he would have listened more carefully when Cole was relating directions.

It was right after Cole had casually stuffed the note in his shirt pocket that his brain went dim. And when the man playfully slapped at his shoulder, he went all stiff inside. But nothing else had happened to cause such mind-numbing fear. Just what had he expected? Reason didn't know and couldn't remember.

The hour was near noon when Satan cantered into the front yard of the Stirrup C Bar. They had made good time even though Reason couldn't recall the exact route they had chosen to get here. His memory lapses were fitful and bothered him more than he cared to admit. He had simply given the horse his head and Satan had done the rest. Secretly he was relieved that the first leg of the journey was over. Now if he could just deliver the message quickly and then track their precise steps home, he should have no further trouble.

Instinctively he tied the stallion's reins to the split rail fence out front and, without a thought of knocking, climbed the porch stairs, and sauntered easily past the screened front door. As if he were walking in his sleep, he passed through the parlor without looking to either side, veered down the hallway to his left, and finally pushed open the door that led into the office.

An attractive young woman with auburn-colored hair was seated at a large oak desk that seemed to overpower her small petite frame, while a tall, lean fellow somewhere in his mid-thirties had one hand on the back of her chair, one hand flat on the desk, and was leaning over her shoulder. Both of them were examining a ledger of some kind with hand-written numbers in long columns printed on the pages.

At his entrance, the woman glanced up. A startled gasp of fright caught at her throat and her hand went straight to her neck as if she were strangling.

"Reason," she breathed. "Oh my God!" The man peered up in surprise.

Hastily Reason threw a glance over his shoulder. Had someone snuck up behind him with a knife when he wasn't looking? There was no one there. The hallway behind him stood empty. So what was the woman so afraid of?

Slowly he turned to face the startled woman at the desk. The man straightened, his composure never once compromised. With an easy grin, he said, "Howdy Reason. Glad you're finally back."

He was lying. Reason could feel it deep in his bones. If he was a dog, the ruff on the back of his neck would have stood stiffly on end. He sensed a rival in this man. But for what? And for who? He didn't know. And cared even less.

"I'm not staying," he finally said in a cold, chilling voice that sounded foreign even to him. "I'm just here to deliver a message."

"From your brother?" the red-haired woman he supposed was Rachel, said.

"Who?"

"Randall, your brother," she patiently explained.

Reason shook his head. "No. Cole."

There was a heavy silence pervading the room for a full minute until, with a sharp tone of impatience, she said, "Well? Where is it?"

"Where's what?"

"The message from Cole you were sent to deliver."

He had forgotten about the note. What a simple-minded fool. Yet how could he concentrate on a thin scrap of paper when that pretty little filly with the blue-green eyes was staring so intently at him.

Now just where had he put it? His right hand raised to slap at his left shirt pocket. The crisp crunch of paper instantly relieved his mind. His first guess was the correct one.

Reaching into his shirt, he carefully withdrew the folded piece of yellow paper, then sauntered closer to the desk and held it out to her.

Tentatively Rachel reached out to grasp the note. Were her slender fingers trembling? Reason thought he must have imagined it. Slowly she unfolded the brief letter and rapidly scanned the contents. When next she glanced up, Reason would have sworn there were tears glistening in her eyes.

"He's expecting an answer," was all he said.

Without haste, she folded the small yellow slip into a tiny square.

"I'll have to think about this." Her voice was husky as she spoke.

Gracefully, she rose from the chair and with a careless sweep of her hand indicated the man at her side. "You remember Joe Steele, don't you?"

Reason's spine stiffened defensively. He didn't remember anyone, much less a man who raised his hackles at first sight. And, although Joe Steele grinned easily at him, he didn't offer any further information.

"No," he finally said.

"Joe's been a big help around here ever since...." She shrugged her small shoulders. "Well, that's neither here nor there." She turned to the man beside her. "That'll be all for today, Joe. And thanks for the help."

"No thanks necessary, Rachel. I'm the one obliged to you. Call if you need me. I'll be right outside." He knew Reason's history. As much as any of them did. Had heard all the sordid rumors whispered among the hands. Mainly that Reason had lost a few marbles somewhere along the way. And he had read the note from Cole over Rachel's shoulder.

With his normal loose-limbed stride, he stepped around the desk and moved up to Reason. Then held out a friendly hand to shake.

"Good to see you again, boss."

Reason didn't move a muscle. Only the direction of his gaze dropped once to Joe's extended hand, then traveled slowly back up to his face. And if Joe Steele hadn't been a hardened gunslinger himself at one time, he might have cringed from the cold, calculating look appearing in Reason's pale eyes.

Slowly his hand dropped back to his side. Reason wasn't about to be friendly. At least not to him.

"See you later, Rachel." He nodded once to Reason then stepped around the man and vanished out the door.

"Awful friendly with the hired help, aren't you, Rachel?" Reason sneered. His tone held a hint of malice that made Rachel gasp in alarm. Why he sounded just like a jealous husband. Yet if he didn't remember her, how on earth could he possibly be jealous?

Reason was thinking the exact same thing. What on earth made him say that? What the hell business was it of his what this woman did with her free time? He held no claim to her. For all intents and purposes he'd sounded like a spiteful, jilted lover.

His gaze slid over the woman still seated at the desk. Not that he wouldn't mind being one, he thought to himself. She was an appealing enough individual with curves in all the right places. That's if you liked that freckled face innocence she portrayed to the public eye while secretly hiding a wanton spitfire nature, far beneath the surface, kind of gal.

"Is there any…" she faltered slightly, "reason why I shouldn't be?"

"I was out of line. Sorry."

Rachel wanted to scream at him. No! You weren't. You were acting just as you should have. But she remembered Cole's note and held her tongue.

Instead she asked, "Are you hungry?" She forced a sweet smile. "Sally's in the kitchen. I'm sure she can whip you up something to eat if you'd like."

He didn't know who Sally was and cared even less.

"No. Thanks." Reason's insides began growing jittery. The air was suddenly stifling in the small enclosed room and he seemed to be having trouble breathing again. His gaze flew longingly towards the open door. If only she'd give him the damn note so he could leave.

"Are you all right? You seem…nervous." When Reason's eyes finally locked with hers, Rachel was horrified to see the state of near panic in the slightly unfocused blue stare of the man that she loved. Wolf's eyes, she used to call them. Now they were the tormented hunted eyes of a wounded animal with a pack of hound dogs at his feet, threatening him at bay.

Her heart almost broke in two. How much of this was she supposed to stand?

She wanted to say the hell with it all, throw her arms around his neck, and kiss him deeply, thoroughly. Be enfolded in his warm embrace in return. Yet she sensed in his current state of mind that he would shy violently away from her, as he had done once before. And that would just about kill her.

Then she recalled the note. *He still doesn't remember. Be gentle!*

He was her husband, dammit! And she wanted him here, by her side.

"I need an… answer," he said haltingly.

"You mean the note?"

Reason slowly nodded.

Be gentle…. Cole's words echoed in her brain.

Ever so slowly Rachel sat back down in the chair. She picked up her pen and dipped the tapered point in the open bottle of black ink.

I understand, she wrote in bold letters across the bottom of the page. Then she blotted the ink, creased the paper once more, and rose from the chair. Nonchalantly, she moved around to the front of the desk.

She paused in front of her husband and held the paper up to him, pressed between two fingers.

"Is this what you're waiting for?"

Reason swallowed hard, then nodded. Her nearness was unsettling, driving him to distraction. She was too close one minute. Then too damn far the next. A sudden impulse made him want to reach out and touch her, to hold her gently within the hungry, lonely span of his arms and then…? Push her away.

He must be insane. Everyone else seemed to think so, the way they all handled him with kid gloves. And now she was probably thinking it too.

"Take it," she offered gently as he was slow in complying. Lightly she tapped his chest with the folded crease of the yellow paper.

Was that all she was offering? Reason could read a clear invitation igniting her sparkling sea green eyes that seemed to originate from deep within. And just the mere thought scared all hell out of him.

He snatched the paper rudely out of her hands.

"Much… obliged," he stammered uneasily. Then he veered around and strode towards the door.

"Reason!" The tone of her voice halted him in his tracks and he turned, unsure of her command.

"Give Cole my love," she said with tears forming in her eyes.

Her husband just stared at her for a brief moment as if at a stranger, before he ducked his head and almost ran out of the room.

"Don't go," Rachel whispered low enough for only herself to hear as she tore into the hall after him. But she was too slow to catch him.

Reason strode past the parlor and out the front door as a man with a deadly purpose. He let the screen door swing shut behind him and then halted in his tracks at the edge of the porch. His lungs felt full to bursting and he stood there gasping for air as if he were having an attack of some kind. A groan of confusion burst from his throat as he braced a hand against a supporting post and tried to still the inward quaking of his limbs.

That had been a close call. The thought ran unbidden in his mind and he almost laughed at himself. What possible harm could a thin slip of a girl named Rachel do to him?

The scraping sound of leather boots on wood planking instantly drew him around. Joe Steele was straightening from leaning his lanky frame against the shadowy front wall of the house. Reason, in his frantic bid for freedom hadn't noticed him lounging there.

"You have the look of a man who's just escaped from an airtight prison cell," Joe drawled conversationally. "Is Rachel all right?"

Reason's back went up from the implied insult that he would dare harm a woman in any way.

"Why shouldn't she be? And what business is it of yours?"

"Rumor has it you're not quite right in the head. And Rachel means a lot to me."

"Just how much is a lot?"

Joe grinned with a wry trace of malice. "Well that depends on her husband."

Reason hadn't once thought of the woman inside as being married, for he felt at times that she was actually making a play for him. And the news threw him for a loop.

"What husband? What depends...?" he finally said when he regained a semblance of his senses once again.

"I guess on whether he wants to stay and work things out? Or cut and run."

Joe had seen the misery in Rachel's eyes over the last ten long months. And it almost ripped his heart out every time she broke down and cried on his shoulder. A man shouldn't ignore a woman like that, no matter what hell he'd been through. And his boss was no exception.

Reason stared long and hard at this man called Joe Steele. He was lean and tough, with keen hazel eyes that saw more than the man was willing to admit. A formidable rival. And why did he get the uncomfortable feeling that this man had already sealed his fate?

"Where's her husband now?"

Joe scoffed insultingly. "You're pulling my leg."

He had heard that Reason was forgetful, but it was impossible, to his mind, that a man didn't recognize his own wife.

Suddenly Reason's mahogany-handled revolver was in his hand, aiming at the man before him.

"Mister, I asked you a civil question."

Joe froze. Every man on the ranch was well aware of Reason's uncanny prowess with a pistol. Joe, more than most. For Joe considered himself the only man on the face of this earth that could beat him in a gunfight if he so chose. But although this particular battle was already stacked against him, Joe wasn't unduly afraid. He knew the man behind the gun. And knew Reason would never fire at a man unless the other stood a fighting chance.

So he said, "A man should never pull a gun on another unless he's prepared to use it."

Then Reason smiled, and Joe saw the hint of madness in his cold blue eyes. Reason was worse off than he thought.

"Now what were you saying?"

Joe hesitated for only the briefest of minutes. Then he said, "I'm looking at him."

Reason's eyes grew round and his jaw dropped open in surprise.

"What?"

And that's when Joe hit him.

His fist caught Reason squarely on the jaw, and knocked him one step backwards. The pistol fell out of his hand to thud on the hard wood floor. Then, before he could recover, a jarring blow to his mid-section made him grunt in pain and another crashing blow to his face spun him completely around. He lost his balance on the top porch step and tumbled headfirst to the ground. By the time Joe got to the bottom of the stairs, Reason was staggering to his feet.

"By God, I ought to kill you for all the hell you've put Rachel through!" And then Joe hit him again.

Reason's head snapped sideways. He went down hard and stayed there.

"Get up!" Joe snarled. When Reason was slow in complying, Joe reached down, grabbed the front of Reason's shirt, and dragged him to his feet. Then he shook him like a dog would a rag until Reason's teeth rattled. But, to Joe's surprise, Reason made not one snarl of protest, nor instigated one single move towards his own defense.

"What's the matter? Forget how to fight too?"

In disgust, Joe pushed Reason away from him. As Reason staggered in a feeble attempt to keep his feet, Joe sauntered back to the porch, retrieved the mahogany-handled revolver from the floor, and as he neared Reason once more, rammed the pistol back into the empty holster.

Then he stepped back with all the stealthy menace of a man who wore a gun and knew damn well how to use it.

"Now, you want to pull that pistol? Go ahead and be my guest."

Reason's breathing was labored as if he had just run a mile-long race. He had raw, red bruises marring both cheeks and along his lower jaw. Blood trickled from a cut lip and his eyes were dull with a glassy sheen. He acted as if he had not heard one word of Joe's deadly challenge.

And, in fact, he hadn't. Reason's nerves jumped almost clear out of his skin when the man called Steele shook him like a rag doll, then shortly afterwards slammed the pistol back into his own holster. And he was mentally bracing himself for another blow, which hadn't occurred yet.

Joe sized up the man standing before him. His limbs were slack. His pale blue eyes were unfocused and he was weaving unsteadily on his feet.

Reason Cordell didn't look like a man about to pull his gun on anyone.

"Did you hear me?" Joe asked quietly.

Slowly Reason raised his head. "What...?"

Then Rachel was bounding down the steps as the screen door banged shut behind her.

"What in tarnation is going on out here!" she hollered to the two men as if they were nothing but a pair of miscreant children.

"Reason, just look at you! And you, Joe, have got some explaining to do!"

Without pausing in her stride, she ran straight up to Reason's side and reached up a hand to touch a reddening bruise on his cheek.

Reason winced hard, then jerked his head away from the gentle touch of her hand. His brain was reeling. What was she doing out here? Had she come out to help her friend, Joe, finish him off? His wife? Inwardly he started to tremble as other, more sinister thoughts crept slowly into his mind.

"You'd better come into the house and let me wash those cuts on your face," Rachel said as he grabbed her husband's left arm and began to lead him towards the stairs.

But Reason abruptly twisted out of her grip.

"No, don't." He raised a shaky hand to his brow, which Joe thought was odd because that was the only place on his face that hadn't been hit. Then, to his further surprise, Reason began stumbling backwards. "No more. Please... don't."

His eyes squeezed shut as if he were in pain, yet he came to a complete halt only when his spine came up hard against his own horse's flanks. Tentatively he reached out a hand, groping blindly for the reins. With one leap he was in the saddle. Then without another word, he reined Satan around and kicked him hard in the sides.

"Well, I'll be." Joe stood speechless with surprise as he watched the black stallion pick up speed and head out towards the flat prairie land beyond. He couldn't have been more surprised if Reason had hit him over the head with a pistol barrel.

Then Rachel dropped to her knees in the dirt with a sharp wail of distress.

"Reason! Please don't go," she shrieked to the wind. "Come back. I love you, dammit!"

And Joe swore from that moment on, that no man, especially Reason, would ever hurt Rachel again.

CHAPTER SEVENTEEN

"I'm guessin' Rachel didn't read my note," Cole drawled from the porch as Reason pulled a lathered Satan up to the rail and lightly swung down. One look at Reason's bruised and battered face was enough to let Cole know the unannounced homecoming hadn't gone as well as expected.

Reason ignored him as he tied Satan's reins to the rail, stormed up the stairs and headed for the front door.

"Hey, what happened?" Cole grabbed Reason's arm as he barreled on by and spun him around. "I'm talkin' to…." The round hard bore of Reason's pistol jabbed him in the side.

Cole froze. His blood turned to ice water in his veins. The look in Reason's frigid blue eyes was equally chilling.

"Easy Reason." He released his grip and dropped his hand to his side. "It's Cole. Remember?"

A thin menacing smile graced Reason's hard jaw.

"I remember," he said. Yet he didn't relax his grip on the pistol. "You sent me to deliver a note."

Cole nodded his head. "That's right. Where is it?" He tried to change the subject.

"I lost it."

Cole swallowed hard. Reason's face was bruised in more places than one. He had a dried cut on his lip and his left cheek was swollen to twice its normal size. Obviously, he had been in a brawl and lost a hell of a lot more than the note.

"Did you see Rachel?" Once again, Cole tried to veer Reason's mind away from killing him.

"Is she my wife?"

Uh-oh. So that's what this was all about.

Cole nodded.

The hard bore of the pistol dug deeper into his unprotected side, and Cole flinched.

"Why didn't you tell me!"

Cole had no plausible excuse. He had wanted to go slow with Reason. Let him find out in his own time. Yet things must have somehow gotten out of hand. Sweat beaded his brow beneath the low brim of his Stetson. He took a stumbling step backwards.

"I thought you would have more fun finding out yourself."

The look on Reason's face was incredulous. "Fun?"

Unbidden images from the past suddenly crept into his mind. Two mountain men leering at him in a sinister way, coming towards him, touching him in ways that made him physically sick. *Don't you wanna have some fun?*

The pistol went off in Reason's hand.

But Cole had seen the deadly display of emotions crossing Reason's face. The dimness entering the clear blue eyes. And he jerked sideways just as the pistol went off.

Before Reason had time to recover, Cole grabbed Reason's right wrist and gave it a vicious twist, then threw a shoulder into his chest, knocking him backwards into the outer wall of the house. He held him pinned there by one hand, while the other rammed the back of his gun-held wrist hard into the wall until Reason's fist finally opened and the revolver clattered harmlessly to the wooden floor of the porch.

A sudden shout from the corral reached Cole's ears and the thud of boots against hard packed soil warned of ranch hands running pell-mell towards the house. Then Randall Cordell flew out the front door and came to a sudden halt. "What the hell's going on out here!"

Cole slowly straightened when there was no retaliatory response from Reason, and then released his arm.

"Everythin's under control." Cole drew a deep breath. "There's no cause for alarm." Yet never once did he veer his gaze from Reason as he spoke.

"Did he just try to kill you?" Randall shouted in surprise at Cole's less than truthful response. A blind man could see that the two men had been fighting over control of the revolver that now lay on the floor between them. "I heard a shot! Dammit, I warned you before about him!"

"It was just a misunderstanding. That's all." Cole turned his head at the sound of running boot steps.

"Is everything okay up there?" Chad Stevens spoke up from the small knot of men that skidded to an abrupt halt at the bottom of the porch steps. "We heard a ruckus goin' on over here and wondered if someone needed help." Chad's gaze roved anxiously over the three men on the porch and from the looks of it, the boss's brother, holding onto a sore right wrist, was the one who ended up with the short end of the stick this time.

"Send them away, Randall," Cole spoke low as he turned to Reason once again. "Before they see things they shouldn't."

"What started all this," Randall growled after the curious group of ranch hands had been sent back to their daily chores. "And when did Reason get back?"

Earlier this morning, Randall had been informed by Cole of his plan to send Reason on a trial-based errand and Randall hadn't felt the need to press him about it. Up until now, Cole had handled Reason with smooth precision and timely intervention and Randall trusted Cole's judgment with regards to his brother's welfare above all other men.

"Just a short while ago," Cole answered honestly. "And it was my own damn fault. I should have warned him about Rachel beforehand."

Reason was still braced up snug against the wall of the house where Cole had flung him, cradling his injured wrist. Although he hadn't instigated any further acts of aggression since the moment he'd first pulled his revolver, he still wasn't over it, Cole knew. The distrust was still obvious in the steadfast gaze and stiff, unwavering form.

"What about her?" Randall sounded puzzled.

"That she was his wife."

"He knows all that. She's been over here enough times even for him to remember."

"Well he didn't. And I sent him over there."

"Are you loco?" Randall was incredulous. "Armed like that?"

"It was a risk. I admit it. But I thought he was ready."

Reason shifted awkwardly against the wall. "...*think he's ready*...?" Where had he heard that dreaded expression before? Three simple words that put fear in his soul.

"Obviously he's not. And I'm not comfortable with the idea of him wandering around with a loaded pistol strapped to his hip until he's over all this. Now get that gun belt off him and lock it up good and tight until he knows what's what around here."

For once Cole agreed with Randall. That had been too close a call. Cole's hand went to his suddenly stinging left side and came away smeared with blood. It was a surface scratch. Nothing more. But an inch or two further and Cole might have bought the farm.

"Hand it over, Reason." Cole held out his right hand, palm up. "You'll get it back soon. I promise."

But Reason backed away from the extended arm.

"This won't be as easy as it looks," Cole warned the man standing next to him. Cautiously he bent down and retrieved the mahogany-handled pistol from the floor, then without shifting his gaze off Reason, passed it wordlessly to Randall.

Randall tucked the troublesome revolver in the tight leather belt at his waist and Reason flinched violently.

"Easy fella," Cole soothed as he took a step nearer. He could see Reason was either ready to bolt like a skittish stallion off the porch, or else go down on his knees before him. And Cole secretly hoped his mindless response would be to flee, rather than crawl.

"He's gonna run, Randall," Cole spoke in that same crooning monotone as before so as not to precipitate any further action on Reason's part. "Fan out so we can catch him before he gets too far."

"Oh for crying out loud. Just take it, for God sakes!" Randall had lost all sense of patience. Without thought, he made an abrupt move in Reason's direction.

Fearing for his life, Reason flattened himself like a pancake against the front wall of the house.

"No," he groaned low. He stared glassy-eyed at the man standing before him as if his brother was a complete and utter stranger.

Randall stopped stock-still. "What's he doing?" he said in awe.

"Stay where you are," Cole ordered, as he flung out a staying arm across Randall's chest. "Don't move. He's hallucinatin' again." Then to Reason he said softly, "You already know me, Reason. I won't lie to you. This here is your brother, Randall.

Neither one of us is going to hurt you."

But Reason wasn't seeing either of them at the moment. He was seeing two hulking mountain men who were stealthily advancing. *Think he's ready, Buck?* In a frantic attempt to flee to safety, Reason started sidling towards the far edge of the porch.

Randall misunderstood. "All we want is your damned gun belt, Reason. Just hand the thing over, will you?" He brushed away Cole's arm and took another step forward. He couldn't understand why Cole was acting so damn laid-back all of a sudden.

Reason froze. His breath caught in his throat. It was too late to run, even if he could. He was back in the corner of the shack again in his mind.

Then Randall did something he would later regret. He reached out and tugged fiercely at the black leather gun belt buckled low at Reason's waist.

"God...no!" Reason gasped and sucked in his breath. His back was already flat up against the wall. There was nowhere to run. He was trapped!

In a useless attempt to block the violent images threatening his sanity, he threw both arms up over his eyes. Then his entire body began to tremble as if he were in the turbulent throes of an earthquake. A gut-wrenching groan came from deep in his throat, and Randall jerked back in alarm. "Cole...?"

"I warned you not to go near him," Cole snapped in anger. "What Reason's been through...."

Then Reason's knees buckled beneath him and he slid straight down to the floor. He bent at the waist and curled up tight as a drum as if in agony. "No, don't. Please...not again. God help me."

Randall glanced at the man next to him as if Cole would explain his last words. But Cole was suddenly strangely silent. The glittering amber eyes seemed to hold a terrible secret that didn't warrant speaking out loud. Dawning recognition hit Randall with the fury of a lightning bolt.

"You weren't going to tell me, were you? That he'd been assaulted in more ways than one."

With an unsteady grin, Cole said, "Guilty as charged."

"How long have you known?"

"Not all that long. A month or so, seems like. How'd you guess?"

Randall's jaw grew tight, not unlike Reason's at times.

"There's not much in this life that would bring my brother to his knees."

Cole shifted uncomfortably on his feet. "One was named Mort, the other...?" He shrugged his shoulders as Randall stared hard at him.

"There were two?" he said incredulously.

After a moment's hesitation, Cole nodded.

"Jesus." Randall ran a hand across his mouth and then around the nape of his neck. With a heavy heart, he turned away from his brother's cringing figure and shifted his gaze towards the barn. Most of the ranch hands had disbursed, going about their separate chores. But a few were still within shouting distance.

"Get him up off the floor, will you?" Randall said gently. "Before he gives the men something else to talk about."

Cole glanced once over his shoulder towards the barn, then back at the man on his knees.

He said, "Get up, Reason."

He may as well have been talking to the wall.

Cole pulled his gun. He hated this part, but sometimes there was no other way to get his attention.

"Look here," he ordered sternly.

Still no response. Reason was buried deep in his own misery.

The blast was loud and sudden as Cole shot a bullet into the wood floor of the porch close to Reason's right knee.

Randall almost leaped clear off the porch. He swore hard, then jerked around all ready to berate Cole for his foolishness, when he saw Reason flinch violently and slowly raise his head.

"Get up, Reason," Cole said again. "You're makin' a spectacle of yourself."

"Did you have to do that?" Randall swore, as Reason rose woodenly to his feet.

"Only as a last resort."

CHAPTER EIGHTEEN

Strong hands grabbed at him and tore at his clothes. The battle-scarred table slammed him cruelly in the face. Something heavy pressed chokingly against the back of his neck holding him in place, and his right wrist that had been twisted behind his back was now wrenched up painfully tight between his shoulder blades.

"No, don't," Reason moaned in his sleep.

Distorted images came at him from all directions. The smell of damp earth, burning wood and unwashed bodies permeated the air. Dark hairy shapes hovered over him, hurting him, again and again.

"We want to hear you groan, boy. Make some noise. Quit holdin' out on us."

Fists pummeled him. The lights went out, leaving him in utter darkness. He was cold. Wet. A deluge of water almost drowned him once again. He couldn't breathe. Muscular arms went around his waist and squeezed hard. He cried out in agony as the pain in his back intensified.

"Now you're talkin'. Do it again, Buck. Until you get it right."

Jesus!

Reason's eyes flew open and he gazed at the dim plastered ceiling. He awoke bathed in a glistening sheen of sweat. His heart hammered wildly in his chest until he thought it would burst clear through his rib cage. His right hand shook uncontrollably as he raised it to his brow.

He was having a nightmare again. That's all it was, he rationalized to himself. The sheets beneath him were damp from perspiration. How long had he been dreaming?

He bolted up in bed. This had to stop! Every night since he could remember he'd awakened this way. In pitch darkness with a scream bubbling in his throat. Dammit, if he had to stay awake for the rest of his life to avoid the gut-wrenching nightmares, then that's just what he'd do.

He lunged out of bed, slipped into his trousers and yanked on his boots. He needed air. Badly. The four walls of his small room were closing in on him again.

As he rushed out into the hall, Cole was just stumbling through his bedroom doorway.

"Thought I heard you yellin' in your sleep again," he mumbled half-awake.

Reason didn't even slow down to answer him. Was every simple move he made, or sound he uttered, a cause for public concern? He made a quick right and ran down the stairs. If everyone would just leave him the hell alone! He burst through the back door and tore out into the night like a bat shot from hell.

"Reason!" Cole was right behind him, but Reason kept on running. He wasn't sure where he was going, just far enough away that the fearful images imbedded in his brain couldn't find him.

"Stop!"

Reason came to an abrupt skidding halt. His chest was heaving so badly he couldn't catch his breath. *Why couldn't they just leave him alone? What the hell kind of animals were they?*

Cole rushed up to his side. He was gasping also from the furious mad dash outside, but now he was wide-awake.

"What're you doin', Reason?" He moved to face him, blocking his retreat. If Reason chose to run again, he'd have to turn around and head back towards the house. "Where you runnin' to?"

"Anywhere away from here," was the answer.

Reason needed space. Okay, Cole could understand that.

"You want company?"

Reason backed up a step. He shook his head. "No."

Cole ran his fingers through sleep-tousled hair. He was under direct orders from Randall not to let Reason out of his sight for a minute. Except when he was sleeping. And now they were both fully awake.

"Well, you're gettin' it anyway. Come on." He jerked his head at the trees beyond him. "Let's go for a walk. Maybe you can tell me about your nightmares. I'm getting awful tired of havin' my sleep disturbed every night. I've heard talkin' helps some."

Cole's deep drawl was familiar to him. Calm and soothing.

Reason sensed he had nothing to fear from this man. But what had happened to the others? The ones that were chasing him? He darted a quick look over his shoulder, but there was no one there. Had he imagined all of it? Again?

Jesus, he had to get a grip. In an unconscious imitation of Cole, he ran shaky fingers through his own dark hair. He couldn't go on like this much longer. Maybe Cole was right. It might help to talk to someone. And who else was there?

"All right." He finally nodded to the man standing before him.

Cole wasn't exactly sure what Reason was agreeing to, but whatever it was, he knew it was a start in the right direction. He stepped to the side and let Reason set the pace. He was curious to see just where Reason would lead him.

He didn't have long to wait. Reason seemed to know exactly where he was going this time. They ended up at the stream where they had once gone fishing.

Moonlight filtered through the leaves of the cottonwood trees casting eerie shadows on the low grassy bank. An owl hooted from somewhere up above. The lone cry of a lobo wolf sounded far away. Reason moved woodenly towards the flat rock where he normally lounged and sat stiffly down on it. Then rested his elbows on bent knees and lowered his head into his hands.

Cole crouched at the river's edge, picked up a smooth-edged stone, reared back his right arm, and sailed the rock out over the water as far as he could throw. He kept watching the undulating surface of the water until he saw the subtle ripples of the stone's splash.

"I almost made it across that time." He turned to Reason with an easy grin.

Reason sat unmoving in the shadows and Cole wondered whether he had heard him or not.

"You want to talk about it?" he said gently.

Cole was damn sure he didn't want to hear Reason's account of his time in the trapper's cabin. He had already thrown up once in this spot and wasn't looking for a repeat performance. But to his instant relief, Reason just shook his head. Guess he changed his mind. And that was fine with him.

Then Reason said, "There were two of them." And Cole's gut clenched.

"One of the men saved my life." Reason lifted his head to stare blindly out over the water as he had done once before. Then slowly he closed his eyes, clenched his teeth, and ducked his head to his chest. "I can't do this," he said with a tight throat.

Cole ran a hand over his face, then slapped himself to full awareness. Damn, now he was the one getting mental pictures. He'd be puking his guts up once more if he wasn't careful.

"Reason, you don't have to..." he started to say, but Reason continued as if Cole hadn't spoken.

"The one who found me was named Buck. The other... Mortimer." Reason spoke slowly, as if each word had to be forced out of his throat with a great deal of effort.

Cole kept silent. He could always put his hands over his ears if things got too bad. Reason wasn't even looking his way anyhow. He'd never know.

"They waited until I was able to stand up on my own. I didn't know what they planned...." Cole saw him shudder violently.

Then Reason shook his head in denial of his own words. "Yes, I did. I could see the hunger in their eyes. But I refused to accept it."

He laughed in a harsh way. "After all they had just saved my life." Then he sobered. "And now I wish to hell they had never found me at all."

Cole swallowed hard. Here was another reason why the man shouldn't regain possession of his pistol until he was fully sane. One that Cole had never thought of before. Reason might decide one day to take his own life. He'd have to keep that thought in mind in case one day he forgot, and Reason blew his brains out for nothing.

"There was not a damn thing you could do, Reason. You're not responsible for the acts of those men. You had a bullet hole in your back, remember?"

Reason's haunted pale blue eyes raised to Cole.

"Oh yeah. How could I forget? They used that against me, every damn chance they could get."

His lips curled in a sullen sneer and his eyes grew cold and hard. He reminded Cole of that lobo wolf he had just heard singing at the moon a short while ago. Wild and untamed.

"I tried to fight them off...." Reason paused in remembrance.

"But I was too damn weak." He shook his head slowly. "And they were just too damn strong."

This time Cole looked away and glanced unseeing out over the water.

"They forced me to do things that...." His voice suddenly broke and he choked. His right elbow had been resting on a bent knee and now he raised that hand to shield his eyes and part of his face.

"Shit!"

Cole sneaked a quick glance over at Reason. He wanted to tell him it's okay. I know the story. You don't need to rehash it again in your mind. But he kept silent. Reason needed to voice his fears out loud. He needed to face his demons squarely and realize nothing had changed because of them. Only then could his mind begin the long road back to normalcy.

Then Reason groaned. "They used me, Cole. Like they would a woman. Only worse." Then as if a damn had burst somewhere deep inside, a muffled soul-wrenching sob shook his lean frame, and he began to cry softly behind his hand.

Cole jerked his gaze back to the river that now blurred before his eyes. Blindly he picked up another rock and threw it far out across the water just for the hell of it. He didn't much care when it finally landed upon the opposite shore. Cole was sick to the depths of his soul for the needless suffering Reason had gone through. And all because of him.

An image of the two tough trappers came unbidden to his mind.

Some men didn't deserve to breathe.

CHAPTER NINETEEN

Cole had been wrong. Spilling his guts hadn't helped Reason at all. If anything he became worse. He shied away from Cole now at the slightest opportunity. If Cole spoke to him and demanded an answer, Reason was back to one-word syllables. He seemed to withdraw further into himself, if that was humanly possible. And Cole knew something had to give soon, or Reason would be lost to them forever.

Leaning across the polished mahogany bar of the Golden Nugget Saloon, Cole reached out and poured himself another beer right out of the tap. They had ridden into town early this morning for a few necessary supplies then, once purchased and tied on the backs of their saddles, Cole had headed for the nearest saloon to quench a long-suffering thirst.

The portly bartender frowned at his actions from the far corner where he was chatting with a customer, but he recognized Cole from his frequent visits in town and knew he was good for it. In response, Cole reached into his shirt pocket and plunked a few silver coins down on the counter in payment for the drink he just poured himself along with a few extra, which seemed to satisfy the man for the moment. Cole had no thoughts of sneaking a free beer. He just didn't care to wait for the bartender to mosey over to him for a refill. He was planning to tie one on today, no matter what.

Keeping tabs on Reason had become his personal chore and moral obligation, and was more than a bit trying at times. A responsibility he hadn't asked for, yet felt hugely guilty about. If only he had ridden home with him from Laramie, then none of this hell would ever have taken place. He raised the glass to his lips and took a deep swallow, then slid his gaze towards the man that stood beside him.

"Want another?" Cole swiped the foam off his lips with the back of his hand.

"Not right now." Reason had his head down and was staring at his half-full glass as if in deep thought. Yet only Cole knew there wasn't much going on behind that vacant stare.

Cole shifted his glance towards the large full-length mirror behind the bar. The place was busy for a weekday afternoon. Five men were seated at a wooden table smoking cigars and playing a concentrated game of stud poker, while a few scantily clad ladies were circulating among the drinking patrons lined up at the bar. Yet there was one man leaning lazily against the far wall, deep in the shadows that worried Cole. The annoying fellow seemed to have an unhealthy interest in Reason's unsuspecting back.

Directing his gaze over his shoulder, Cole could have sworn the man grinned. Then the fellow pushed away from the wall just as a pretty bottle-blonde girl, not a day over twenty, brushed up against Reason's right arm. He felt Reason's entire body tense beside him.

"Howdy handsome," she smiled. "What's so special about that warm beer in your hand? You've been starin' at it for ten minutes now. I've got somethin' else you can look at that might be of more interest to ya."

She wasn't bad either, Cole had to admit. With her painted-up face, wide brown eyes, and bright yellow curls, she looked like a store-bought china doll. But she wasn't speaking to Cole at the moment, and the man she was interested in acted as if he had suddenly turned to stone.

"Are ya deaf, honey?" she asked simply, as she traced a well-manicured fingernail up his dark-sleeved arm. "Cause if you are, I know some sign language that could help. I had a friend of mine," she went on, "that couldn't hear a train whistle if he was standing right next to the station." She smiled seductively. "And we never had no trouble communicatin'." She peered up at him and batted her curled black eyelashes at him. But when she saw she wasn't getting any response, she said, "Well, if you'd rather have one of the other girls, I can arrange that too."

"He's not interested," Cole said from Reason's left. Then he leaned sideways across the bar so he was facing her and grinned in his girl chasing, devil-may-care way. "But I might be so inclined."

She smiled sweetly at him, but the sudden sound of men scraping chairs against the scuffed wood floor in their haste at retreat, drew her head around.

"Cord?"

Reason jerked at the coarse, slightly mocking sound of his name issued from a stranger close behind him and, without once raising his head, drew in a deep ragged breath. Cole glanced once more over his shoulder to see the man who had been lounging against the far wall, now standing less than ten feet behind Reason. And "Cord" was the handle most gunslingers used to challenge him with when they were scouting up trouble.

"Stay put, Reason," Cole whispered low. "He won't shoot you in the back. You're unarmed, and there's just too damn many witnesses."

"Turn around, boy," the man sneered. "I'd like to have a word with you."

The man was whipcord lean to the point of being gaunt. He had a scar running diagonally down his left cheek and he had a missing front tooth that a fella noticed when he smiled. Against Cole's wishes, Reason turned to face him.

"Where's your pistol, Cord? That Colt .44 I hear you favor?"

Reason was silent. His missing gun belt was obvious. He didn't feel the need to comment on it. The blonde-haired young girl slid hastily away from his side and out of immediate danger.

"Never heard of you strolling around town without packing a gun on your hip before," the man went on. "I've been waitin' a long time to run into you. Sure hope you're not turnin' over a new leaf. First you turn down the ladies, then you face me without a gun in your hand? Tsk, tsk," he made a clucking sound with his tongue. "What is this world comin' to?"

Reason reached back and braced both hands on the curved brass rail of the bar. Only Cole saw that they were trembling.

With the intent of avoiding trouble, Cole pushed away from the bar and slapped Reason on the shoulder just hard enough to grab his attention.

"Come on, we're through here. There's other places we can go to wet our whistle. This one's sort of lost its appeal."

"Hey, hold on there," the stranger made a furtive move in Cole's direction as he started to head for the door. "You stay out'a this if you know what's good for ya."

Then Cole grinned and when Reason made no move to follow, turned to face the man squarely.

"Well now, I was never much good at book learnin'. So I guess some folks don't consider me too bright. But I do know what would thrill me to pieces right now would be to beat the living crap out a jackass like you!"

The stranger's gun was in his hand before Cole could blink.

"You've got a big mouth for someone slow on the draw," he said. "Just how would you like it if I shoot a few holes in you for fun?"

"Define the word 'fun'," Cole snapped in reply, fearless of the man before him. "Only a coward would shoot another man for sport."

Suddenly Cole became aware of Reason's labored breathing beside him. The trembling in his hands now spread to his arms. Somehow, he had to get Reason out of there fast, or else divert attention from him. For if word of his instability happened to spread among the varied up-and-coming gunslingers roaming the Wyoming territory, looking to make a name for themselves, he'd be putty in their hands. And many wouldn't give a damn whether he wore a gun strapped to his hip, or not. They'd shoot him on sight.

"Are you callin' me a coward?" the stranger shouted in awe. "You've got some balls for a man that won't pull his own gun."

"You've already got me covered. What damn good would it do?"

Slowly the man holstered his revolver. "Any time you're ready, fella." He grinned with that unnerving gap-toothed smile.

Cole was caught in his own trap. He knew full well he was no match for the man standing before him. He was a ranch hand by nature, not a fast gun like Reason. But he had backed himself into a corner with his own words and now there was only one way out. And Cole had never been a patient man.

He jerked his hand towards his revolver, closed his fingers around the worn mahogany butt, and had almost cleared leather when the stunning blow of a bullet plowed deep into his chest. Cole stumbled backwards against the brass rail of the bar as the crashing sound of the man's discharging pistol sounded loud in his ears. A woman screamed shrilly in the distance as the room tilted out of focus and as Cole's hand lost his grip, the revolver dropped easily back into his holster. He grabbed onto the bar for support and swayed there a brief minute, gasping for breath, before his knees buckled beneath him and he slid to the floor on his back.

"Reason..." he gasped as all sound began to fade and the room grew dangerously dark.

Reason never moved so much as an inch. His back was still braced against the bar. His mind a muddled fog of confusion mixed with outright fear.

The stranger's aim shifted back towards the man he knew as Cord.

"Your friend just bought the farm," he sneered. "Don't you even give a damn?"

Reason was only half-listening. Everything had happened too damn fast to comprehend. One minute Cole was standing next to him, planning to leave. The next, gunfire erupted right in his face and Cole was lying flat on the floor.

Bought the farm? Is that what he said? Slowly Reason's eyes swept over the man he knew as Cole lying so deathly still near his feet. There was an ugly raw and gaping hole that had ripped through the front of Cole's blue shirt at his left shoulder, while a dark red stain slowly seeped across his chest. Cole's normally sun-tanned pallor was now ashen and already the man looked dead to Reason's eyes.

Then the stranger moved forward until he was only a few inches from Reason. The gaunt, scarred face peered at him as if he were a strange specimen unknown to man.

"I've heard about fellas like you. That lost their nerve. Never met one until now." Casually he holstered his pistol and grinned. "What's it feel like, being on top of the world one minute and then flung to the bottom of the heap the next, I wonder?" he sneered. Then he drew back his fist and slammed Reason deep in the gut.

Reason doubled up in a rush of pain from the unexpected blow, while air escaped his throat in a grunt of denial. His hands instinctively raised to his belly in an effort to protect himself from further punishment. Now this was something he could understand, being savagely beaten for disobeying a direct order.

The next blow came up under the left side of the jaw and

snapped his head around. Brooking no resistance, his body twisted sideways and he fell, face forward, against the top of the bar. *Jesus, not again.* The smoothness of the mahogany wood felt cool against his aching cheek, but the stranger wasn't through yet. A strong, bony fist grabbed the scruff of Reason's shirt and he was dragged backwards and violently wrenched around. Another blow to his gut made him jerk hard and gasp out loud. The last blow to his unprotected face made him stumble backwards, trip over Cole's prone form and fall sprawling to the floor where he stayed, docile and weary, gulping for air.

"There's not much left of you is there," the stranger sneered. "You're not even worth my effort."

Then the stranger stepped triumphantly around both fallen men and sauntered casually towards the door.

Reason was the first to come to his senses. His jaw ached incessantly and his belly hurt to the point of nausea. He blinked awake only to find a golden-haired angel peering down at him with dark doe eyes.

"Are you okay?" she asked with an anxious frown.

Unsure of the answer, Reason struggled to rise, but his legs seemed to hamper his progress as if they were tangled up over something, or someone. Then he saw him.

"Cole?"

Instantly he was on his knees beside Cole's prone form.

"What happened?" he said to the pretty little blonde thing kneeling next to him. Without further thought, he ripped open the torn and bloody shirt to expose a raw and gaping hole near Cole's left shoulder, then slipped off the blue bandanna Cole wore around his throat and folded it into a pad. He pressed the material deep against the wound to staunch the bleeding and was relieved to see Cole flinch, then groan in protest of the rough handling.

"What do you mean? Don't you know?" the girl said. "You were the cause of it all. That fella who just left here wanted you to draw, but you weren't wearin' any gun. So he took his frustrations out on this poor innocent soul." She lightly brushed Cole's forehead with her hand in a gentle caress. "Is he dyin'?"

"Not if I can help it. Somebody get the doctor," he yelled over his shoulder to whoever would hear.

"Already sent for," the bartender said from above. "He should be here soon."

"Cole? Can you hear me?" Reason asked softly.

Cole's dark eyelashes flickered once and then he blinked up at Reason. "What happened...?"

"Mercy, is that a standard response?" the girl laughed in a nervous way. "Doesn't anyone in this dump pay attention when someone's shooting at them?"

Then Cole shifted on the floor in a poor attempt to rise and his breath whistled between clenched teeth.

"Don't move. Stay down. Someone just went for Peterson. Who did this, Cole?"

Cole's amber eyes peered up at Reason in a suspicious squint.

"Hell, am I hurt so bad that you're finally shocked back to your senses?" His head fell wearily to the side. "Just bury me deep, Reason. I don't want the coyotes fightin' over my remains."

"You're not going to die, Cole. Unless you bleed to death for spite. It's a shoulder wound. Missed your heart by inches. Now just tell me who did it and I'll let you be."

"For cryin' out loud, didn't you see...?" he started to say, when a deep voice shouted from the window. "The fella you're lookin' for is just crossin' the street."

"Much obliged," Reason said rising. "Take over here," he said to the girl. "I'll be right back." His hip felt unusually light when he began to move and when he glanced down he saw why. Dropping down to one knee, he unbuckled the gun belt strapped to Cole's waist.

"I'm just borrowing this for a minute," he said when Cole glanced up with a question in his eyes. Reason slid the belt gently as he could out from beneath him.

"Where do you think you're goin' with that?" Cole said, as Reason rose to his feet.

"I've got a debt to pay." Reason slapped the belt around his waist, tied the holster to his thigh, then checked the chambers to find they were fully loaded. Cole never got off one shot.

"Are you crazy?" Cole yelled, then winced hard. "Dammit he is, you fool." He answered his own question as Reason headed for the door.

"Somebody stop him," he shouted, then swore at the sudden sharp pain in his chest. "He doesn't know what in the world he's doin'," he gasped. "He's not even wearin' his own gun!"

"Seems to be doin' all right for himself," a man spoke from the window. "He's out in the street bracin' the fella that shot ya."

Reason adjusted the heavy gun belt low on his hip as he ran out the front door of the saloon. His brain was still a bit frazzled and cloudy in areas, but his mind was dead set on revenge. Cole had taken a bullet meant for him. That's what the girl said. He wasn't exactly sure why that thought angered him so, or exactly how it had happened with him standing right there, but it sure as hell did. Now if he could just spot the fellow....

Glancing rapidly in all directions, he stepped out into the street. A thin, reedy fellow with a well-oiled tied down holster was just gaining the sidewalk across the way.

"Hey! You! With the fancy gun belt!"

The gunslinger froze with one foot already on the walkway, the other still in the dirt of the street. Then slowly he swiveled to face his adversary.

It was the same man. Reason would have bet his life on it.

"Were you looking for action?" Reason shouted. "Because if you are...." He raised his arms far out from his sides, so the gap-toothed fellow could easily see he was armed.

"Well, now. Ain't this a surprise. You finally come to your senses? It must be Christmas in July."

In one fluid motion, the man dropped to a crouch and brought up a pistol that fairly leaped to his hand with the speed of a striking rattlesnake. Flames shot from his gun as he fired three times in rapid succession, yet not one bullet met its mark.

Acting on pure instinct alone, Reason had begun his draw as the man dropped to a crouch. But the butt of Cole's pistol felt foreign to his hand. The grip was too stocky and the balance was way off. And there was no time to make hasty adjustments. A split-second before the stranger's gun drew level, Reason dove to the ground and rolled to his right as fast-flying bullets whizzed over his head and thudded into the front wall of the saloon. He heard glass shatter and men curse behind him. Then, in one breathless moment and with the easy grace of a mountain cat, he rolled to his feet, judged distance against the excessive weight of the pistol, and fired one shot in return.

The man jerked in surprise. His pistol fell, forgotten to the ground. With both hands, he clutched at a wet, red stain spreading rapidly across his chest. He staggered once, then dropped to his knees in the dirt. And there he stayed, his eyes glazing over with pain coupled with the first promise of death, as Reason holstered his revolver and casually sauntered up to him.

"What's your name, Mister? I'll see it's written properly on your tombstone."

"Fess Jackson. I don't understand...." He coughed as fluid began building in his lungs. "A minute ago...." He glanced up at the gunslinger he knew as Cord. "Are you the same man?"

A muscle bunched in Reason's tightly clenched jaw.

"I certainly hope not."

CHAPTER TWENTY

By the time Reason strolled once more into the saloon, Doc Peterson was already kneeling beside his latest patient. Cole's face was screwed up in pain and a clean rag lay clenched tightly between his teeth. As the doc cautiously probed the bloody hole in the wounded man's chest with a slim metal instrument, Reason could plainly hear Cole's muffled groans of protest above the cheerful banter of the fast-gathering crowd.

Two men were holding him down. One at his head, holding his shoulders, and another at his booted ankles. But still Cole thrashed dangerously beneath them.

"Dammit, if you don't lay still I'll quit right now," Peterson warned, kneeling across Cole's left wrist in an effort to calm the injured man's flailing movements. "You always were a troublesome patient along with that partner of yours, and some things just don't get any better with time. If you're gonna bleed to death, then I'm just wasting precious minutes here. I've got a young woman about to deliver twins any second now. And she needs my help just as much as you do. Now what's it gonna be, young fella. Are you gonna behave? Or do I walk!"

The front of Cole's shirt was in bloody tatters in an effort to expose the bullet-laden wound for extraction, and both his chest and face held a sheen of nervous perspiration. He seemed weary to Reason's eyes even though he kept struggling against his human bonds in a near-frantic, unceasing, manner.

Without conscious thought, Reason shouldered through the small knot of curious onlookers circling the injured man and knelt, near the doc, by his side.

"Simmer down, Cole," he said soothingly, trying to instill a sense of calm in the overwrought man. "Peterson's just trying to help. It'll be over in a minute if you just try to relax and let the doc finish what he has to do."

At the sound of the familiar, husky voice Cole knew so well, his pain-glazed amber eyes slowly opened and his fearful glance swept rapidly over the strangers crowded above him with a frenzied purpose. Yet only when his searching eyes finally dropped lower to focus on Reason crouched beside him did his movements abruptly still and his body grow limp with obvious relief.

Peterson gave a sharp crow of victory. "Ha! Now we're getting somewhere. Don't you go anywhere Cordell, until this sucker's out. I don't aim to be working here all damn day."

The doctor knew these two men well. Knew the close-knit bond the two men shared. Why, he once swore he had taken enough lead out of both their hides over the years, to load a cannon. And it looked like he wasn't through yet!

Cole flinched as the doctor once again began his careful probing and a short groan caught deep in his throat. But within seconds Peterson pulled a flat piece of metal out from the small bloody hole in Cole's chest.

"Got it!" He laughed. "That little devil. Now that wasn't so bad, was it," he snickered smugly.

Cole made a muffled, frustrated, response in reply. Without thinking of the consequences, Reason leaned over and removed the gag so he could be clearly heard.

"Not for you," Cole snapped churlishly. "I wonder how you'd like it if…." Cole never had the chance to finish.

Peterson hastily snatched the cloth out of Reason's hand and rammed it between Cole's teeth once more.

"I'm not finished yet," he ordered sternly, then winked conspiratorially at Reason. Reaching behind him, he uncorked a half-full bottle of whisky and then proceeded to pour a quarter of the contents all over Cole's injured shoulder. Cole jerked hard and banged his head against the floor in the process. His face twisted in a painful grimace and he made a guttural sound of protest deep in his throat. Reason knew from experience that pouring whiskey on an open wound was a necessary evil and a fiery sting you never forgot. But thankfully, within seconds, Cole's body went limp and he mercifully passed out.

"A few of you men cart this fella to my office for me so I can get on to my other patient," Peterson called out a few minutes later as he rose to his feet, "and I'll give you free medical advice for a month."

"Make it a year," someone laughed from within the group, "and you've got yourself a deal." A few men chuckled as Reason moved automatically to help. But suddenly the blonde girl was there, blocking his view, along with his efforts.

"Your friend will be all right," she smiled sweetly at him. "But I'll still be lonely. Buy me a drink?"

As Reason started to move around her, she placed the palms of both her hands on his chest and slid them sensuously down to his waist.

Reason sucked in a deep breath. His gut tightened automatically at her gentle touch, and this time not in fear or disgust, but in actual desire.

"I can't," he said. "I have to make sure...." He glanced over her head in time to see his blissfully unconscious friend being carried out the bat-wing doors by three helpful strangers.

"Just one," she crooned softly. "And then you can go if you want. I promise." Her small body obstructed his retreat and her hands now slid around his back as she pressed her soft shapely curves against his own hard frame.

A slow smile crept across Reason's boyishly chiseled jawline and he shrugged helplessly.

"I guess one couldn't hurt."

Sliding an arm around her small, trim waist, they moved as one to the bar. There he ordered another beer for himself and when she nodded, a tea-ladened whiskey for the lady. Spying an empty table in the far corner he carried the drinks over and spread them out on the table. But when he went to take his seat, she slid into his lap and positioned herself comfortably across his rock-hard thighs.

"I hope I'm not too heavy," she grinned coyly, flinging a bare arm across his shoulder, as Reason smiled back. Once again, she had outsmarted him with no amount of effort on her part.

"Can you reach your drink from here?" Reason teased. "Or should I order you another."

"No, this is just fine."

My stars, the girl was thinking to herself, *this man has the most startling black-lashed clear-blue eyes she had ever seen.*

135

When he stared at you, he seemed to look right through a girl all the way to heaven and beyond.

"You sure are a handsome devil," she giggled. "Anyone ever tell you that?"

Suddenly Reason wasn't seeing the blonde-haired, brown-eyed vixen that was seated before him any longer. This woman was a few years older with titian feathered bangs and a mane of thick wavy hair. Sea green eyes blazed angrily at him from beneath pale brows. *"Reason! Come back! I love you, dammit!"* Those few short words seemed to echo again and again in his brain.

Reason blinked, and the young girl, once again, came vividly into focus. His conscience leaped. What the hell was he doing sitting in a saloon with a barmaid on his lap? He was a married man. Wasn't he? Cole said he was.

"I have to be going," he said. He tried to guide her gently off his lap. But she was having none of it. Her hands clung to his shoulders like a dangling kitten on an expensive drape.

"But you just got here," she pouted. "At least be gentlemanly enough to wait until I finish my drink." She took the tips of her fingers and ran them lightly down his cheek.

A shiver of lust so strong he flinched, shook him to the core of his soul. *God, how long has it been since he'd lain with a woman*, he wondered silently to himself. Too damn long, judging by his reaction to this determined female.

"I know you want me," she whispered in a husky, sensuous voice as she leaned closer and her soft cheek brushed against his own bristled jaw. Her feathery breath tickled his ear, the scent of cheap perfume tickled his nose and Reason groaned low in his throat. "I can feel it." She shifted slightly on his lap. Then she took her hand and guided his face to hers when he would have glanced away.

Peering deep into his passion-glazed, slightly unfocused, pale blue eyes, she sighed.

"I'm yours, if you want me. Take me upstairs?" Then she opened her mouth and pressed her warm soft lips against his.

Reason had lost the battle. He met her willingly, halfway. His right hand caught in her hair at the back of her head and he thrust his tongue deep into her hot, moist mouth. The left hand he slid around her waist, pulling her to him as tightly as he dared. Then as he plundered her mouth with his own, his left hand slid up her side to curve beneath her soft rounded breast.

God, he had been too long without a woman. And this girl was just too damn willing.

CHAPTER TWENTY-ONE

By the time Reason made his way downstairs two hours later, he felt as if he had been scrubbed, rinsed, and wrung out to dry. Mariah's lush curvaceous body had been all over him and they had made love more than twice in the short time he had been upstairs, and in a number of unusual ways. He ran a shaky hand over his face as he bellied up to the bar and ordered a fresh beer. *Had sex ever been that good with his wife,* he wondered? He gulped half a glass down in one shot, then swiped at his lips with a sleeve the way Cole had recently done. He didn't know, for he couldn't for the life of him remember.

But although Mariah had been loving and sweet, and the only sexual partner he could mentally recall, he knew something was missing. He didn't have that contented feeling of complete satisfaction afterwards. Well, maybe satisfaction was a little far-fetched and too strong a term. For she satisfied him in every possible way. An unconscious smile creased his chiseled jaw in remembrance. Yes, indeed.

"You better not let Rachel see you grinning like the cat that ate the canary. She'd know right away what a bastard like you was up to."

Reason's insides turned to ice and he sobered quickly. Not only at the mention of his wife's name in a place where God-fearing women were forbidden, but from the threatening tone in which the warning was issued. Slowly he glanced up at the mirror over the bar.

That fellow from Rachel's ranch, Joe Steele, stood next to him caught in the act of raising a glass of beer to his lips. Furious hazel eyes locked and clashed with clear blue in the mirror beyond the bar. Reason was the first to look away.

"Can't a fella grin once in a while without someone taking it the wrong way?" Purposely, Reason stared back at his own guilty reflection, unwilling to instigate a fight with the Stirrup C Bar's hired hand. Besides, it just could be he was right.

Steele took a deep swallow, then placed his mug on the bar top.

"Depends on what he's grinning about. Now his partner just got shot up some from what I hear. So it damn well can't be that." He turned sideways to face Reason, just as Cole had done earlier. "Must be something else." He paused. "And here she comes now. And judging by the radiant expression on her face, she's looking for more of the same."

Reason froze, refusing to take the bait and glance in Mariah's direction. But he could smell her musky scent as she neared him and when she placed a familiar hand on the back of his shoulders, he didn't once flinch in surprise.

"Who's your friend, Reason?" she said pleasantly.

He was caught, red-handed, and he wasn't about to make excuses for himself to this man. He remained silent, yet he drained the rest of his beer in one shot.

"Joe Steele is the name, ma'am," he grinned with all the cunning of a rattlesnake to Reason's mind. "And may I say I admire your cologne. You smell like roses after a rainstorm, and you both reek of it!"

Reason could feel the heat of shame creeping up his neck and flaming his cheeks red. Damn this man. He hadn't liked him from the start.

Mariah gasped at his rudeness.

"Reason, who is this bore?" she snapped. "Friend, or not. I can have him thrown out of here in a dance hall minute!"

She was feisty. Reason had to give her that. And when she wanted something, she knew exactly how to get it. But Reason wasn't looking for any more trouble. He had already killed one man today, and Cole had gotten hurt in the process. Slowly he turned to her.

"It's all right. I'll handle this. Why don't you go mingle for awhile. I'll catch up with you later."

"Sure sugar. Don't be too long." She smiled in that sensuous way she had, then reached up on tiptoe and lightly kissed Reason's lips.

Reason didn't bother to move out of the way. Why should he? The cat was already out of the bag. Steele must have seen him go upstairs with her earlier, and he had probably been counting the minutes until Reason came back down.

Mariah moved away from his side and began to mingle among the other men as she was being paid to do. When Reason finally met Steele's glittering hazel eyes, the man had the audacity to grin.

"When you're finished your beer," Steele snarled insolently. "I'd like to see you outside."

CHAPTER TWENTY-TWO

Reason took his own sweet time. He ordered another brew and when that was finished, he signaled for a third. But although he paid for it, the last one he left untouched. He figured he was numb enough for whatever Steele had in mind. And he had dawdled long enough.

He had barely cleared the doorway when a tap on his left shoulder drew his head around. The blow to his face felt like he had been kicked by a mule and he went flying backwards, tripping over the leg of a chair and landing on his back on the hard wooden boardwalk. Bright spots of light danced before his eyes. The world reeled around him like a dog chasing its own tail. The sounds of the street faded out, then in again, as if his hearing was dangerously impaired.

"That was for Rachel," Steele growled low. Then he reached down and hauled Reason to his feet by the lapels of his shirt. "And this is for me." Pain exploded in Reason's belly and he retched. Then another slamming blow to his face jerked his head sideways, and he went down in a sprawl once again.

"Get up you son-of-a-bitch and fight me like a man!"

But Reason wasn't about to move a finger, even if he had heard. Harsh sounds buzzed annoyingly in his ears. The world grew dark as pitch. There were large, menacing shapes looming before him. Laughing at him. Taunting him. *"Come on, pretty boy. Don't you want to have some fun?"*

Reason threw both hands up over his eyes as he writhed on the sidewalk in a vain attempt to flee the frightening mental images imbedded deeply in his mind.

"No!"

"Aw, that little trick ain't gonna work no more," Steele said, as he grabbed Reason by the shirt and once more dragged him to his feet. Then he slammed Reason backwards against the hard wall of the saloon. "By God, if I had my way, I'd kill you right now," he snarled. His hands fisted in Reason's shirt, his work-hardened forearms pinned Reason's chest and shoulders to the wall. "But if Rachel ever found out she might never speak to me again. So I reckon I'll just have to beat you half to death instead."

Again a solid fist caused pain to explode violently in his belly, and then another, and another. When the blow connected with his jaw once again, Reason went down with a groan for the last time.

By the time Reason regained consciousness and opened his eyes, he was surprised to find his aching body stretched comfortably out upon a soft downy mattress instead of the hard planked sidewalk he remembered landing on. A pink floral spread lay beneath his back with matching ruffled pillows scattered strategically about the bed.

Obviously a woman's room and one that seemed vaguely familiar. But who's? When he attempted to raise himself up, a blinding headache dropped him right back down to the pillows beneath his head. The faint scent of roses was in the air coupled with the musky aroma of recent lovemaking. Oh, shit! He was back in Mariah's bedroom on the second floor of the Golden Nugget again. How the hell did he get back here?

Hastily he threw his denim-clad legs over the side of the bed and struggled to sit up. Instantly the room spun wildly around him. Nausea hit him like a ton of bricks and he lurched out of bed, stumbled towards the wide-open window on the left wall, leaned far out over the sill, and retched the contents of his stomach into the narrow, darkened alleyway below.

When he was through, he leaned his back against the window frame and groaned softly. Great, now he smelled of raw sex, cheap perfume, and stale beer. He needed a bath. Badly. But that would have to wait until later.

His senses reeled as he began to stumble his way back to bed, but his knees buckled beneath him before he got halfway there. He hit the floor hard on his face and the jarring jolt almost made him retch again. But this time he couldn't get up. His belly hurt and his head throbbed unmercifully. Instinctively he rolled to his back in a vain attempt to rise and abruptly passed out.

The second time he awoke Mariah was there by his side.

"You gave me such a fright," she said as if she were scolding a wayward child. "Whatever made you get out of bed this morning? I only went downstairs to grab a bite to eat and when I came up here, you were sprawled out on the floor. I thought you were dead," she shouted at him. "I had to have Dominic pick you up and put you back into bed. Don't ever do that to me again!"

"Don't worry. I won't." Reason's voice sounded muffled as if he spoke with a handful of marbles stuffed in his mouth. And he didn't dare ask who the hell Dominic was. Slowly he swung his legs over the side of the bed and sat up.

"Where's my boots," he said as the room spun around him once more.

"Right there, next to you on the floor. But you can't get up yet. You need to rest before you get back on your feet."

Reason ignored her and with a muffled groan slipped on his boots. Then he rose from the bed, stamped his right heel down, turned, and said, "I'm already on my feet. Where's my gun belt?"

She nodded over her shoulder. "Over there by the door."

Reason managed to saunter casually to the dresser she indicated, grab the belt off the top and slap it snugly around his lean hips. Cole's buckle was worn and a little tricky, but he finally managed to clasp the thing on. His black Stetson was lying on the same bureau and he placed it on his head, tugging the brim low on his brow.

He hesitated with one hand on the doorknob and turned to Mariah.

"Thanks. For everything." Then he opened the door and stepped out into the hall.

The saloon was quiet when he stumbled down the stairs that afternoon. Yet even those few patrons scattered about the room eyed him strangely when he staggered over to the bar and ordered a beer.

He was surprised when the bartender refused to serve him.

"I think what you need, young fella, is some wholesome food

from the looks of you. And that you can find in the café across the street.

Reason nodded the best he was able. "You might be right." But when he reached the sidewalk, instead of the café, he headed directly towards Peterson's office.

"What the hell happened to you?" Peterson's eyes were huge as if he were witnessing a catastrophe first-hand. He leaned far back in his chair and squinted at the newcomer as if to assess the damage to the man. "You look as if a herd of stampeding buffalo ran all over your face."

"If you think that's bad, you should see the rest of me," Reason said with a tight grin.

"Sit down boy," he indicated an empty chair before his desk. "And let me have a look at you." Peterson rose to his feet, but Reason held up a staying hand.

"I appreciate your concern, but I'm here to see Cole."

"Oh him. Another one. Between the two of you fellas I could retire a happy man."

"I think it's already too late for that old timer," Reason said with a wry grin that hurt like hell when he finally managed to accomplish it.

"Smart ass," Peterson growled under his breath, as he regained his seat. "Second door on your right."

"Much obliged."

Cole was propped up in bed with plump pillows piled high beneath his head when Reason strolled into the room. His ruined shirt was gone, while a stark white bandage circled his chest with a knot tied at the left shoulder. He appeared to be sleeping peacefully and Reason was reluctant to wake him. But as the door clicked shut behind him, Cole slowly opened his eyes, blinked, then frowned his way.

"You look like...."

"I know, I know." Reason interrupted. "Like a herd of buffaloes ran all over me."

Cole grinned. "I was gonna say long-horns." Then he sobered. "Who did all that work on your face? I don't recall you bein' so beat-up before I finally passed out. But I could be wrong. Did that weasel-faced gunslinger slam you with his gun barrel instead of shooting ya with it?"

"No. He won't be causing any more trouble."

"Figured that. I heard the gunshots from the hard floor of the saloon. Gotta admit I was kind of worried until I saw those damn blue eyes of yours starin' me down once again." He drew a deep breath as if it was an effort to speak. "Then who...?"

"A fella by the name of Joe Steele."

Cole's eyes widened in surprise. "Joe? What's he got to do with all this?"

"He'd been in town yesterday. All the commotion must have drawn him to the saloon. Somehow he saw me go upstairs with Mariah. He was waiting to challenge me about it when I came back down."

"You mean that pretty little blonde filly?"

At Reason's nod, Cole whistled softly between his teeth. "Well, that explains it, I guess."

"Explains what...?"

"Aw, nothin'. Joe gets carried away sometimes when it comes to Rachel."

Reason squinted at him. "I thought she was my wife? Just what is their relationship anyway? I suspect there's more going on between those two than I care to hear about."

"Well, you're probably right about that. But I wouldn't know," Cole hedged innocently.

"I think you're aware of a lot more than you let on. Now are you going to tell me? Or do I have to find out the hard way, once again?"

Cole grew uneasy. He grabbed the corner of the blanket and pulled it up to his chest as if to remind Reason he was a sick man. Then he shrugged, and winced. "Okay you win. I guess I've known for some time that Joe and Rachel had become pretty close, what with the running of the ranch and all. Damn, it's only natural that he would feel protective of her, if you know what I mean. And since you've been away so damn long.... Well, hell. Who can blame her?"

"He's in love with her."

Cole snorted derisively. "Always has. That's no news."

Reason moved towards the window and stared into the street.

"Go on."

"That's about it, I guess."

That wasn't good enough for Reason.

"Just how far do you think they go?" He recalled walking into Rachel's office and seeing the two bent over the desk, studying some numbers written in a book. Their startled, almost guilty, expressions as he stepped unannounced into the room. As if he had interrupted something he had no business seeing.

And Steele had the nerve to confront me over Mariah, Reason fumed. *When all along he was secretly bedding my wife!* Reason's world went red with rage. He barely heard Cole say....

"I'm sure there's nothing serious going on. But, well, they are alone a lot. And they rely on one another to see the work gets done as it should. And Jocelyn dotes on Joe. She always has.

"Jocelyn?"

"Hell, you don't remember anything, do ya? She's your daughter."

CHAPTER TWENTY-THREE

Reason couldn't eat a bite. Between his split lip, his jaw all swollen and sore, his queasy, aching stomach, and this latest bit of news, he threw down the fork in a fit of disgust and pushed the mouth-watering plate of steak and home fries far away from him. He should have ordered oatmeal, soup, eggs, or any other soft food if he actually expected to swallow a damn thing, he thought grudgingly.

A bowl of sour-tasting gruel suddenly appeared in Reason's mind, along with the dirty bearded faces of two demented mountain men leering lustfully in his direction. In a heart-thudding panic, he kicked back the chair and rose unsteadily to his feet.

"Is anything wrong, sir?" A middle-aged waitress said as she turned towards the clean-cut young man that had just risen from his seat. His thick wavy dark hair was slicked wetly back behind his ears as if he had just come from the bathhouse down the street. He was a welcome addition to the café, a man that stood out far above the rest of the slovenly hard-case miscreants that sometimes ate there, and she wondered if his order had left something to be desired.

"No. It's all right." His voice trembled slightly as he ran his fingers through his damp hair. For a minute there, he had almost lost it again. Would he never be whole? He thought Mariah had gotten him over the hump, so to speak, but now he guessed he was wrong.

"I can get you something a bit easier to chew," she offered noting his bruised face and swollen lip. "Some soup, maybe?"

"Thanks, I'm fine." He drew a crumpled bill out of his pocket, threw it on the table, and left without waiting for change. He'd eat later, tomorrow, next week, next year. Who cared? No one.

147

And yet he had a daughter. Rachel must have cared enough for him at one time to give him an heir. *"Reason, I love you, dammit!"*

It hadn't been that long ago she'd shouted those condemning words at his fleeing back. When had she changed her mind? And why did the thought of her sleeping with that fellow Steele hurt so damn much?

He recalled the silent invitation in the moist green eyes the day he had turned tail and run straight out of the room and through the front door of the Stirrup C Bar like a cowardly rat, afraid to face up to a host of responsibilities that he couldn't for the life of him recall. The same day Steele had felt the need to pulverize some sense into him with his fists the first time.

"Reason, I love you!" He hadn't seen her since. She must have grown disgusted with his abandonment of her and turned to Steele for the comfort and pleasure she wanted and needed from a man.

Just as he had turned to Mariah.

But, regardless of the facts, she was still legally his wife! Not Joe Steele's. And as far as he knew, she never once saw fit to file for divorce throughout the long months of their estrangement. Maybe he should ride out to the ranch once again and try to fix things between them. If she would only give him half a chance, maybe he could remember the way it used to be. After all, he loved her enough to marry her, didn't he?

He squinted up at the sun. Now just what direction was that ranch in? He couldn't seem to remember. Maybe he should just ride out and give Satan his head like he did the last time. But from town he might automatically head back to Randall's Stirrup C, instead of Rachel's.

He'd ask Cole. He'd know.

Cole knew, but he wasn't talking.

"I don't think it's a good idea, Reason. The timing is all wrong, it's too soon. You're still forgetful at times. And I don't want you butting heads again with Steele without me around. There's no sense pushing his buttons without just cause. We need him to help Rachel run the ranch while we're not there. And he almost killed you twice, are you forgettin'? Wait until I'm on my feet and we can go together. You probably don't remember much about him, but of all the damn gunslingers in this world, I think he's the one who could take you down."

Reason had no choice but to abide by Cole's wishes. Anyway, what was the all-fired hurry? He still had Mariah standing by whenever he felt the need for female companionship.

But somehow that thought didn't set well with his conscience anymore and, until he made things right one way or the other with Rachel, he planned on avoiding the Golden Nugget as much as humanly possible.

He was on his way to check on Satan boarded at the livery stable on the edge of town that afternoon, when someone shouted his name.

"Mr. Cordell?"

Reason jerked around, the palm of his right hand automatically reaching for the butt of Cole's pistol. He was leery of anyone calling him anything after that business in the saloon yesterday. And he was still sore as hell in places, and wasn't up to another fight of any kind. But this man wore a silver star pinned to his vest and Reason began to relax.

"Didn't mean to startle you, Mr. Cordell," he said genially. "I know you must be a bit jumpy after all the events of yesterday. By the way, there was a five hundred dollar reward out for that man you shot. As soon as it comes in off the stage, I'll let you know."

"Send it to his next of kin," Reason said. "I'm not claiming any part of it."

"Oh, well fine. In that case, I will," Sheriff Brannigan stammered in surprise.

"See you around then." Reason turned to continue on his way.

"Uh, there is one other thing."

Reason halted. What now? Slowly he turned to face the man with the badge once more.

"That fella in my cell. Joe Steele. What do you want me to do with him? He works for you, I take it? Do you want to press charges for assault?"

A wide smile began to take shape along Reason's bruised jaw. Maybe this wasn't such a bad day after all.

"Would it mean a jail term?"

"It's entirely possible."

Reason hesitated. He glanced down the semi-busy street, stalling for time and then back to the lawman again. This unforeseen set of circumstances opened up a whole new world of possibilities. With Joe Steele safely out of the way, he might have more of a chance at winning back the distant affections of a badly neglected wife.

"I'd like to see him first."

"Sure. Stop by around four. I should be back by then." He tipped his hat. "Good day, Mr. Cordell."

"It sure is, Sheriff."

CHAPTER TWENTY-FOUR

Reason was there at a quarter to four. He was anxious to make sure that the lawman hadn't been lying to him. Or that he had dreamed up the whole damn story. But when he reached the brick building with the bars on the windows due west of the main part of town, the man with the badge was already there waiting for him.

"You can go right on in," the Sheriff said. "But first, I must ask you to leave your weapons with me."

Reason shucked Cole's gun belt without a second thought, then handed the works over to Brannigan.

"All right?"

Brannigan nodded. "You got fifteen minutes."

Reason grinned to himself. *He'd only need five, if that.*

Joe Steele was lounging on the cot with the brick wall at his back and an arm carelessly resting on a raised knee, when Reason strolled by the barred cell and came to a halt.

"Afternoon," Reason said matter-of-factly, yet he couldn't stop the smug grin spreading across his face.

Steele slowly glanced up. "Figured you'd be by one of these days," he drawled. "If only to gloat."

"I just had to see this with my own eyes," Reason purred. "Are you comfy?"

"Can you eat yet?"

In a self-conscious action, Reason reached up and tugged the brim of his Stetson hat lower in a vain attempt to hide his bruised and battered face. Well, he had him there. Deliberately he changed the subject.

"Brannigan wants to know if I'm pressing charges."

"Well are you?" The question was spoken without a trace of bitterness, just a mild sense of curiosity.

"Why shouldn't I?"

"I know what you'd like to do is throw away the key."

Reason squinted at Steele through the slotted iron bars. Just how well did they know each other? This man seemed calm and confident even behind the caged door of a locked prison cell. As if no harm could possibly come to him. Worst of all, he seemed to know just what Reason was thinking. And Cole had hinted only this morning if it ever came down to gunplay between them, that they might be evenly matched. Well, actually Cole said that Steele might take him. The only man on God's green earth that could.

Abruptly Steele rose off the cot and began pacing the small confines of the cell. He ran a hand through his straight brown hair. Then he halted in the middle of the cell, hooked his thumbs in his belt, took a deep breath, and stared down at the hardwood floor beneath his feet.

"Look, maybe I was a little out of line the other day," he admitted somewhat sheepishly. "I came into town for supplies and a quick beer, not to find you...."

Shit, he was doing it again. Getting himself all worked up over Rachel. He ran a hand over his mouth, and tried to soften his words. "You and that blonde...." He glanced helplessly at Reason through the iron bars of the cell. "It was just a shock to me, that's all."

"Let me get this straight. Am I hearing an apology coming out of your mouth?"

"As close to one as you're ever likely to get."

"Maybe that's not good enough."

Steele's eyes widened in surprise. Then he nodded as if all hope was gone.

"Okay. I guess that's my answer then."

He strolled back to his cot, threw himself down to the thin mattress, then tilted his brown Stetson over his face.

"Have a nice day, boss."

Reason fumed at this man's calm acceptance of his own fate. And he hated the idea that Joe had summarily dismissed him like a servant with a few simple words. Why did this man seem to bring out the worst in him?

"Get up! I'm not through with you yet!"

Steele didn't move, yet he said through his hat, "I'm listening."

"What would it take to get you to stay the hell away from my wife!"

With the tip of one finger, Steele pushed the brim of his Stetson up over his eyes and peered at Reason as if he hadn't heard him right. Then he swung his legs over the side of the bed and sat up.

"Probably your comin' home and resuming your duties on the ranch would do it," he drawled honestly.

Reason shook his head. "I can't do that. Not yet."

Steele ducked his head and glanced down at the floor. His next words seemed forced from his throat.

"Then maybe I should quit."

"...*Jocelyn dotes on him. We need him at the ranch, Reason...*"

"You can't quit," Reason said. "Cole thinks we need you."

Steele laughed without humor. "Cole thinks...?" He jerked his head up. "What about you?"

"I think Cole's the better judge right now."

"Oh, you do!" His eyebrows raised in a smug way. "Well, you're probably right about that."

He rose off the cot and stepped up to the edge of his cell. Then reaching up, he curled his fingers around the vertical iron bars. His keen hazel eyes seemed to be sizing up the man standing before him.

Probably for the measurements of a coffin, Reason thought disgustedly. And he began to grow uneasy under the man's close scrutiny.

Then Steele said bluntly, "I'm just curious as to exactly what moment in hell did you finally lose your nerve?"

Reason swallowed hard. Where had he heard that recently? Seemed like only yesterday someone else had insulted him right to his face. Then a picture of the gunslinger he had killed loomed large before him. Hadn't he said something similar, shortly before he died?

"Better watch what you say," Reason warned low.

An insulting sneer creased Steele's narrow jaw.

"What're you gonna do about it if I don't?"

The truth was, Reason couldn't do a damn thing about it at the moment. They were both unarmed, and Reason still wasn't over the beating he took yesterday from Steele's fists. And Steele damn well knew it.

"I can wait until you're free, find my own gun belt, and meet you in the street."

Joe was at a sudden disadvantage. He hadn't expected that much sand in Reason's answer. Nor the roundabout challenge. After all he had just beaten the man senseless yesterday, and Reason hadn't once raised a hand in his own defense. Yet something Reason said rang a warning bell in his mind.

"What do you mean, find it? Is your holster lost?"

Reason appeared suddenly confused to Joe's eyes. He blinked twice as if trying to focus on a picture in his mind that had escaped him. Then he shook his head.

"No. I don't think so."

Steele's eyes widened once again in surprise. What was wrong with this man? The Reason Cordell he knew was a tough-as-nails gunslinger with an insouciant, often cocky, confident manner that made sane men think twice before bracing him. The man standing before him now couldn't remember where he had misplaced his favorite pistol.

"Think?" Steele said aloud. "You don't...think so?" He couldn't believe his ears. Had he hit Reason in the face once too often? But no, he was like this when he first came back to the ranch, when he had strolled in the door of Rachel's office as if he still lived there. If a man couldn't remember his own wife, then what hope did he have of recalling much of anything else?

"What the hell happened to you while you were gone? You get kicked in the head by that wild stallion of yours and lose your mind?"

Steele watched Reason take a careful step backwards. For a minute, Joe thought he was leaving, but instead Reason just stood there. Then Reason shook his head and his eyes grew slightly glazed.

"No, he didn't...."

Reason ducked his head. He reached out behind him and groped for the wall as a blind man would reach out to get his bearings. Finding the solid partition beneath the palm of his hand seemed to calm him somewhat, yet his breathing was unusually erratic and harsh. Almost exactly like the scene in Rachel's yard, right after Steele had braced him, when he had blindly reached for his horse.

Then Reason raised a hand to his eyes, and Steele could plainly see his fingers tremble.

"What's ailing you, man?" Steele exclaimed in awe. "Are you having a fit of some kind? Maybe you should see a doctor."

Slowly Reason brought his hand down from his face to straddle his left hip as if to keep his hand from shaking. But the right hand remained glued to the wall as if he was supporting it.

"It's nothing," he finally said.

"Sure looks like something to me," Steele argued. "Maybe Peterson could give you a pill or something to fix you up. Your memory loss could prove fatal for a man with a well-known reputation like yours."

"It almost did yesterday when I used Cole's revolver instead of my own."

"Yesterday? Were you the one that left that dead man lying in the street?"

Reason nodded and Steele grinned.

"I should have known."

CHAPTER TWENTY-FIVE

Reason left five minutes later. Although nothing was settled between him and Steele, he sensed the man had cooled off somewhat in his misguided feelings of avenging Rachel's honor. And Reason's temper also tapered off, although the bruises still remained."

"Let him out," he told Brannigan after retrieving Cole's pistol and rushing through the door towards the street. He didn't care to linger long enough to answer further questions.

He ran into Cole half a block away. His left arm was cradled in a white sling to ease the stress on his shoulder and he kept glancing right and left as if he were searching for someone, or something. Then a big stupid grin lit up his face as he saw Reason heading straight towards him.

"There ya are," he drawled easily. "Was worried about ya."

"Why? You're the one all shot up. And why aren't you still in bed?"

"Aw, Peterson kicked me out. He said I was doin' nothin' but givin' him a heartache and wastin' precious bed space. That cantankerous old coot." He chuckled beneath his breath. "Thought I'd go and get a beer. Never got a chance to finish the last one. Wanna join me?"

Cole seemed pale and a bit gray around the eyes to Reason's mind, so he stifled the urge to ask directions to Rachel's place once again for fear Cole would insist on riding with him. And, after all, what else was there to do?

"Sure. But just one. And this time I'm wearing the belt until I get my own back."

Cole smiled. "That might not be such a bad idea, since I've already proved I'm not too handy with the damn thing anyway."

The saloon was empty this time with only a few cowhands lingering at the bar. Reason had just raised his glass to his lips when a small blonde head suddenly ducked beneath his arm. Large brown eyes and tempting red lips smiled up at him.

"Missed you," she said softly.

Cole choked on his beer. Swallowing hard, he slammed the glass down on the bar, then swiped his mouth with the back of his right hand.

"Dammit! Remind me not to guzzle so damn fast," he said to no one in particular by way of explanation for his odd behavior.

Mariah peered at Cole with a puzzled frown, then reached up, drew Reason's head down and whispered something in his ear. Through the mirror behind the bar, Cole saw Reason smile as his arm dropped naturally around her. Then he gently shook his head. But instead of leaving she only grew more insistent. Cole swore in his mind that if he didn't know where Reason left off, he wouldn't have known where she began, she was that close. Then she murmured something again and Reason closed his eyes, dipped his head, and gently nuzzled the top of her blonde head with his lips, breathing her name.

"Is he at it again?"

The softly sneering voice came from Cole's left and the suddenness of the sound startled him for a brief minute. Then, when he saw who the man was in the mirror, he turned towards his left and grinned. "Oh, it's you, Joe."

Steele ordered a beer, but gone was the normal carefully controlled substance of the man. He looked as if he could spit bullets at any minute.

"Somethin' on your mind?" Cole questioned.

"This is gonna take some getting used to, I see." Joe spoke as if to himself. He grabbed the mug the bartender had just placed before him, raised the glass to his lips, and proceeded to drown himself in the foamy brew. Then he slammed the glass down on the mahogany bar much as Cole had done minutes before, and licked his lips.

Reason's head slowly turned at the sound. He raised slightly unfocused pale blue eyes in Cole's direction. Then Cole felt Reason grow deathly still.

"Come on, sugar. You sure you don't want to go upstairs?" the blonde's voice carried over the men at the bar as she wiggled suggestively against him. "I can feel you're lyin' to me."

"You don't waste a minute, do ya," Steele sneered. He shifted slightly sideways to face Reason and, in the process, freed his holster for easy access.

"Stay out of this, Steele," Reason said coldly, while his right arm was still wrapped around Mariah's slender back. "What I do is no concern of yours."

"Well, now, I surely will," he said, his voice dripping with scorn. "But you don't mind if I take notes, do ya? I expect Rachel will want a full report of my stay in town when I finally get back. Just one thing." His hazel gray eyes grew as cold as his name. "How do you spell Mariah?"

Reason's right arm dropped down to his side and he moved to face the man who had slyly challenged him.

"Who's Rachel?" Mariah peered up at Reason in a squint.

"Why that's his wife, honey," Steele answered before Reason had a chance to defend himself. "Didn't you know he was married?"

Mariah's brown eyes grew even darker as she pierced Joe with a determined stare of her own.

"It don't matter a hill of beans to me if he was," she stated. "If he chooses to be in my bed rather than the woman who wears his ring, well, that's just fine with me."

Cole shot Reason a quick glance over his right shoulder. The man reminded Cole of a stray wolf caught raiding the hen house and staring down the twin barrels of a double-gauge shotgun. Cole was glad he was positioned in the middle of the squabbling pair of jealous rivals. He knew neither man would shoot through him to get to the other. At least he damn well hoped not.

"Take it easy, both of you," Cole said evenly. "Joe, why don't you finish your beer and get on home. It seems to me you must be long overdue by now."

"Well I aim to, Cole. Just as soon as I'm done here."

Then Reason growled behind him, "Step aside, Cole. You're blocking my way."

"I ain't movin'." Then Cole reached for Joe's glass, drained the rest of his beer in one swallow, and plunked the empty mug back on the bar. "You're done, Joe. Now I suggest you scram, before you have two men to contend with, instead of just one. And don't think this sling is gonna slow me down any."

All three men standing there knew Cole's threat was an idle one. A good hard whistle would blow him over at the moment, much less one punch. But he was making a stand for Reason's benefit and letting Joe know which way the wind would blow if push came to shove.

"You'd take his side over Rachel's?" Steele said in awe. "Why just look at him. Even he knows he's guilty as sin."

Cole didn't need to look twice. He'd already seen the haunted pale blue eyes, and it wasn't a pretty sight.

"If you knew the whole story you might cool your hocks a bit," Cole added.

Reason suddenly spoke Cole's name in a low, warning snarl.

"Don't worry. I won't spill nothin' you don't want folks to know."

"There's not a thing you could say that would change my mind," Steele growled low. "Actions speak louder than words in my book."

"Yeah, well it was a few actions that...."

"Cole!" The loud, threatening tone of Reason's voice made Cole hesitate. "You've said enough." Reason gently pushed Cole to the side, then stepped forward in his vacated space. "Besides, I don't think Steele's interested in hearing any more long-winded stories at the moment."

"You're so right about that!" Then Joe backed up a few steps and fell into the casual, yet deadly, gunfighter's stance that Reason knew so well.

"Looks like you ain't gonna learn no other way," Joe sneered with all the confidence of a man who knew what he was about.

But Cole wasn't about to be denied. He moved forward and threw his right arm across Reason's chest in order to stall any further action by either party.

"Look, nobody's drawin' on anybody today. Joe, I'm givin' you one last chance to move on outta here, or you're gonna be lookin' for a new line of work tomorrow. You know damn well you don't wanna kill Reason. You're not foolin' anyone. You couldn't do it years ago when you'd been paid damn good money to, and you're not about to do it now. Hell, I know you're mad.

And maybe you think you have just cause. But go stick your head in the horse trough out front and cool off before you end up doin' somethin' we'll both regret."

Reason shoved his arm away.

"Dammit, Cole. Keep out of this." But when he glanced back at Steele, some of the fire seemed to have died down in the slitted hazel eyes.

A tight muscle bunched in Steele's cheek, yet he made no further threats.

Then to Reason's surprise he said, "Maybe you're right. I sure as hell don't want to start riding the grub line again."

His glance slid once over the pretty blonde girl at the bar, then back to Reason.

"I reckon a man's got the right to dig his own grave as deep as he wants, without someone coming along all ready to push him in it."

Then he flicked the rolled brim of his hat with two fingers in a mock salute, turned and slammed out the swinging bat-wing doors of the saloon.

CHAPTER TWENTY-SIX

Reason awoke in a cold sweat. Where the hell was he? The moonlit dark four walls of the room seemed vaguely familiar to him. He started to roll out of bed, but instead bumped up against a slender silk-clad body with shoulder length pale blonde hair. She sighed in her sleep, which caused Reason's heart to skip in his chest. In a panic, he switched direction and abruptly stumbled out the opposite side.

"What's goin' on?" A match suddenly flared and the bedside lamp burst into a low flame. Replacing the glass chimney, Mariah sat up in bed and rubbed at sleepy eyes.

"Reason?" She glanced at him. "You look like you've just seen a ghost. Come back to bed, honey. I'll warm you up real good."

Oh, shit! He was in Mariah's bedroom again. And all he had on were his socks. He ran a shaky hand through his sleep-tousled hair and searched on the floor for his clothes. His denim trousers were in a heap by the foot of the bed where he had thrown them and, with all due haste, he slipped them on.

"Are you goin' somewhere?" Maria asked in surprise. "It's the middle of the night."

"Where's Cole?" he said as he stamped into his boots, then slipped into his shirt.

"That fella you were with? The one in the sling?"

"Yeah, that's the one."

"I think he's in twelve, with Cheryl."

Reason paused in the act of stuffing the tail of his shirt into his tight-fitting pants.

"Cheryl's twelve?"

"Room twelve, silly. You're not fully awake yet."

She was right about that. And just where was he going in such a rush? There was no fire that he knew of. That nightmare had thrown him off balance again. Slowly he sat down on the edge of the bed.

Instantly Mariah had her arms wrapped tight around his chest, her bare breasts pressed intimately against his back, and she was nuzzling the side of his neck by the left ear with her warm, moist tongue.

"Why you're trembling," she whispered in surprise mixed with sheer delight. "And I know just the thing that'll cure it."

Twenty minutes later Reason had his arms crossed beneath his head and was staring at the cracked plaster designs running every which way across the ceiling. Silently Mariah rose up from the bed and slipped into a pink cotton robe, then lit a ready-made cigarette with a match from a metal box she kept on a nearby table.

Reason slowly slid his eyes over her small, but shapely, figure outlined by the soft material of her robe. Not bad for a saloon girl. And she sure knew how to please a man. Yet frown lines appeared on her brow as she blew out a lungful of smoke and stared fixedly at the wall behind the carved wooden headboard above his head.

She was mad. Reason could sense the anger building up inside her with each exhale of her lungs.

"What's wrong, Mariah?" he grinned mischievously. "Weren't you satisfied?"

"You know I was," she said curtly.

"Then why the frown?"

If looks could kill Reason would have been a dead man.

"I don't mind you havin' a wife," she said coldly. "But what I do mind is when you bring her into my bed."

Uh-oh. Reason rolled out of bed and slipped into his denim trousers.

"What do you mean?" he asked as he did up the buttons of his pants.

"You called me Rachel!"

Reason stood there half-dressed and stared at her across the broad expanse of the room. He didn't bother to deny it. He hadn't recalled saying her name, but if she said he did, then he must have.

"I'm sorry."

"You damn well should be." Then she lifted her cigarette-filled hand to her face and started to cry.

Reason padded to her side in socked feet. He placed both hands on the back of her small shoulders.

"Look, I never meant to hurt you," he said softly. "And I'm damned sorry if I did."

"Just get out," she sobbed behind her hand. "You're always half out the door anyway."

Without another word, Reason backed away. He found his boots where he had thrown them earlier, and stamped his heels down into the soles. Then he picked his shirt up off the floor, slammed his hat on his head, grabbed Cole's gun belt and headed for the door.

He paused before room number twelve, fully dressed. Softly he tapped on the door.

"Cole?"

He didn't want to wake the house. When there was no response, he slowly turned the handle.

A candle had burned down to almost nothing on the dresser, setting off a warm glow within the room. But Cole was fast asleep with a pretty little brunette snoring on his good shoulder.

"Cole?" he whispered softly. Then "Cole!" a trifle louder and sharper.

Cole jumped awake. "Reason? What…?"

He started to rise a little too fast and suddenly he yelped out loud and grabbed for his bandaged shoulder. He fell back to the mattress with a groan. The brunette had been jostled awake in the process and now she sat up, blinking at Reason standing in the doorway.

"What are you doing here, Mister? I thought you were with Mariah?"

"Yeah, so did I," Cole grumbled. Then he gradually slipped out from under the shapely brunette, rose to his feet, and faced Reason. "I take it you're ready to leave?"

Cole was already half-dressed. He still wore his blue denim's and white socks. He reached down and snatched up his shirt from the floor.

"Whenever you're ready," Reason answered. "I'll be waiting

downstairs."

A good half-hour later Cole finally brushed up next to Reason at the bar.

"Took you long enough," Reason said good-naturedly. "What'd you do? Go back for seconds?"

An easy lop-sided grin spread across Cole's face.

"Can't let the well run dry. If the lady's willin', then so am I. Beer," he said to the bartender passing by. He sipped at the brew placed before him, then glanced slyly at Reason. "What happened upstairs? She finally kick your sorry ass out?"

Reason reached for his warm beer. "Yup."

"Aw, you're lyin', right?"

Reason took a deep swallow, then said, "A word of advice. Don't ever call the woman you're sleeping with by your wife's name."

Cole whistled low and raised the beer to his lips.

"That'll do it every time."

Reason wanted to ride out. Cole wanted to sit in a hand of poker. When Reason threatened to leave without him, Cole finally conceded.

"I already made that mistake once," Cole growled, as the two of them strolled along the darkened boardwalk towards the livery stable at the outskirts of town. "And look what happened. I ain't makin' the same one twice."

Reason almost asked what happened? But then he remembered a ramshackle cabin in the woods and he stopped dead in his tracks. Two shaggy, unkempt backwoodsmen advanced towards him in the dark. Their dark beady eyes bright with lust. *"You hold him down, Buck, while I.... Dammit! I said hold him! He's got spunk, you gotta give him that. Even though he's all tied up like a neat little package. Hit him again if he won't listen...."*

"Reason? Reason! Snap out of it!" A strong hand grabbed at his shoulder from out of the dark. Shook him violently. Before he knew what he was doing, the revolver at his hip was suddenly in his hand. He aimed it straight at the dark figure before him. And fired!

Cole gasped in pain and surprise as a red-hot fire sliced through his belly like a knife and the bark of a six-gun sounded loud in his ears.

"Aw Jesus, no!" he swore as his knees buckled beneath him and the sidewalk reared up to slam him full in the face. He had thought Reason was getting better.

He had just made a humongous mistake!

CHAPTER TWENTY-SEVEN

When Reason awoke, he found himself seated on the worn edge of a badly rumpled cot, staring down at his hands while his elbows rested on bent knees. An unfamiliar scuffed and dirty hard-planked floor lay beneath his booted feet. He was fully clothed and unhurt, yet he shook his head in dismay. This wasn't the Stirrup C. Nor Mariah's tidy little bedroom. Just where the hell was he now?

Disoriented and confused, he dragged his bewildered gaze higher and was shocked to see the iron bars of a locked prison cell surrounding him on all three sides. Slowly he rose to his feet and glanced around at the gray-mortared walls behind him in a state of sheer horror. By God, he was in jail! How the hell did he get here?

Try as he might, he couldn't remember a thing from the time he and Cole left the saloon until now. Now? What time was it?

His eyes flew to the small barred window behind him. Still dark as pitch outside. And where the hell was Cole?

Why hadn't his so-called partner already sprung him out of this hellhole? His bail couldn't be all that much. Had Cole gone back to play poker after all and lost every damn dime he owned? But, more importantly, what the hell could he possibly have done to land himself in jail in the first place? And why couldn't he recall a Goddamn thing?

Footsteps shuffled lazily across the wood floor beyond the far wall, and frantically Reason glanced around to get his bearings. Dammit, this was the exact same cell Joe Steele had been caged in. Now that conceited, jackass of a fool was free as a bird on the wing and he was locked up like some common criminal.

Was he? The thought jumped unbidden to his mind. Had he killed someone last night without so much as blinking an eye? Why did the sound of distant gunfire ringing in his ears seem to warn him of danger? Panic flared like wildfire in his chest. He had to know.

"Hey! Anybody out there?" he shouted out loud.

Someone heard him, for the boot steps changed direction and came clomping heavily towards the back wall. Then Sheriff Brannigan made an entrance and sauntered casually up to his cell door.

"You finally come to?" he said with a suspicious squint to his eyes.

Reason's mind started to ease. He'd been unconscious, that's why he couldn't remember anything. Maybe he was jailed for something simple as drunk and disorderly conduct. Could be Cole had gone back to play poker like he thought, and he had returned to the bar and tied one on. The only thing is he didn't feel headachy or sick as if he were nursing a hangover. And rarely did he ever consume enough beer to get pie-eyed drunk.

"How long was I out?'

"You never was."

"What do you mean? I don't understand."

Again Brannigan squinted at him, frowning. "Don't you remember anything?"

"About what?"

"Last night."

"What about it?"

"There's a man dying over at Peterson's office right now because of you. Are you saying you don't recall shooting him?"

Reason's heart started thudding rapidly against the hard-muscled wall of his chest. Suddenly the simple act of breathing became troublesome. What was he afraid of? He'd shot men before with just cause.

"Dying?" Reason repeated. "No, I…. Who?" Dammit, why couldn't he keep two simple thoughts together. He ran his fingers nervously through his hair. The Sheriff had said "last night." He'd lost twenty-four hours that he couldn't recall.

"Where's Cole?" he finally voiced the nagging fear that had been secretly haunting him since he awoke.

"He's the man you shot."

The cell went dark. Distant blurred, shadowy images fled rapidly through Reason's mind. Someone shouting at him, shaking him. A flash of light. The deafening blast of a revolver....

A low moan of despair reached his ears as if the sound had traveled a great distance. He knew he was swaying precariously on his feet and that he'd go down in a minute if he didn't do something fast to prevent it. Blindly he reached out for support and as his left hand connected firmly with the cold iron bars of the prison cell, he grabbed on for dear life.

God, no! It couldn't be true, his mind screamed in silent denial. Why would he do such a terrible thing like that? To Cole, no less.

Gradually the room lightened and Brannigan, once again, came clearly into focus. The lawman was peering at him strangely. Was this another bad dream? Nightmare was more like it.

Reason swallowed hard. "What happened?"

"Don't know. The poor fellow never regained consciousness. And you weren't doing any talking either."

Brannigan drew a deep breath and then went on. "All I know is that I was making my final rounds for the night and heard a shot. When I got to you, your pistol was still gripped tight in your hand and you were staring out into the night like you were in a trance of some sort. Your friend was lying unconscious at your feet." He hesitated. "Oddly enough, I had to pry the pistol out of your hand in order to get it away from you, for you didn't seem to want to give it up easy. But, other than that, you didn't give me an ounce of trouble when I cuffed and arrested you on the spot, then sent a man for the Doc. Are you saying you don't recall a thing?"

Reason didn't bother to answer. Unwilling to face the truth, he stumbled backwards until his legs came in contact with the hard wooden edge of the cot and he sat down hard.

"Are you sure it was me?" he said in a soft voice, almost as if he were talking to himself.

"Your revolver was still warm. And recently fired. There was only one shot. One bullet was missing from your pistol. Just how much did you have to drink last night?"

"Not nearly enough." Reason dropped his head in his hands and moaned softly beneath his breath. There was no sense asking anything more. The whole incident was cut and dried. He had killed the one man in the world that he trusted. The only one he would dare call a friend if push came to shove. And now he would pay dearly for it. He'd hang by the neck as he justly deserved.

Reason laid on the rumpled cot in that jail cell for five long days and six lonely nights. He wouldn't talk to a soul and totally ignored anyone that dared speak to him. Coffee and bread he existed on, refusing to touch any of the other more palatable foods on his plate as if the appetizing aromas made him physically ill. Mariah came to visit him every day in an effort to bolster his mood. But even she proved no exception to his own rule. He would throw an arm up over his eyes and turn his face to the wall whenever anyone asked him a simple question.

In the dead of night, when the world was still and darkness filled his cell with shadowy images from the past, he moaned in his sleep; other times he trembled as if he were an unweaned mongrel pup caught out in a raging blue norther. Sometimes both.

On the sixth day, he was finally put out of his misery. Brannigan shuffled down the hall, jangled a set of long keys in his hand, twisted one in the lock of his cell, and swung the door wide.

"You're free to go, Mr. Cordell."

Reason blinked. Twice. Slowly he sat up on the cot and swung his legs over the side. His hair and clothes were rumpled to the point of no return, he needed a shave badly, and he reeked of sweat mixed with outright fear.

"What do you mean?" he stammered in a state of confusion, his first spoken words in almost a week. "You can't just...." He rose to his feet. "I killed a man in cold blood."

"Seems your friend didn't die after all, like we thought. He's a hard-headed cuss I've heard tell, and wouldn't take 'no use' for an answer." He chuckled beneath his breath. "The doc says he shook hands with the devil and even he didn't want that ornery fella in hell with him. So he threw him back to the river of life like we would a small fish in a stream, just to annoy us all."

Euphoria flew through Reason's mind and made his knees grow weak with relief. Cole had made it! Against insurmountable odds. Reason had been extremely lucky this time. But what about the next?

Brannigan jerked his head at the door. "Let's go."

"What about assault charges?" Reason stubbornly insisted. "I can't just walk out of here scot-free."

The Sheriff squinted at him the way everyone else did when they glanced at Reason lately.

"Mister, sounds like you want to be locked up."

What Reason really wanted at the moment was to get his hands on a pistol and blow whatever was left of his brains out. Even he didn't trust himself anymore, especially around people he cared about. What was to stop him from snapping again? But there was one thing he had to do first. He had to make sure Cole was all right with his own eyes.

When Reason was slow in responding, the Sheriff added, "There's to be no charges made against you. Mr. Dansing made that perfectly clear when I spoke to him this morning. Now are you coming out of there? Or do you want me to send for lunch?"

CHAPTER TWENTY-EIGHT

"I'm surprised to see you here," Peterson growled as he eyed the subdued young man over the top of his spectacles, standing humbly before his desk with his hat in his hands. "That must have been one humdinger of a fight you two had. I sure hope she was worth it."

"She?"

"You know. That little saloon gal you were fighting over." He squinted at Reason much the way the Sheriff had done. "That's what Cole said anyway. That you had a fight over a woman."

Reason remained silent. There was no woman. That much he was certain.

When Reason refrained from comment, Peterson added, "Well, go on back. You know the way. That's what you came for, isn't it? To see Cole?" He eyed the pistol at Reason's hip, then shrugged. Those two young coyotes might kill each other one of these days, he figured, but he doubted today would be the day.

Motivated by guilt, yet dreading to face the man who had befriended him above all others and was now suffering miserably for it, Reason made his way down the hall to the same room Cole used once before and, with the tips of his fingers, gently pushed open the door.

Cole was lying on his back, his upper body once again propped up by large soft-looking pillows. Only this time he was fully awake and his attention shifted towards the door as it slowly creaked open.

Wary amber eyes watched the dark-clad man standing in the open doorway, taking full measure of the deadly gun belt still strapped low on Reason's hips. He was unsure of Reason's intentions, yet brazenly said, "Come on in. Don't just stand there."

171

His voice was weak and a sheen of perspiration dotted his forehead.

As Reason began to close the door behind him, the sudden panic that leaped to Cole's face made him reconsider, and he left the door wide as he stepped nearer the bed. Reason's agitation was obvious as he fiddled awkwardly with the rolled brim of the black Stetson in his hands. Then he cleared his throat loudly as if he had a fishbone stuck in it.

"Everyone tells me I shot you." Reason's voice was husky and raw. "Is that true?"

An ironic sneer began to crease Cole's jaw, and a joke formed in his brain, but one look at Reason's haunted blue eyes changed his mind.

"Yeah, I reckon so."

"There was no woman, was there." Reason spoke as if each syllable was an effort.

"No, there wasn't."

Reason's lips curled in scorn aimed solely at himself.

"That's what I thought."

An intuition of horror leaped in Cole's gut that had nothing to do with his injury, nor fear of the man standing before him. Reason looked like a man that had nothing left to live for.

Hastily Cole added, "Look, I knew the score. How you jump at shadows and all." He hesitated as a brief spasm of pain crossed his face, then went on more slowly. "I shouldn't have lunged at you like that. I lost my head for a minute there. Don't go beatin' yourself up about it. I'm gonna be all right. It was just a scratch after all."

For the first time Reason's eyes strayed down Cole's professionally bandaged shoulder to the trim gauze trappings wrapped tight around his waist. A dark red stain near Cole's middle was the only thing that marred the purity of the bandage itself.

"You call that a scratch?" Reason's hardened gaze raised to Cole's amber eyes. "I call that an awful close call. Too damn close."

When Cole remained silent, Reason asked. "How do you feel?"

"I won't lie to you. I've been better." He chuckled softly, then winced hard. "Truth is it hurts like all the fires of hell."

Reason swallowed down the sudden tightness in his throat.

"Is there anything you need? That I can do…?"

"Yeah. I was waitin' for you to ask." Once again a fleeting bolt of pain shot across Cole's face and he grunted softly as if the simple effort to speak was getting beyond him.

"Name it!"

Cole squinted up at him just like all the others had done. He hesitated, then said, "I'd like my gun back, if you don't mind."

Reason stared at him long and hard. Was Cole afraid he'd shoot him in bed next? Or had the man instinctively guessed his next move.

"Are you afraid I'm going to end it all?"

"Hell no! It's just…." Cole had spoken too fast, almost as if he already knew the answer to Reason's question. And now it was too late to try and cover up the lie. He could read the mistake in Reason's keen pale eyes. "Okay. You got me. Tell me I'm wrong. If you can."

"I can always buy another gun."

"Well, you're damn sure not using mine." Gone was the levity of earlier. Cole was dead serious.

"All right." As if reluctant to do so, Reason slowly unbuckled the heavy belt, bent to untie the rawhide thong from his thigh, then tossed the whole works on a nearby chair. "Satisfied?"

"For the moment."

"Anything else?"

Cole winced. He had shifted slightly and was instantly suffering for it. He swallowed hard, then said, "Pull up a chair."

Reason eyed the one Cole's gun belt was on.

"Not that one. The one by the door."

Cole could read his thoughts before they were spoken aloud.

Reason did as Cole asked. Then he just stood there, waiting by the bed.

"Now sit!"

Reason's dark brows raised in surprise.

Cole answered the unspoken query, "You're gonna stay here in this room with me, until I'm back on my feet, or dead! Whichever comes first!"

CHAPTER TWENTY-NINE

It was hard for Reason to watch Cole in pain, day after day, knowing he was the cause of it all. And the moments were worse when Peterson would come in to change the bandage. But all things heal with time and after a few more days of total bed rest, Cole was back on his feet. A bit shaky and unsure, but upright.

"Can't keep a fool down," Peterson grumbled good-naturedly as he grudgingly gave Cole the okay to leave. "But I want to see you in a few days just to make sure everything's healing as it should. No riding, roping, or shenanigans until then. You hear me?"

"Yeah, yeah," Cole humored him, shrugging into his recently sewn and freshly washed blue checked shirt. "Whatever you say, doc."

"And you," the doctor turned to Reason. "Lay off the hard stuff. I don't want to see either of you fellas needing my medical expertise for, say," he rubbed at his chin with a finger, yet there was a decided twinkled in his eyes, "at least another six months. Got it?"

Reason slowly nodded. This was no laughing matter. At least not to him. And surely not to Cole.

"Good," Peterson said, as he turned to storm out the door. "Now get the hell out of here. And stay out!"

Five days later, they were back in the saddle heading for home when they came to a sharp fork in the trail. Reason pulled the anxious black stallion up short. Suddenly he knew where he was, and the path that led to Rachel.

"You go on ahead," Reason said, "and take it slow. I'll catch up with you later at the house."

"Like hell." Carefully Cole drew his bay around to face him.

"Just what are you plannin' on doin'? Visiting Rachel?"

"What if I am?"

"Then I'm ridin' with ya."

Reason shook his head. "Uh-uh. I'm goin' alone."

"Over my dead body. And that can be easily arranged because...." Suddenly he grabbed at his waist with a free hand. He let out a short grunt of pain, "uhh," and half-doubled over the saddle. "Damn!" He peered at Reason out of the corner of his eye to see if his stunt was working. From the look of anguish on Reason's face, it was.

"All right. All right! Don't get all worked up over nothing. We'll take it slow, then."

Gingerly Cole sat up in the saddle and grinned.

"Now you're talkin'."

Joe Steele just happened to be standing on the front steps with one foot on the porch talking to Rachel when Reason and Cole cantered slowly up to the house. The hired hand's back grew ramrod stiff at Reason's approach, yet he remained silent. And Rachel just stood there, staring at the oncoming riders as if neither man meant a thing to her, although her heart was fluttering like a startled sparrow's wing at the mere sight of her dark-clad husband.

Reason pulled the black to a halt as Cole drew up beside him.

"Mawnin' Joe. Rachel." Cole said pleasantly to the pair on the porch.

"Cole," Rachel acknowledged, as Joe nodded in reply. Then her eyes slid furtively towards Reason.

"I'd like to have a word with you, Rachel," Reason said.

"Is that so?" she said with a haughty air. Then paused. Reason was afraid she would refuse him, when finally she added, "Well, come on in then."

She led the way into the house as Reason slid easily from the saddle. He seemed in no hurry as he scuffed up the stairs, but as he drew near Steele, he hesitated.

A deadly challenge was thrown from Steele's cold hazel eyes to Reason's clear blue ones. *Hurt Rachel once more and there'd be hell to pay!*

Abruptly, Reason pushed past him.

Rachel turned into the study where he had last seen her, and Reason followed her there. By the time he cleared the doorway, she was already seated at her desk with a pen in hand, jotting a figure in the ledger that lay opened before her.

"State your business and be quick about it. I'm quite busy here," she stated with a no-nonsense attitude. She wasn't going to make this easy for him.

"Rachel...." Reason's dark Stetson was suddenly in his hands. "I'm sorry."

"Sorry?" She peered up at him, and Reason saw fire in her emerald eyes. "Sorry," she repeated again as if he had just uttered something funny. She tossed the pen to the ledger, rose from the chair, and abruptly moved to the front of the desk with her arms crossed over her chest to face him. "Just what, exactly, are you sorry for?"

Reason could see she had plenty on her mind so he remained silent, determined to let her have her say.

"For losing your memory?" She laughed, and the sound wasn't pleasant. "Well, that can be explained, I guess. Although no one felt the need to let me in on that little secret until I was half out of my mind with worry."

"For walking out on me when I needed you? But then I should be used to that by now. You come and go here like a swinging door was installed in the front of this house. Just like always. I must not have what it takes to hold you."

"Rachel...." Reason tried again, but she cut him off with a simple wave of her arm.

"Or are you sorry you married me in the first place. After all I'm not that petite little blonde that you seem to favor in town now, am I!"

So Steele had told her. He probably couldn't wait to run back here and spill his guts. And that's what all this pent-up anger was about.

Once again, fiddling with the brim of his hat, he stared sheepishly at the floor. "Let me explain...."

"You don't need to say a thing." She boldly stepped up to him, her small hands in fists at her sides. If she planned on decking him, Reason wouldn't lift a finger to stop her.

"I was worried sick when you were gone last year. I couldn't eat, couldn't sleep, for months. And then when you were found I was so relieved."

Reason slowly glanced up and there were tears in her beautiful sea green eyes.

"All right, so you didn't know me. Or anyone else for that matter. I didn't care. I was just so thankful you were alive and safe. Nothing else mattered. I knew you'd come around eventually. But this...!"

Reason swallowed hard. This apology was going to be tougher than he thought.

"She means nothing to me, Rachel."

"That makes it all the worse," she shouted. "How dare you go to bed with some cheap whore down at the saloon while I was home all that time waiting for you to come to me!"

Reason's jaw tightened and his eyes grew hard. This wasn't all his fault. And he refused to take full blame.

"Be honest with me," he sneered coldly. "You weren't waiting alone."

The flat of her hand caught him stingingly on the cheek and he winced in surprise.

"How dare you say that to me!" She snarled with all the pent-up hostility of a woman scorned. "Do you think I was sleeping with one of the ranch hands?"

The fierce glare in Reason's condemning pale blue eyes was her answer.

"Who? Tell me, damn you! Just who do you think it was? Mulgrew? Anderson? Peters?"

Reason didn't know any of those names.

She kept on. "Oh, I admit Jimmy Peters is not a bad-looking fellow," she smiled slyly, then shrugged. "But he's got a girl in town that he visits every now and then. And he's not a man that deliberately goes out of his way looking for trouble. Unlike some that I know." Then she was brazenly silent, waiting.

"Joe Steele."

Her eyes grew overly large in her face. "Joe?"

Reason nodded.

"Why do you think...? Well, that's just ridiculous," she stammered self-consciously.

"Is it?"

Her chin came up defiantly. "Why ever would you think that?"

"I've seen the way he looks at you."

"How could you possibly," she snapped. "You're never around!"

"I was here last month, when I delivered that note."

A decidedly unfeminine sneer shaped her soft lips.

"Oh yes. The note. How could I forget? You must have been here a good…let's see now." She tapped her finger to her chin and lifted her eyes to the ceiling as if she were thinking hard. Then slanted her angry eyes back at him. "Five minutes?"

Reason grew uncomfortable. Had he been wrong in accusing her of something he had no proof of? She didn't act one bit guilty. But then why should she? He'd been gone a long time. And none of this was her fault.

"Because he's in love with you."

That silenced her. Slowly she turned back to the desk and resumed her seat. Bracing her elbows on the green felt blotter, she sifted her slender fingers through the auburn curls at her temples.

"Don't tell me you didn't know," Reason insisted.

"I knew." Then she glanced up. "But that doesn't mean I slept with him."

"But you wanted to."

Once again, she rose to her feet, and Reason was glad the desk stood between them.

"I'm a married woman, in case you've forgotten," she snapped. "And Joe respects that fact."

A smug smile creased Reason's jaw. "Joe again?"

She slammed her small fist down on top of the desk.

"What do you think I am? A damned saint?" Her chest was heaving in anger. "I'm a woman. With needs and desires. And a forgetful husband. One who doesn't even know I exist most of the time. Or care a whole hell of a lot!"

"I care."

"Like hell you do! You don't remember me. You had to be told you even had a wife!"

It was true. And Reason couldn't deny it.

Then he heard the whisper of a sound behind him, and a small voice said, "Daddy?"

Reason's gut twisted as if he had suddenly been knifed in the back. Slowly he turned to face the open doorway, and glanced down.

A small child in a pink nightgown that reached to the floor stood inches before him. Her large black-lashed clear blue eyes peered up at him with all the innocence of youth. She had sleep-tousled dark wavy hair that reached her shoulders and was clutching a stuffed toy bear tightly to her chest that had seen better days.

You have a daughter named Jocelyn, Cole had said. The eyes peering up at him were like looking in a mirror.

Slowly Reason dropped to one knee to meet the child at eye level.

"What did you say?" he questioned softly.

"Are you home for good, Daddy?" she replied. Her thumb went to her mouth and she sucked on it nervously. Many months had gone by since she had last seen her father and she became shy as he stared at her.

"That depends on your mother," he said in a husky voice that even he didn't recognize.

He peered over his shoulder at Rachel.

Tears trickled down her freckled cheeks and she was softly crying behind her hand.

When Reason stepped out the front door a few minutes later, Cole was relaxing on the top porch step and Steele was leaning a shoulder against a white support column. As Steele turned at the sound of the screen door opening behind him and saw who it was, he pushed himself upright and veered to face Reason. Both men before him had unanswered questions showing in their eyes.

"I'm staying," Reason said to Cole, prepared for an argument.

Instead Cole nodded. "All right. Maybe things can start getting back to normal around here."

"Don't be too hasty," Reason said. "There's still a lot Rachel and I have to discuss." Then he slid a glance in Steele's direction. "Go ahead. Say it. Before you bust a gut."

"If she's crying...!"

"Do you want to go in there and hold her hand?"

"Somebody should."

Reason jerked his head towards the door.

"Be my guest."

Steele remained where he stood.

"That's a husband's privilege."

"Are you applying for the job?"

A small sneer creased Steele's jaw. "Can't just yet. But I'm hoping a vacancy will open up soon enough."

"Easy, Joe." Cole spoke from his seat. "Give them a chance to sort things out before you go jumpin' in and…."

A pretty blonde woman in her mid-twenties came around the corner of the house with a basket of folded laundry in her hands. Her footsteps faltered for a moment as she spied the men on the porch, but then she boldly walked past them while a small boy playfully tagged at her heels.

"Cole." She nodded indifferently as she passed him by and went on into the house. The boy, however, gave a loud whoop of delight and began climbing all over the man seated on the top porch step.

"When did you get back? Ma said you weren't never comin' home. What in tarnation took you so long!"

Cole laughed and ducked his head as the boy tried to get his father in a headlock.

"Easy there, pardner," Cole chuckled. "I'm a sick man. Ow, watch it. That hurts." Abruptly, the boy ceased pummeling his father.

"Are you all right? What do ya mean, you're sick. Are you gonna die?"

"Nope. Not today anyway." Cole grinned good-naturedly at the tow-headed boy with the same unusual amber eyes as himself. "And hopefully not tomorrow."

"Cole?" Reason asked in a state of confusion.

Cole glanced up once, then said, "Oh, I forgot. You don't remember, do ya." Then he grinned. "This rascal here is my son, Nicholas Jr. And that woman who just passed us by with the sunny disposition," he said sarcastically, "is my wife."

CHAPTER THIRTY

Dinner that evening was a living hell. Both Jocelyn and Nick had eaten earlier and been put to bed, and so there was just the four of them at the dining room table.

Sally made a meal fit for a king, yet the silence around the room was fraught with tension. The only words Sally uttered to Cole after his yearlong absence was "please pass the salt." Even Cole had nothing to say for once and sullenly picked at his food.

And Rachel was no better. Bright spots of color fused her cheeks and her sea green eyes were cold and hard as chipped emeralds. Reason had the idea that she was simply biding her time, waiting for the right moment to give him the tongue-lashing he deserved.

All four of them seemed to breathe a sigh of relief when supper was over. Rachel and Sally rose immediately to clear the table and do the dishes. Cole decided to hit the hay, for he was worn out and sore from the long ride home, and Reason headed out to the front porch for a breath of fresh air. He wasn't sure which room was his anyway, or whether he'd even be welcome in it.

The warm spring night was hot and sticky. Insects buzzed in the trees, and the mournful cry of a coyote howling at the moon split the serenity of the evening. A match flared over by the corrals as one of the hands lit a smoke, and Reason wondered if Steele was watching the house. Slowly he backed up into a chair and sat down hard in the shadow of the porch, then rubbed a weary hand over his face.

What a mess his life was in. Had it always been this way between him and Rachel? This vast chasm of tension and distrust that now separated them? Somehow he doubted it. They had made a beautiful daughter between them. There must have been love once. Then why in hell's name couldn't he recall it?

The coyote yipped and howled once more searching for his mate, and Reason felt as lost and lonely as the bone-chilling cry sounded.

A sudden squeal of rusty hinges alerted Reason to a presence that just stepped out onto the porch. Rachel's slim form dressed in a cool cotton dress let the screen door close quietly behind her, then stood outlined from the light within the house against the darkness of the damp night air. She seemed to be searching for someone with her eyes, far beyond the shadows of the porch.

"Reason?" she whispered low.

"Over here."

Slowly she turned in the direction of his voice.

"Why are you sitting over there in the dark?" she demanded softly.

"Is there something wrong with it?" Reason replied in the same impatient, yet subdued, tone of voice.

"No. It's just…. You startled me."

Casually, she moved towards the edge of the porch, whipped her skirt up beneath her knees, and sat down on the same top step that Cole had vacated earlier. Reason could see the pert outline of her face as she peered into the vast darkness of the night. He wondered if Steele was watching her too, from the corral.

Without turning towards him, she said, "Why'd you come back?"

"It's where I belong, isn't it?" he said, and his heart seemed to skip a beat, waiting for her answer.

"Only if you want to be here."

When there was no response, she turned slightly towards him. "Do you?"

His eyes stung for just a brief moment. Then he said, "Yes." *More than you know*, he wanted to add. Yet he remained silent, unsure of his welcome.

"I'd like to ask you something, and I'd like an honest answer." She drew in a deep breath as if the question was hard for her to utter out loud. Then said, "Why did you go to her, and not to me."

The insects buzzed louder in his ears. Or was it just so damn quiet on the porch? He could hear himself breathe.

"She was there," he said simply. "You weren't. And I didn't

know how to find you."

"You didn't look very hard," she accused, and Reason heard the catch in her voice.

"You're right. I hate to admit it, but it's true." He hesitated for a guilty split-second. "And I could have turned her down. But I didn't." There was a heavy silence between them before Reason said, "When did Steele tell you?"

"He never did. Jimmy Peters was in town that day with Joe. He's the one that saw you go upstairs arm in arm with that two-bit slut."

"Don't call her that."

Reason's response was automatic. Mariah's soft words and gentle touch had filled a need that Reason hadn't even known existed until the moment she offered herself to him. And he couldn't help but be surprised that Steele hadn't ratted on him after all.

"You'd defend her? Against me? Are you telling me you have feelings for this saloon girl?"

"It's over, Rachel. You're my wife. Forget about the past."

"That didn't answer my question much."

Reason was silent. He thought he had.

"I'm curious about one other thing. If Joe hadn't mentioned you were married, would you have recognized me at all?"

Yes, he wanted to say. He had found her attractive the day he delivered Cole's note. But that wasn't the same as remembering your own wife.

"I didn't recall anyone at the time," he replied in all honesty. "I didn't even know my own name. There's still too many holes in my memory. Even now."

"I know. I saw you with Jocelyn." She peered out into the night, then glanced back at her husband. "What happened out there, Reason? What terrible event made you forget everything that you once held dear."

Uh-oh. Here it comes. He knew she'd be asking him about it sooner or later. He'd hoped later. He felt the trembling begin in his hands that soon spread to other parts of his body.

"I don't want to talk about it."

But she wouldn't take no for an answer. "The only way we can patch things up is if I can understand a little of what you went through. Your brother told me you were ambushed on the trail coming home, shot up something awful, and left for dead. I almost passed out on the floor when he told me. But you didn't die. You survived against all odds. What happened Reason? Did someone find you? Help you? If they did I'd like to thank them."

"No! God, no!"

The night suddenly turned ominous. Dark figures lunged at him in his mind. Reason leaped up from his seat, tripped over the chair behind him and backed up until he was in the far corner with the palms of his hands pressed hard up against the wall.

Rachel leaped up from the step in alarm. "Oh, my Lord! What's wrong? Are you having an attack of some kind?"

Reason was breathing as if he were suffocating, unable to draw air into his lungs. His pale blue eyes stared fearfully out into the night as if some huge horrid beast was all ready to pounce on him and chew him up alive.

"Reason, what is it? Should I get Cole?"

"No, please...." He started to say. Then threw both arms up over his eyes as if to block out a terrible image in his mind, or else ward off a blow. "Don't...."

"All right, I won't," Rachel cried, confused and disoriented by Reason's odd behavior. She had seen him like this once before in the yard after Joe had lit into him. But she thought he was over all that. "Is there anything I can do?"

Reason moaned low in his throat. "Don't...touch me."

"Well, you don't have to worry about that," Rachel said in a huff of indignation. "If that's what you want, you've got it."

Suddenly a familiar deep drawling voice spoke from the bottom steps of the porch.

"Is anything wrong, Rachel?"

Rachel's pride was stung deep. Reason was her husband and he didn't want her touching him. So be it!

"Reason's acting funny again and doesn't want my help," Rachel stormed. "I'm going in to bed. Maybe you can talk sense to him. He's not making any to me." She turned on her heel and stormed into the house in a huff.

Steele glanced over at Reason cowering against the far corner of the house. Twice already he'd seen him like this. Once in this very same yard, and once at the jail. And he didn't know what the hell to do with him any more than Rachel did.

Against his will, he climbed up the steps to the porch and sauntered over to Reason.

"What the hell's wrong with you, boss?" But Reason didn't seem to hear a word he said.

In order to gain his attention, Joe grabbed Reason's wrists and forced them down and away from his face. He wasn't much surprised to feel Reason trembling beneath his hands like a newborn foal on shaky legs.

"No, don't." Reason moaned softly, deep in his throat.

"Don't... what?" Steele shouted. And when there was no response, he released his wrists, grabbed him by the shoulders, and shook him until his teeth rattled. "Talk to me, man. What's wrong?"

"Don't... hurt me," Reason finally groaned.

Steele was so shocked he almost dropped him. But instead he hung on like a pit bull with his jaws clamped tight around an enemy's jugular.

"Do you know who I am?" Steele shouted. "Look at me," he yelled when Reason didn't answer. "Who am I?"

Gradually Reason looked up and fear glistened in his pale blue eyes.

"Buck...?" he said softly.

"Who the hell is Buck?"

Suddenly Cole was there, by Steele's side.

"What's goin' on out here, Joe? You were hollerin' loud enough to wake the dead. Reason? What the hell are ya doin' in the corner?"

"He's having a fit of some kind," Steele said. "And he just called me Buck."

Cole didn't seem much surprised to Joe's eyes. Did he know more than he was letting on?

Buck and Mortimer. Weren't those the two names Reason had once confided to him? Cole had been hoping he'd heard wrong. Now he knew he hadn't. Reason was in a bad way again.

"Let him go, dammit," he said to Joe. "You're not helpin' him any." Then to Reason he said, "Easy fella, it's Cole. Nobody's gonna hurt ya none. Take it easy now."

But when Steele released him, Reason sank straight down to

his knees with a muffled groan.

"What the hell started all this?" Cole turned to Joe for an explanation.

"Don't look at me," Joe replied in a testy way. After all he'd only been trying to help. "Rachel and him were out here having a conversation of sorts, and then I see Reason suddenly jump out of his chair like it bit him in the ass and stumble backwards into this here damned corner."

Ignoring Steele, Cole went down on one knee. "Reason, it's Cole," he repeated again. "There's nothin' to fret about. You're home, with your family. Why don't ya get up and we'll go inside and grab a cup of coffee. I think there's still some left in the pot. If not, then I'll make some more. What do ya say?"

Cole's voice seemed to soothe Reason to Joe's eyes.

"Cole?"

"Damned straight it's me. And everythin's all right now. Come on. Get up, will ya?"

Cautiously, Reason lifted his head. He saw Cole right away for he was at eye level with him. But Steele he had to look up at. Then he swallowed hard.

"What am I doing…?"

Cole grabbed him beneath one arm before Reason could finish the sentence, and he motioned for Steele to get the other. Between the both of them they helped Reason to his feet. But immediately upon rising, he shrugged out of their grip and stumbled back against the wall.

"Easy now," Cole soothed. "We were only tryin' to help you up, Reason. Now how about that coffee? Joe, could you stand a cup?"

Steele was more than confused and a trifle curious as to Reason's odd behavior. And Cole seemed to be the only one who could handle him in this condition. Maybe he could learn something useful in his future dealings with the man.

"Don't mind if I do," he said with a wry grin.

CHAPTER THIRTY-ONE

The three men sat alone at the kitchen table with a cold glass of milk in each of their hands. The coffee was all gone and Cole wasn't sure where Sally kept the grounds anymore. She was always moving things around. Reason was lounging in his chair with his legs stretched out before him and crossed at the ankles, staring down at the scuffed toes of his boots. While Joe Steele kept glancing his way every few seconds, wondering what worrisome course of action his boss would instigate next.

"Either of you fellas care to fill me in on what's goin' on around here?" Steele asked with an honest amount of curiosity as his attention shifted to Cole.

"Reason had some trouble while he was headin' back from Laramie last year," Cole said, as he tapped the fingers of his right hand restlessly against the table's smooth top. "And it still shakes up his mind at times."

"What sort of trouble?"

Reason was still and silent seated at the table, and Cole wondered whether he even heard them at all.

"Let's just say the kind no man goes lookin' for."

"That tells me a lot," Steele sneered as he raised the tall glass of milk to his lips.

"That's all you need to know," Cole stated, sitting up straighter in his seat. "Anythin' more and I'd be betrayin' a confidence. Just let it be known that if you or I had suffered through the hell he did, we'd probably both be actin' the same way right now, or worse."

"I doubt it." Steele's smug grin was annoying to say the least.

"Well, maybe not you," Cole admitted. "And maybe not me. But it sure knocked the stuffin' out'a him."

"What're you plannin' to do about it?"

Good question. Cole shifted his attention towards the man seated across the table from him.

"Reason, are you hearin' any of this?"

Reason's head jerked up. "What?"

"That's what I thought," Cole grumbled half to himself. "What's it gonna take, I wonder, to get you through this nightmare from hell." Cole voiced an idea that crept into his mind. "What if we go after those two, Reason? You wanna do that?"

Reason came to life within the blink of an eye. He jumped up from his chair much like he did earlier on the porch. "Are you crazy?"

"Now that's real funny comin' from you," Cole said softly. "I'd laugh if you weren't so dead serious."

"What two?" Steele said in confusion.

"The two men that…."

"Shut up Cole!"

"If he's goin' with us, then maybe he should know why."

"He's not going anywhere. And neither are you!"

Cole leaned far back in his chair. "Okay. It was just a thought."

Reason breathed a sigh of relief and found his seat. "Besides, I couldn't find that place again if I tried."

"I might," Cole said with a smug trace of confidence. "I have a vague idea where I found you."

"What the hell are you two talkin' about? Found him where?"

"Steele, why don't you go back to the bunkhouse where you belong," Reason growled low.

Joe grinned. "Well, I would. But I'm finding this conversation awful interesting. And I'm curious about one thing. Who is this fella called Buck?"

Reason froze. His insides turned to ice. Then he shifted an accusing stare at Cole.

"Just what the hell have you been telling him!"

Cole raised his arms, palms out from his sides in an innocent gesture.

"Don't go blamin' me. You're the one who called him that. I heard you plain as day."

"Me? Called him…? You're lying!"

Steele sucked in a deep breath. One man didn't go around insulting another like that in his book. And if he did, that fellow was looking for pure trouble. But Cole just took it with a grain of salt.

"God's honest truth," Cole swore. "I heard Joe ask you point blank as I came out on the porch just a few minutes ago, who you thought he was. And you said, Buck."

Reason glanced over at Steele with a look of sheer horror written all over his face.

"I said that?"

Joe nodded firmly.

Reason clapped a hand over his mouth as if he could call back those very words.

"My God!"

"That clinches it." Cole rose to his feet and started towards the front of the house. "Wait here, I'll be right back."

There was an unhealthy silence shifting subtly between the two men left at the table, but within minutes Cole was back. Without a word, he threw Reason's black leather gun belt and mahogany-handled revolver on the table before him that he had retrieved from his own saddlebags in his room.

Reason slowly glanced up. "What's this?"

"We're goin' after them, whether you're with us, or not."

"Who's we?" Steele asked suspiciously.

"You and I. Any questions?" He directed his words to Steele, but his eyes were on Reason as he spoke. A sick sense of dread shone in the pale blue eyes facing him, yet Reason remained silent.

"Yeah. A few. Just where we going?" Steele asked in reply.

"To repay an old debt that's been long overdue. Now get some sleep. Both of you. We leave at first light."

CHAPTER THIRTY-TWO

Cole didn't have the trouble he figured on finding the path that led into the mountains where he first found Reason. Two days later brought the three men directly to the lightning-split oak tree Cole recalled from memory. But the cabin was another story.

Suddenly Cole pulled up short. "I think it's just over that rise of pine trees yonder. Come one, Joe. Let's get down and take a look see."

All three men dismounted, but when Reason moved to follow, Cole immediately raised a hand and pushed at his chest.

"Not you. You stay with the horses. There's no sense all of us shouting a welcome at the same time. Besides, if we should happen to get into trouble, you'll be our back-up plan."

Reason knew Cole was only trying to spare him the misery of facing those two men once again, but his idea did make sense.

"Why don't you stay here then," Reason argued. "You're the one who's already hurt. And we all know you can't hit the broad side of a barn if you had a double-barreled shotgun placed in your hands."

Cole chuckled. "Aw, I'll be all right. But thanks for the vote of confidence anyway." He slapped Reason companionably on the shoulder. "Besides, I have Joe here. And he's faster than both of us on a good day."

He winked at Reason to ease the sting of his words.

"Just don't panic if you hear shots. We don't plan on takin' them quietly. Only," he hesitated ever so slightly, "if we're not back within the hour," Cole shrugged, "maybe you should just ride out and we'll catch up when we can."

At Reason's sharp look, he added, "That's just a precaution now. I'm sure everythin's gonna work out just fine. Don't worry.

We've got the element of surprise on our side. Just keep the horses quiet and out of sight, will ya?"

Then he nodded to the man next to him. "Come on, Joe. Let's get this job over with. Sally was kind of warmin' up to me before all the ruckus on the porch started. I'm kind'a anxious to get home and see if the fire's still burnin' for me."

He smiled in that wild, reckless way he had that made all the ladies swoon. And Steele just shook his head and laughed. Then with a brief wave, both men disappeared into the dense covering of the woods.

Reason remained with the horses, and found the chore wasn't half-bad as he thought it would be. Truth was, his legs sort of refused to carry him further on their own power anyway. And he was secretly thankful Cole had sensed his inner reluctance and refused to allow him to participate in this particular raid. For he was damned sure he didn't want to set eyes on either of those two mountain men again in this lifetime, or any other.

Reason led the horses farther into the shade, then hunkered down to wait. His insides were in a turmoil and his hands trembled slightly as he raised one to shield his eyes from the sun. Anxiously, he mouthed a silent prayer that both men would return safe.

When Cole and Joe topped the rise, Cole couldn't believe his eyes. There was the ramshackle old cabin just as he remembered, with the falling down barn and the broken corral. And there on the porch sitting there calm as you pleased and smoking a corncob pipe was the trapper Reason knew as Buck.

Cole grinned in a confident way. "There he is. One of them anyway. You see any signs of the other?"

Joe's keen hazel eyes swept the surrounding trees and dense forest around them.

"No. Do you?"

"He could be out huntin'. Or he could be still in the shack. I'm not second-guessin'. Let's split up. You take the left. I'll mosey around to my right. Whenever you're ready, you can brace the one on the porch. I'll keep you in plain sight at all times, and I'll cover your back when you make your play."

Joe nodded and instantly moved out. This was what Reason

was so worried about? This was going to be easier than taking a Sunday stroll on the sidewalk in Sheridan.

Cole immediately cut to his right. He was alert and ready for trouble, and wasn't taking any unnecessary chances with these two uncivilized mountain men. He'd seen the size of those brutes close up and felt the power in their hands. And for two illiterate trappers, they seemed to possess all the innate cunning of the animals they killed for a living.

The woods were thick and dense with growth. And Cole had to step careful so as not to make any undue noise. Even so, branches rubbed against his shirt and trousers with a whispering, rustling sound, and no matter how careful he stepped, every so often the soft snap of a broken twig beneath his boots could be clearly heard to his overactive ears.

Suddenly Cole froze and listened hard. Had he heard something in the woods behind him?

He turned halfway around, his pistol already in his hand, but there was no one there. Just the gently swaying needles of a bent pine.

He was getting a bad case of the jitters, he scolded himself firmly. Then he chuckled. He was acting as jumpy as Reason.

It must be the imminent threat of gunplay that was shaking him up so badly, he figured. Handguns were never Cole's choice of weapon to begin with. He was a ranch hand, plain and simple. He never had the nerves of steel that both Reason and Joe had when it came right down to killing a man. And he never would.

Another sound of a twig snapping behind him made his nerves almost leap clear out of his skin. Something was out there. He knew it in his gut.

Something big!

CHAPTER THIRTY-THREE

Steele sat on his haunches on the opposite side of the cabin, and peered through the leafy coverage of a large prickly bush before him. There was still no sign of the other trapper, and no trace of Cole. But Joe didn't expect to see his boss anyway, until the moment he stepped out into full view of the clearing beyond him.

Cautiously he eased the pistol from his hip. The man was still on the porch in a rickety old chair, blowing smoke rings into the air as if he hadn't a care in the world. Joe wondered if this was the fellow named Buck that Reason had seemed so damn afraid of. He didn't look so threatening to Joe. Okay, so the man was a big fellow. You could see the way he filled out the chair almost to the breaking point. And the massive legs stretched out before him reminded Joe of the trunks of giant oak trees. Yet any man could be brought down with a single bullet between the eyes, or centered straight through the heart. And Joe was confident in his abilities as a marksman.

With the easy natural grace and quiet stealth of a fast gun for hire, Joe slipped out from the cover of the trees and strode boldly into full view of the porch. Without taking his eyes off the man, Joe raised his revolver chest level and aimed the weapon smack dab in the middle of the fellow's left suspender.

"Don't move. I've got you covered."

The man didn't flinch. Not one muscle. And Joe had the uneasy sensation that the trapper had known he was out there all along. And if he had, then where was the second man? And where the hell was Cole?

Slowly the man laid his hand-filled pipe on one bent knee.

"I'd put that pop gun down, boy, if I were you," he said

calmly. "Unless you want your friend to get hurt some."

The man was bluffing. Wasn't he? Joe suddenly grew edgy. He threw a quick glance over his shoulder and breathed a sigh of relief. There was no one in sight.

But there should have been. Cole was supposed to be backing his play. Just where the hell was he?

His question was answered when Cole burst into the clearing from the opposite direction with his hands held shoulder high, palms out. His cheeks were smudged with dirt and he was hatless as if he had been in a recent struggle of some kind. Then another large man came out behind him with a rifle aimed at the small of his back. He prodded Cole roughly onward with the hard bore of a Winchester when Cole came to a complete and sudden halt.

Joe swore beneath his breath. This wasn't good. He felt that both he and Cole had underestimated the intelligence of the trappers and now they might pay dearly for it. A sick queasy feeling began forming in his gut.

"Put it down, boy," the man on the porch said again, as he calmly raised the pipe once more to his lips and sucked contentedly on the wooden stem. "Now you see what I mean?"

When he removed the pipe from his mouth and blew out another round of smoke, Joe adjusted his aim and squeezed the trigger. He blew the corncob bowl right off the stem. The gunshot blast sounded loud in the clearing, and the man in the chair jerked in alarm.

"See what I mean?" Joe said, just as calmly.

Then he heard Cole gasp. Joe darted his eyes in his boss's direction, only to see Cole wince in agony. The man's large beefy left arm was now wrapped tight around Cole's middle, squeezing him hard against his own large body, while the steel bore of the rifle rested snug against his right temple.

"Cole? You all right?" Joe shouted across the clearing in confusion. Why the hell was he in so much pain? He knew Cole wasn't up to par when he and Reason had returned to the Stirrup C Bar, but he'd never been told by anyone exactly why.

The big man grinned and squeezed Cole again. And Cole threw back his head and gave a sharp yelp of agony.

"Seems he's hurtin' some in the middle," the man holding Cole said. And Cole groaned softly in response.

"Let him go," Joe yelled across the distance. Cole looked as if he was going to pass clear out. "Or I'll shoot!" Joe still had his revolver trained on the man on the porch.

"You shoot and I'll snap his spine like a twig," the man behind Cole sneered. For emphasis he jerked his arm back once more. A bubble of agony caught in Cole's throat and he would have gone straight to his knees if the man hadn't already been holding him up. Cole's world suddenly grew dark.

"Shoot, Joe. Shoot to kill," he groaned softly as his knees trembled and began to buckle of their own volition.

But instead Joe slowly lowered his arm to his side.

"Now drop the pistol, boy," the man on the porch said.

Joe let his fingers grow loose and dropped the revolver to the dirt. The man on the porch still hadn't moved from the chair. Then he chuckled softly as if at some private joke.

"Bring them on in, Mortie. And let's find out just what the hell these boys are made of, and what they're doin' so damn far from home."

Reason heard the gunshot just over the hill and he jumped to his feet. Instinctively his hand reached for the revolver strapped to his side. But there was no further sound, and the soft whispering silence of the surrounding woods told him no more.

Cole had warned him there might be shots. And not to be alarmed if he heard them. But there was only one shot fired, not two. One shot couldn't bring down two men.

He was starting to get a bad feeling in his gut and he wondered why in the name of hell he had ever let those two men go after the woodsmen alone. They were too evenly matched, two against two. And Buck and Mortimer were in their element. A third man might have made all the difference in the world. But it was too late now for regrets. Whatever happened had already occurred. And all he could do now was wait and hope both men got back to him in one piece.

He waited, he paced. An ice-cold sweat broke out over his entire body as the minutes slowly ticked by and there was still no sign of either man. Something was wrong. They should have been back by now. The gunshot had sounded over twenty minutes ago.

Reason swore softly beneath his breath. He pulled his revolver and checked the fully loaded chamber for the tenth time, it seemed. Then abruptly re-holstered his pistol. He wasn't waiting any longer. Cautiously, he slipped into the thickest part of the woods.

Reason traveled instinctively in an easterly direction until he finally came to the short rise overlooking the cabin. Here he had a clear view of the yard below. The tumbledown shack. The broken-railed corral. But the place appeared empty. There was no one in sight.

Although the day was cool, beads of sweat trickled in his eyes as he ducked back out of sight of the cabin below. His gun hand trembled as he swiped at his brow. He swore softly beneath his breath and ground his teeth in frustration. His brain rebelled at what he had to do.

Cole and Joe hadn't come back. That meant they were still down there. Probably inside the run-down shack along with the two backwoodsmen.

His insides were so jittery he wanted to vomit right there on the spot. But he didn't have time to be sick. The job now fell to him to make sure both men got out of there alive and in one piece. For if it hadn't been for him, both Cole and Joe wouldn't have been down there in the first place.

Slowly Reason backed up. He'd approach the cabin from a different angle. One where he could move closer and not be so clearly visible. He was focusing so intently on the cabin below, he didn't pay much attention to where his feet were landing.

There was a sudden clank of metal as pain sliced into his right leg like sharp jagged knives, causing him to cry out loud and pinning his foot to the ground. He lost his balance and fell on his side his teeth gnashing in pain as the steel jaws of a cougar trap bit deeply into his calf, clear through the thick leather shaft of his boot. He laid there gasping for breath and unable to move, wondering if his leg was broken. It sure as hell felt like it. For every time he twitched, the steel teeth grated nauseatingly on bone.

He cursed himself a fool for not paying attention to where he was going. After all, the men were trappers, weren't they?

Why hadn't he remembered that?

CHAPTER THIRTY-FOUR

"Mort? You reckon we should rough him up some? I doubt we'll get any answers this way. He looks as if he's plumb passed out."

Joe was seated on a straight-back chair, same as Cole, with their hands tied cruelly behind their backs, their ankles roped to the hard wooden legs. Only Cole was seated more towards the center of the small room, the main focus of attention, while Joe's chair was braced up against the sidewall. But although Joe was fully aware of every word being uttered, Cole had his head down as if he were blissfully unconscious.

Then the man called Mort stepped alongside Cole's chair, grabbed him by the hair and snapped his head backwards. Cole winced, but refused to open his eyes.

"Aw, he's just play-actin' like an ol' possum," Mort said. "He's as wide awake as we are." Mort leaned over and breathed in Cole's face. "Aren't you, boy?"

The man's fetid breath made Cole grimace in disgust and jerk his head to the side.

"See there?" Mort crowed with delight. "What'd I tell ya." Then he leaned once more over Cole. "Sing, boy, like a canary. Tell us what we want to know and we won't hurt you more'n we should. Now what're you doin' back here noseyin' around and bringin' trouble with ya."

Cole remained silent. He was as alert as any man in this room, but he'd be damned if he'd tell these bastards a thing. Reason was still out there. Alone. Cole's fervent wish was that Reason had hopped on Satan when they hadn't returned within a reasonable amount of time and lit out for home. But there was no way of knowing what Reason would do next. And there was no way in hell he'd say anything that would send these two mangy critters out after him.

"He ain't talkin', Buck." Mort released the handful of Cole's dark hair and watched his head fall down to his chest once more. "What do you reckon we'll do with him now?"

Buck shrugged innocently. "Make him."

Morty laughed in response, then walked around the chair to face Cole. He lifted Cole's chin, then slapped him hard across the face with the flat of his huge hand. Joe winced, as Cole's head snapped sideways. But Cole never uttered a sound. Then the big man swung back and whacked him fiercely on the opposite cheek.

Cole jerked so hard he almost fell sideways, dragging the chair with him. A soft groan issued from deep in his throat, while a thin stream of blood trickled from the corner of his mouth and ran down his chin.

"You're a tough one, huh?" Mortimer leered. "Well, we got ways of dealin' with your kind." Then his hand went to Cole's throat and he gently squeezed.

Cole choked. His eyes flew open and he struggled for breath.

"Now are you gonna talk? Or do I crush your windpipe."

Cole's face began turning various shades of purple. Bright spots of light danced before his eyes, and he was teetering on the edge of blackness, when Joe shouted, "How the hell do you expect a man to answer, when you're strangling him to death, you damn fool!"

Buck chuckled as he leaned a hip against an old battle-scarred table.

"He's got a point there, Morty, old man. Just what are you tryin' to prove?"

Mortimer grudgingly released him and Cole's breath came out in a rush. His chest heaved uncontrollably as he drew fresh air into tortured, deprived lungs.

"Guess I got a little carried away," Mortimer sneered. Then he lifted Cole's head once more with two fingers clamped to his chin, and silently assessed his chiseled features. "He's not quite as pretty as the other one was," he said. "But he's not all that hard to look at neither. What do you say we have a go at him? It's been a while since we had any fun. And I'm getting might hungry."

Cole jerked his jaw out of the man's hand. He had heard bits of conversation sift through his oxygen-starved brain and ringing ears, and he wasn't liking any of what he was hearing.

"Keep your filthy paws off me," he groaned. "You'll have to kill me first."

"Is that so?" Mortimer sneered and leaned over Cole once more. He raised a huge hand to Cole's face and patted him gently on the same cheek he had slapped him minutes before. Cole flinched hard and Mortimer laughed. Then the man reached down and ripped open the front of Cole's shirt. A gasp of fear escaped Cole's throat and he sucked in a deep breath.

"Look at me," Mortimer snarled.

Cole deliberately ignored him, choosing instead to stare down at the rough planked floor. Then Mortimer slammed him once more in the face with the flat of his hand so hard his neck almost snapped completely in two. Cole was only barely coherent when Mortimer brought his head around to face him once more.

"Now, look at me," he ordered firmly

Cole's amber eyes were glazed with fear and pain, yet slowly he raised his head to meet the crazed, beady eyes of the trapper.

"Now, that's a good boy," Mortimer sneered. Then he reached for Cole's red-streaked neck once again.

Cole's spine stiffened and his breath caught in his throat. Mentally he braced himself for further anguish. Only instead of violence, this time the man's touch was a gentle caress, and his knowing leer...? Gut wrenching. Cole eyes lost focus as Mortimer's hand slid lower beneath his blue shirt.

He'd rather be hit.

Reason had tried to free his leg. Tried to spring the unyielding steel jaws of the trap with his bare hands. Once he even managed to split them apart a few inches. But when his leg jerked instinctively, in a premature bid for freedom, his sweaty grip slipped on the trap itself. When the steel teeth snapped back and bit deeply into his torn and bleeding leg a second time, Reason cried out in agony, then fell back to the ground with a deep moan.

That was the last straw. He was done for and he wouldn't be trying that stunt again, ever. He simply didn't have the strength, the leverage, or the stomach, to accomplish such a feat. He had heard stories of frantic animals chewing off their own limbs to escape the torturous clutches of a steel trap. And now he knew why.

Reason's breath was harsh and ragged. How long had he lain here? Hours? Minutes? He'd lost all track of time. The tops of the tall pines surrounding him blurred against the blue sky.

What had happened to Cole, and Steele, he wondered. There had been no sign of them at the shack. Were they even alive?

Blood soaked his pants leg, ran down the inside of his boot to drench his sock, and, like a river meeting a dam, puddled at the sole of his foot. If the steel-blade knife he kept in the leather shaft of his boot hadn't partially obstructed the steel snap of the trap, his leg would have shattered like fine china upon impact and become even more mangled than it already was. Even now he knew it would be days before he could put weight on it again. If ever.

His heart beat frantically in his chest like the wings of a caged bird. He knew it was only a matter of time before Buck or Mortimer checked their traps and found him. And once more he would be at their mercy. His body jerked involuntarily at the thought and pain shot straight up his leg to his brain. He couldn't let that happen. Not a second time! He'd kill himself first.

Without another thought, his hand slid towards the familiar mahogany butt of the pistol at his side. A sense of inner peace ran fleetingly across his mind, and he realized an easy way out. He had planned to end it all anyway, right after he had been let out of jail. But Cole had anticipated such a move and proceeded to distract him from it. But this time there was no one to stop him. And now he had even more of an excuse to take his own life than ever before.

Slowly he eased the revolver out of the holster at his hip and rested the steel barrel across his chest. Now, if he only had the guts to pull this off, in a few measly seconds all pain would be gone forever. The nauseating, debilitating agony of his torn and bleeding leg, the violent nightmares that left him breathless and trembling with each new dawn, the loss of his memory and with it his wife.

Although taking the coward's way out went against the grain to his mind, there was only so much hell a man could stomach in life. And he figured he had suffered more than his fair share.

Drawing a deep breath, he slowly eased the hammer back with

his thumb and began to lift the heavy steel bore to his temple.

But he didn't count on company.

"Hold it right there!" The loud booming voice came from out of the woods.

Reason's frayed nerves leaped in alarm and he clenched his teeth in agony at the resulting pain in his leg. Before he knew what was happening, the pistol was roughly snatched from his hand. Slowly he glanced up, then gasped in fear.

A large bulky shadow loomed between him and the sky. The barrel of a rifle, aimed straight at him caught the glinting golden rays of the sun. Crooked yellow teeth grinned down at him, and a hauntingly familiar, "Well, lookit here," made his gut wrench in full-blown panic.

"Oh shit," he moaned helplessly as he flung an arm up over his face in an attempt to block out all sight and sound from his awareness. His haunting nightmares were coming true all over again.

"I caught me somethin' bigger than a rabbit this time," Buck sneered.

"Welcome back, Reason. Me and Morty sure been missin' ya."

CHAPTER THIRTY-FIVE

It was Joe Steele who told them where they left Reason. He simply couldn't stand the sight of the gut-wrenching tableau being enacted in front of his eyes a moment longer.

Cole was trembling like a six-point quake was rocking his chair and he couldn't seem to tear his eyes away from the man standing before him when Morty's hand slid sensuously down Cole's bare chest and over his ruined bandages to the tarnished brass buckle at his waist. Only then did Cole gasp and try to wrench away once more. Another hard slap almost rendered him unconscious.

"I said look at me, damn you! I wanna see the fear in your eyes." He grabbed Cole's jaw once more in his meaty fist and shook his head violently.

Cole moaned aloud, both from pain and fright. Then, as if resigned to his fate, his glazed amber eyes lifted once more to the man who stood grinning maddeningly in his face.

"Now that's better," Mortimer chuckled. "By the time I get through with you, you won't know which end is up."

He reached for Cole's brown leather belt once more, and that's when Joe finally spoke up.

"Hold it! Just let him be, damn you. And I'll tell you whatever it is you want to know."

So he told them exactly what they were doing here, hoping to settle an old score…and where they had left Reason, just over the ridge. It just about killed him to give in to those brutes, but he couldn't stand to watch them torment and pummel Cole a moment longer. And he didn't know how much more abuse Cole could stand and still survive.

Now if it was him they were after, he probably could have

handled whatever paces those damned jackasses put him through. But instead they seemed to enjoy taking their frustrations out on an already injured man. And it tore his guts up to witness a virile, fearless man, one he called a friend, reduced to a shivering mass of molding putty.

Yet he realized his mistake shortly after the one called Buck stormed out the door with a rifle in his hands and Mortimer sat back down at the table.

"You got a big mouth when you shouldn't." Cole slurred his words through a badly swollen jaw and a bloody split lip without turning around.

"I was only trying to save your damned neck," Joe growled back. "And that's the thanks I get?"

"They're gonna do what they want with me anyway," Cole said, weary beyond belief. "You blabbin' your mouth off is only gonna delay things, and bring another poor sucker into the picture."

Mortimer laughed like a hyena to Cole's mind.

"You got that right, boy. And I'm sure gonna enjoy takin' you down when Buck gets back with your friend. Then we'll see just how tough you really are."

Only a short time later, Buck burst through the door of the shack lugging, as easy as a lightweight sack of cotton, a limp and barely conscious Reason over his right shoulder. He went straight towards a thick pallet of hides by the far wall and dropped his heavy bundle right on top. Reason gasped as his back hit the makeshift mattress with a thud and then groaned as someone grabbed at his throbbing right leg.

"We might have to cut that boot off," Buck said to his partner in crime.

Cole had swiveled his attention to Buck in time to see Reason flinch in pain.

"What the hell did you do to him now, you sick bastards?" he snarled, forgetting for the moment his own misery in regard for his friend.

Buck glanced over at him then grinned.

"Boy, you wound me, you surely do," he said with a chuckle.

"I swear I didn't touch him, except to free him from the sharp claws of one of my cougar traps."

A quick glance at Reason's right leg gave testimony to Buck's words. Cole noted the mangled boot along with the enormous amount of blood soaking through the right leg of his trousers.

"Is it broken?" he asked in a worried voice.

"Don't rightly know. He sort of hollers every time I go to touch it." He grabbed Reason's boot at the ankle and gave it a sharp tug.

Reason gasped and flew halfway up to grab desperately at his right knee. "You-son-of-a-bitch!" His face screwed up in a grimace of agony before he finally fell back down to the furred mattress.

"See there? What do you think?"

"Untie me and let me take a look," Cole shouted in a fit of anger. "You're as gentle as a stampeding buffalo caught in a prairie fire. He could bleed to death while you two just stand there and watch."

"Naw, you're just tryin' to trick us," Buck said slyly. "Me and Mortie'll fix him up, don't you worry. Just like we did last time." He turned towards his friend. "Get me that whiskey bottle, Mort, over in the corner, and here," he reached in the waistband of his trousers and withdrew Reason's revolver. Then threw it at Morty.

"Put that somewhere safe. The fool was all ready to blow his brains to Kingdom come when I found him. Now that would have been a pure waste, if you ask me. I can think of a lot more useful things for him to do."

Cole's gaze met Joe's. Neither man needed to utter a word. They both knew Joe had unwittingly saved Reason's life by speaking up when he did. And not a moment too soon, it seemed. But what price would Reason have to pay for his salvation this time? Would he have been better off if Buck hadn't found him at all?

"Come here, Morty, and hold him down while I cut this damn boot off."

Reason didn't even put up a struggle when Mortimer grabbed both wrists and pressed them firmly into his chest. But he yelped out loud when Buck began to savagely saw at the leather with a large skinning knife. In a fit of frustration, Buck threw the knife to the floor.

"This ain't workin' worth a damn. I can't cut this thing. I'll end up sawin' his whole leg off. I'm gonna pull it off him. Hold him tight now, so I can wiggle it off."

Reason threw back his head and groaned as Buck tugged viciously at his boot, but finally his foot was free. His white cotton sock was drenched in blood, as were his denim trousers. Buck tore open the leg of his pants to expose three raw, gaping, and bloody holes on one side of his calf and two on the other, where the trap had grabbed and held around the knife in his boot.

"I don't think it's broken. Wiggle your toes, boy."

"There see," he crowed with delight, as Reason jerked his foot in a purely reflexive action, a scant two inches. "I was right. Give me that whiskey."

Cole winced as Buck poured the amber liquid directly over Reason's lacerated and bleeding flesh. He heard Reason gasp in surprise, saw his body jerk convulsively, then his taut muscles went limp.

"Reason?" Cole called out, worried at the sudden silence coming from the bed.

"Aw he just blacked out. Don't fret none. He'll be good as new in a few hours. Then we'll have us some real fun."

They doused Reason's leg one more time, then bound the injury with a clean white bandage that Cole wondered where on earth they had dug that up from, for everything else in the shanty was covered in a thick layer of dust. Then Mortimer turned to Cole.

"Now where were we, boy? Before we got interrupted, that is." He grinned a wide, gap-toothed smile, then rubbed suggestively at his crotch. "I got me an itch here, and I'm thinkin' maybe you could scratch it for me."

"Go douse yourself with kerosene you got an itch. You're probably crawlin' with vermin anyway," Cole snarled in his usual insolent way. Yet when Mortimer began moving in his direction, Cole's eyes grew large in his face and he swallowed hard.

"What do you think, Buck?" Morty said. "You wanna give me a hand?"

"Aw, why the hell not. I prefer the cute little fella over here," he indicated Reason with a nod and rubbed at the denim-clad knee. "But this one's out cold." He rose off the floor. "Anyways he'll keep until later. You want I should untie him?"

Joe watched the nonchalant exchange between the two burly mountain men and a clear picture of Reason's troubles this past year formed in his mind. So this was what all that hell was about. Reason had been gone, what? Almost a month? That was too long a time.

He watched Cole's chest begin heaving with anxiety and knew exactly what the two men were planning. His gut twisted in mindless revulsion and he began to desperately saw at the ropes binding his wrists. But they were tied too damn tight. Then he saw Buck bend and retrieve his skinning knife from the filthy floor, move towards Cole, and cut through the bonds at each of Cole's booted ankles. Then he severed the rope tying his hands with one upward slice.

Cole jumped up like he was shot out of a cannon at his sudden release, and began backing away from the two men advancing towards him. But when he came up hard against the edge of the crudely built table, he could go no further. Mortimer lunged for him, and Cole skillfully twisted out of his grip. But the wound in his belly must have screamed out a protest, for he staggered, let out a short groan and clutched at his waist.

Mortimer was on top of Cole in an instant and his bulky weight dragged them both down to the floor. Cole gave the man a sharp jab to the ribs and managed to roll out from beneath him. But when Cole started to rise to his feet, Buck grabbed his arms from behind.

"Oh shit!" Cole swore as he tried to twist himself free once more. But this time the man's arms held fast.

Then Mortimer was standing there before him.

"That was a real good try. Real good. But I'm tired of playin' right now. I want some action, and you're gonna be still while I get it."

Without another word he drew back his fist and slammed Cole hard in the gut.

Cole's world turned dark. Stars twinkled before him as agony exploded at his waist. He'd been hit in the exact same spot where Reason's bullet had landed just a few short weeks ago. His knees buckled and even Buck couldn't keep him upright. He landed on the floor with only a small whimper of protest. He hurt too badly to barely utter a sound. All he had strength left to do was breathe. And the way he was gasping for air, he wasn't even doing that right.

Then suddenly someone was above him. Climbing all over him. Hands tore maddeningly at his clothes. Strong fingers reached around him and fumbled at the buckle at his waist. He felt his trousers yanked open.

"No, don't," he moaned softly. "Please! Jesus...don't!"

CHAPTER THIRTY-SIX

Reason hadn't passed out as everyone thought. Shortly after Buck left his side, and when he deemed it safe, he slowly turned his head to see Cole leap out of his chair as if it caught fire with him in it. The look of sheer panic in his amber eyes was a palpable thing as Cole began to edge backwards towards the table.

Now those two horny bastards were after Cole, Reason raged silently to himself, closing in on him like two mangy coyotes salivating over an injured three-legged rabbit. He had to do something to distract the men and prevent them from achieving their goal.

His eyes flew about the room searching for his pistol. In his crippled condition, he was of no use to anyone without it. His knife, still wedged in his boot on the floor, wouldn't be good enough to stop either man. He knew Buck had tossed the Colt to Mortimer, but where had he put it? Then he saw the mahogany-handled butt of his revolver lying on a high shelf near the door.

Couldn't have been further away, he thought disgustedly. He needed a rope and a prayer to retrieve it. Yet without that gun, he didn't have a chance in hell of trying to stop what was going on here.

As Mortimer wrestled Cole to the floor and all eyes were on the struggling pair, Reason silently surged to his feet. His right leg almost buckled beneath him, but he had been expecting that, so when the moment came he simply shifted his weight. But when he tried to take a step forward, his leg collapsed beneath him and he went down on one knee. His damaged leg simply refused to support the slightest bit of weight.

Dammit, if he had to crawl to the door by inches, he would. But there wasn't enough time to make that heroic effort.

He saw Cole once again on his feet and, held in place by Buck, take an unhealthy punch to the belly. Saw his body stiffen in pain, his swollen jaw clench tight as a drum, and his face screw up in utmost agony. Then, as Buck released him and stepped back, watched Cole drop straight to the floor on his face, while Mortimer followed him down. Buck had moved sideways to give the fumbling men on the floor more room and was so busy watching the proceedings he had unconsciously placed his back to Reason and didn't think once of turning around.

Reason's gut rolled with nausea as he saw Mortimer tear at Cole's clothes like a wild thing and wrench open the front of his jeans. He heard Cole plead for his release, then swear in horror.

His eyes flew to his pistol. It was now or never!

He scrambled to his feet and hobbled as fast as he could to the wall. Then, reaching up, grabbed his gun off the shelf, turned and aimed the bore of the weapon straight at Buck's broad back. But Buck wasn't the man he wanted at the moment. And Mortimer was protected by the table and safely out of sight.

"Mortimer!" Reason yelled at the top of his lungs.

Buck suddenly swiveled around and Mortimer lifted his head in surprise over the top of the table. Reason shifted his aim. And fired!

The blast was loud and sudden. Mortimer reared back in pain and surprise. His arms flung out from his sides and he stumbled backwards as a large, purpling hole appeared in the middle of his forehead and blood mixed with brains burst out the back of his skull. Then he fell backwards to the floor, his body jerked once, then stilled, his eyes staring lifelessly up at the rustic ceiling.

Reason couldn't seem to catch his breath. His heart pounded erratically in his chest from rage mixed with exertion, and his right leg was killing him from the effort of supporting his own weight. On top of it all, he was weaving dangerously on his feet. Yet he leveled the pistol towards Buck anyway and tried to steady himself the best he could.

"Don't shoot!" Buck raised his hands high in the air. "I'm unarmed," he shouted, amid the sudden deafening silence in the small room.

Reason hesitated a split-second too long.

Buck lunged down, grabbed Cole about the waist, and lifted

him up to snug his back crushingly against his own chest. A large skinning knife appeared in his right hand from the belt at his waist, and the razor-sharp tip he dug deep into the base of Cole's throat.

"Now put the gun down, boy. You don't want your friend here to get hurt any more than he already is, now do ya?"

Cole's glazed amber eyes found Reason.

"Don't...listen to him...Reason. Shoot!" Cole groaned weakly. But as agonizing pressure was put on the arm around his waist, Cole winced hard, choked, then remained silent. Only his harsh and tortured breathing broke the strained silence of the small room.

Reason's arm was shaking from the weight of the pistol and concern over Cole's safety. Even if he had a clear shot, which he didn't, and fired, would he be able to nail Buck? And not hurt Cole in the process? He wasn't sure, and the way his hand was trembling from weariness, he doubted it. But if he didn't do something, then all three men would die here today. And one wrong move of that sharp blade at Cole's throat would seal his fate forever.

Suddenly he had no choice in the matter. Steele had somehow worked his way free of the ropes binding his wrists and ankles. Abruptly he rose up from his chair and flung the useless bonds aside.

"Buck! Look here," he yelled as he darted swiftly to his left.

Instinctively Buck shifted his stance to compensate for Steele's move and Reason knew this was the best chance he would ever get. Without another thought, he fired at the suddenly exposed side of Buck's large head.

Reason flinched at the ear-splitting blast of his own revolver, and was terrified to glance at the damage he had wrought. If Buck had jerked wrong, Cole had bought it, and no force on the face of this earth would be able to bring him back.

Buck staggered, the bullet entering right through the brain just above the left ear. His hands dropped to his sides, and his large bulky body reeled drunkenly sideways. Cole hit the ground before he did.

But Cole was alive, and Buck had died on his feet. Slowly the man came crashing to the ground.

The fool had played right into Steele's hands. Joe rushed over to Cole who was curled up on his side, gasping for breath.

"Take it easy now. It's all over. You all right?"

Cole slowly opened amber eyes fraught with pain. He swallowed hard, nodded once, then said, "Reason?"

Steele jerked around. Reason had staggered backwards, braced his back up against the wooden front door, and was now sliding down to the floor. Joe squeezed Cole's shoulder, then headed over to Reason.

"How you doing, boss?" he said with an easy grin as he dropped to one knee by his side.

Reason peered up at him with a tremulous smile bordering on exhaustion.

"Think I've been better," he gasped with effort. "But I can't remember when." Then he slowly collapsed on his side to the floor and passed out.

CHAPTER THIRTY-SEVEN

Joe let loose the two swayback nags from the corral and set fire to the shack. He moved farther back towards the shelter of the trees to watch the hellish flames lick at the clear blue fringes of the mountainous sky. The cabin went up like a tinderbox of dried wood and straw. Thick black smoke soon marred the purity of the pale white clouds scudding softly across the heavens. Steele's eyes stung from the caustic aroma of burning wood coupled with the southerly direction of the wind.

"And that's the end of that," he said softly to himself.

"Couldn't happen soon enough for me."

Cole shifted uncomfortably on the ground. His back was braced hard up against the sturdy trunk of a tall pine, while Reason lounged further to Cole's right.

"I gotta admit I thought I was a goner back there," he added slowly. "If Reason hadn't gotten his hand on that pistol when he did, then I might have easily...." He choked on his own thoughts, then ran an abrupt hand over his mouth as if to shut himself up. Some things didn't bear vocalizing out loud.

He could still recall Mortimer's dead weight heavy on his back, dragging him down to the floor, all too clearly. The sickening sound of the tearing at his clothes. The struggle, the pawing, the pain. The savage guttural grunts of untamed lust, too close to his ears to be healthy. The helpless, gut-wrenching sensation of a stranger's callused hands groping bare skin in places where they shouldn't made Cole shiver among the reflected heat of the flames. His stomach heaved violently. Abruptly he leaned to the side and retched on the ground.

Joe shot a sympathetic look Cole's way, then squinted at Reason.

"How the hell did you accomplish it anyway? I thought you were out cold at the time. You sure looked like you were. What were you doing, faking it?"

The fiery yellow-gold flames that were now embracing the sky, reflected back in Reason's pale gaze.

"Cole's not the only one who can put on an act when he wants," he grinned in a weary way, then slid his cool, wolf-like eyes over the man heaving violently on his left.

"What do ya mean?" Cole gasped and swallowed hard. Then he drew a deep, ragged breath, sat up straight, wiped his mouth with the torn sleeve of his shirt, and glanced over his shoulder in Reason's direction.

"Remember almost a week ago when we rode out of town and hit that fork in the road? And all of a sudden you fell over your saddle when I wanted to ride over to Rachel's alone?"

Cole couldn't help the slow grin that spread across his jaw.

"So?" he bluffed although his stomach was still teetering dangerously on the point of nausea.

"I knew you were only fooling," Reason said with a grin, glad he was able to switch Cole's unbridled thoughts towards something less destructive. "You were play-acting solely for my benefit."

"Then why'd you give in so damn fast."

"Because you were so damn good at it. I was afraid you'd hurt yourself further, simply by trying to prove a point.

"Are you telling us you were conscious all the time they were pouring that red-eye all over your sore leg?" Joe said with a tinge of awe.

"After that one brief outburst I couldn't control?" Reason swallowed hard. "Yeah. I had to make it look convincing, or else they wouldn't have bought it."

"That was some acting," Joe sneered with a renewed sense of respect for the man resting only a few yards from his feet.

"I didn't say it was easy." Reason couldn't seem to be able to tear his eyes away from the towering flames before him. He had seen the situation in one glance after Buck had slammed him to the floor. Saw Cole and Steele both tied to chairs with ropes preventing all movement. And he knew somehow he had to prevent Buck from restraining him also. At the moment he was unfettered and that's the way he wanted it kept. If both men thought he was unconscious and therefore not a threat, Buck might not feel the need to bind him also. And it had worked. Because if it hadn't....

Dark images from the past suddenly leaped unbidden to his mind. The fear, the struggle, the pain. Two men holding him down, hurting him far beyond the invisible boundaries of human decency. The cruelty. The sheer and utter helplessness of it all....

Reason brought a hand up to his face and gritted his teeth hard. But the heart-rending sobs bubbling up in his throat wouldn't be denied. Finally with a sharp gasp and a violent shudder he let loose all the misery and suffering his soul had endured over the last long months and cried brokenly behind his hand.

Cole turned his attention back to the fire. He knew the hell Reason was going through in his mind. But for a few more tense and trying moments back in that shack, Cole might have been doing the very same thing. He had thought he would have been strong enough to overcome anything those two sons-of-bitches could throw at him, but when push came to shove, Cole was no better than any other sane man in an abnormally violent situation.

Joe watched both men on the ground reacting to the turbulent soul-searching scenes being played over and over again in their minds. He could see the tears of helpless mortification escaping beneath Reason's tense fingers, could see the muscular shoulders trembling out of control, and hear the stirring sobs of misery and suffering no man should have to endure.

He watched Cole's sun-tanned face turn pale, and his sightless amber eyes stare at the fiery yellow flames of the cabin before him with a wild sense of fear and abandonment, knowing the very same thing that was tormenting Reason's brain, could also have happened to him in a heartbeat.

Mistakenly, Joe thought that he, too, would have been able to withstand their violent assault and come out unscathed. But simply seeing them go after Cole so savagely, broke every firm resolve he ever owned.

Only Reason had saved them. By the man's sheer determination to help his friend in need, regardless of his own suffering; and by Joe himself, sawing through those damned ropes on a sharp corner of the chair in time to distract Buck, and give

Reason a clear shot.

And, thankfully, Reason was man enough to act on it.

Because if he hadn't..... By the time those two backwoodsmen were through with Cole, they would have been coming for Joe.

A shiver of fear ran up his spine as Joe tore his gaze away from the men on the ground and once more centered his focus on the blazing inferno growing in strength before his eyes. *Fire was cleansing. Maybe the flames would purge their souls,* Joe thought in an inspiration born of hope, as the wind shifted and thick black smoke once again stung his eyes and bright orange flickers of heat danced in a blurry haze before him. Neither man deserved the dark impulses that ran unhindered through their tortured minds.

Not one of them thought about the missing five thousand dollars that could, or could not, have been found hidden by the two mountain men in the shoddy reaches of the now burning shack.

Steele had completely forgotten about it.

Reason couldn't remember ever having the money at all.

And Cole just didn't give a damn!

CHAPTER THIRTY-EIGHT

They took their time riding back to the Stirrup C Bar. Cole didn't feel well enough to sit a saddle long, and Reason's leg was paining him something fierce, even though Steele had cushioned the injury with a cut-up piece of an old saddle blanket roped around his ankle to keep his calf from rubbing on Satan's side. To make matters worse, Satan shied at a rabbit halfway home and Reason had fallen right out of the saddle.

Joe Steele breathed a sigh of relief five days later as they rode into the ranch yard at a slow lope and pulled up at the porch. Cole had kept up an almost constant chatter all the way home when his nausea allowed, while Reason had suffered in absolute silence. If one tended to peer closely at the sullen and strangely fearful man, you would have thought he was heading straight for his own execution, instead of towards his own home, to a place of comfort and solitude, where he rightly belonged.

Sally was waiting on the porch when they rode up to the house and she raced to Cole's side as he gingerly swung down.

"Did everything go as planned?" Only Sally was informed by Cole before the men had left, exactly where they were going and what they planned to do, even though he had deliberately neglected to say why.

Rachel was nowhere in sight and that, to Reason, was an omen in itself. Cautiously he swung down, yet couldn't stifle the groan that leaped to his throat when his right foot touched the ground. Steele was suddenly by his side.

"Let me give you a hand," he said, one hand bracing Reason's arm by the shoulder, while Cole was busy lying to Sally that everything had indeed gone according to schedule.

Reason tensed. Now that they were back on home turf, all the old jealous emotions, and hostile rivalry between him and this man flew at him in a rush. This man was in love with his wife, and as far as he knew, the feelings were more than reciprocated.

"I'm fine," Reason snapped, a little too quickly.

Steele noted the cool and distant look in the pale blue eyes, and released him. Yet Reason limped badly as he tied Satan's reins to the rail.

"You sure don't look it," Steele answered with his slow, deliberate drawl.

Then Rachel was out on the porch. Her questioning eyes flew first to Joe Steele, then to Reason, then back to Steele.

"Is everyone all right?" she asked her foreman.

With a sinking feeling in his gut, Reason knew the battle was lost before he had even begun to fight.

"Yeah. Some of us are a little banged up, but nothing that can't be overcome with time," Steele answered nonchalantly. Then as Cole and Sally climbed up the steps arm-in-arm, Steele snatched up the reins of all three horses.

"I'll take these fellas over to the barn. Maybe you should go inside, get something to eat and rest that leg," he said to Reason who remained silent and unmoving. Then he clucked the horses in motion. Both Reason and Rachel watched Steele's back, rather than each other, as he sauntered casually towards the barn with the horses in tow.

Rachel was the first one to move. "I'll see if Sally's getting anything ready," she said in a cold, no-nonsense attitude, then turned her back and slammed the screen door shut with a bang.

Reason watched the space where Rachel had stood for a few more minutes before he finally limped to the porch stairs and carefully lowered himself to the third step from the bottom. So her main concern was for Joe. He had seen her eyes go first to him. Why did that brief little demonstration of caring and devotion surprise him so? Who was he fooling? Himself? That she loved him just a little?

Then the screen door squeaked open and soft bare feet padded across the planked floor to stop a few inches behind him.

"Daddy? Are you crying?"

Reason hadn't realized that he was, yet he swiped the back of his hand across his eyes for good measure before he slowly twisted around.

Jocelyn stood there in small boys' pants and a plaid cotton shirt to match, cradling that raggedy old toy bear in one arm once again. Her soft pale eyes were bright in her face, and the long dark lashes only enhanced their keen intelligence. Dark curls fell in ringlets to her small shoulders, and her angelic heart-shaped face reminded Reason of a pixie.

"No, I wasn't," he lied with a smile.

"It's all right if you was," she said matter-of-factly, with all the studied grace of a grown-up. "Mommy cries all the time."

Reason glanced down and away. Because of him, he knew with all certainty. Because Rachel was not free to follow her heart. She was trapped in a loveless marriage to a man that not only couldn't remember her, but didn't even recognize his own daughter when she stood right before him.

"Maybe I can do something about that." He glanced at Jocelyn once more. There was no denying she was his daughter, even if he had wanted to. She was his spitting image, yet in a childish, feminine form.

"I'm glad, Daddy. Because I get so sad when I see her cry."

Reason's heart almost broke in his chest. He held out a hesitant hand to her, and she instantly went to him. She threw her small arms around his neck and dropped down on his lap with a jolt. A soft puff of pain exploded from his throat as she landed hard on his injured leg, but when she cuddled up against his chest, she was soft as a kitten, and his arms went instinctively around her.

"Don't worry, sweetheart," he said, kissing the top of her dark little head. "Daddy will find a way to make things right."

CHAPTER THIRTY-NINE

That night after another tense supper, Reason curled up in an old wicker chair out on the front porch. It was hot and stifling inside the house anyway, Reason argued to himself. Besides his presence wasn't wanted inside any more than an ornery rattler coiled up beneath a warm stove would be.

As soon as Rachel and Sally left the table to put the children to bed, Reason made his escape. Funny way of putting it, Reason laughed to himself as the cicadas buzzed a soothing tune from the pitch-dark trees surrounding the house and barn. One would think the Stirrup C Bar was a prison, instead of a home, the way he was acting.

More like solitary confinement, Reason mused. Seeing Rachel every minute and not being able to speak to her, or touch her in ways he only dreamed about, was becoming sheer torture. There seemed to be an invisible brick wall built between them that neither one cared to breach.

And just what would he say to her if he tried? That he loved her? Wanted another chance to make things right? Was he crazy? The woman he needed and desired above all else was deeply involved with another man. He had been torn apart from her too long in his mind and she simply turned her affections to another, infinitely more caring, suitor.

Divorce was out of the question. He could never willingly sign papers that would give another man free rein over his wife. She hadn't asked him to yet, although he knew the day couldn't be far off when she would.

And he couldn't just ride away again and leave her in limbo like he did once, years before. They were legally bound to one another this time. By a court of law. At least that's what everybody told him. He remembered none of it.

There was only one other option open to him. One that he had already considered twice, but was thwarted each time he tried. Once by Cole. And the other by Buck.

A shiver ran up his spine, just thinking of the backwoodsman he had finally killed. Well there was no one to stop him this time. Cole was with Sally, and Buck was dead. He was still wearing his gun, and he already knew how to use it. But he wouldn't shoot himself here, on the ranch. Jocelyn might ask uncomfortable questions about the gunshot, both now and in the future. He didn't want to upset the child unnecessarily.

He'd ride out tomorrow. Find a nice spot under the shade of an old oak tree. Set Satan free. And get the job done right this time.

He slept fitfully in the chair. The violent dreams must have come back to haunt him in the wee hours of the morning, for Reason awoke with a start when the chair crashed sideways landing him on the porch floor.

Reason hit the boards hard and went sprawling on his back. He laid there stunned for a moment in the dark, with one arm flung randomly over his eyes, until the fast-paced fluttering of his heart along with his ragged breathing became normal once again. Then he rose to his feet, righted the chair, and moved deeper into the shadows. From there he dropped to the floor on his side, snugged his back up against the front wall of the house, cushioned his head on an arm, and finally fell into another tormented, fitful sleep.

...Joe Steele loved Rachel. Reason loved Rachel. Rachel loved Joe Steele...I love you, dammit!

Reason moaned out loud.

Cole found him there the next morning. In fact, he almost tripped over Reason's booted feet when he sauntered out the front door.

"What the hell...?" He swore softly as Reason blinked awake. "What are ya doin' lyin' out here on the floor? A bed getting too damn soft for ya?"

Reason jerked to full awareness and rose painfully to his feet.

"Was there something you wanted?" he growled in annoyance. He had planned on waking up before anyone else and leaving before dawn, but he had overslept.

"Rachel was worried. You never came in last night. She asked me to go look for ya. And stop starin' at me like I got two heads or somethin'. If you don't believe me, ask her!"

Cole was lying Reason knew, yet he decided not to make an issue out of it. The faster he was out of here, the better it would be for everyone involved. So he ignored Cole's sarcasm and, instead, asked a question of his own.

"Do me a favor?"

"Sure. What is it?"

"Saddle Satan for me?"

Cole squinted suspiciously at the man standing before him.

"What for? Ya goin' somewhere?"

"Is it any of your business?"

Cole stood firm. "You want your horse saddled? Then you tell me where you're goin'."

Reason ground his teeth together. He'd do the job himself, but he didn't think he could walk all the way to the barn. His leg was paining him something awful, and abnormal chills ran up his spine. One minute he was hot, the next shivering in his boots. He had to think of a plausible explanation fast.

"I'm going into town, if you have to know."

"To see Peterson?"

Reason quickly grabbed at the straw Cole had inadvertently thrown.

"Yeah, that's it."

"The leg botherin' ya?"

"Some. Maybe he can give me a dose of that horse liniment he uses on unsuspecting patients."

"Good idea. I'll ride in with ya." Cole started down the stairs.

"Cole!" Reason's voice halted the man before he could take one step further. "I'm going in alone."

Slowly Cole swiveled to face him. His eyes flew to Reason's holster, then he fiercely shook his head.

"No. You're not!"

Reason began limping towards him. "Forget it! I'll saddle Satan myself."

A tight grin creased Cole's face that never quite reached his eyes.

"All right. Ya can if you want. But I'm still ridin' in with ya."

Reason seethed all the way into town. He had been caught in a web of his own deceit. And now he had to make a fair showing at Peterson's to put Cole's mind at ease.

Damn the man! Always butting in where he wasn't wanted. And cynical to a fault. Why, it was almost as if Cole had second-guessed him, once again, and knew he was planning to take his own life.

Reason shook his head. He must be getting paranoid on top of everything else. There was no way in hell Cole could guess what he was up to. Besides, there was no rush. Any hour of the day would do just fine. He'd bide his time, maybe hit the saloon later on and get Cole drunk enough so he could slip out of town without drawing undue attention to himself.

Only then could he accomplish his final, fatal mission.

"Want another round?" Reason said with a tight-lipped smile as he leaned against the bar in a futile attempt to shift the worst part of his weight off his throbbing right leg. It was a normal Saturday night and the saloon was packed. "I'm buying."

Cole sneered out loud, then squinted at his friend in the full-length mirror behind the bar.

"If I didn't know any better, Reason, I'd swear you were deliberately tryin' to get me drunk." He slid his amber eyes towards the dark-clad man besides him. "Now you wouldn't be doin' that to a friend, would ya?"

"You've got a damn suspicious mind," Reason snapped back. All attempt at humor had flown. Cole was on to him. Damn his hide. "Why would you think that?"

"Well…." Cole's gaze flew innocently about the busy room. "You didn't come in here for a quick roll in the hay. You made that pretty clear to Mariah just a few short minutes ago, and she's still in a huff about it. And, though you're already over your usual one beer limit, you haven't touched a drop of your third. Yet you still insist on buyin' another round." Cole grinned disarmingly and veered his slightly glassy gaze towards the man standing next to him. "Now I know I've already had my fair share and by all rights, you should be chastising me for it by now. Instead, you want to buy me still another. What else should I think?"

"I think you're already drunk," Reason said with pure disgust in his voice.

"But not enough for what you have in mind. Is that it?"

Reason shot him a quick look, but Cole just grinned widely in response and abruptly changed the subject.

"Damn good thing we rode into town when we did," Cole kept on. "Peterson said another day or two and that infection could have spread so bad the whole damn leg might have had to be sawed clear off." He paused and studied the familiar frown lines on Reason's face. "Funny you don't seem all that concerned about it. Why didn't you tell me earlier your leg was givin' you trouble?"

Reason grabbed at his glass and almost drained it, he was so fed-up with the days' events. Then he slammed the half-empty mug hard on the bar.

"Wasn't bothering me all that much," he snarled, then licked at his foamy lips. Anyway what did it matter? He would just add a missing limb to the growing list of grievances in his mind. Just one more excuse for a quick bullet to the brain. That's if he could get rid of Cole for one blasted minute.

"Look why don't you go round up that black-haired wench that keeps glancing your way. You've already broken her in once before. I don't plan on riding back until morning anyway."

"You can't. Peterson forbade it. In fact you shouldn't even be on your feet now."

How did this discussion revert back to him again? Reason had been trying to divert Cole's attention away from himself and once more had failed miserably.

"What about poker? There's a game going on in the corner over there." Reason threw a hasty glance over his shoulder. "Looks like there's an empty chair, if you want to jump in, I don't mind."

Cole grinned. Reason didn't play cards if he could help it. This was just another excuse to get rid of him.

"Broke," he cut in sharply, before Reason had a chance to build up steam.

Reason gnashed his teeth together in silent rage. How the hell was he supposed to elude this annoying shadow? Every option he suggested, Cole turned down flat.

"If money's a problem, I can stand you a few bucks." He'd give Cole every last dime he had in his pockets, just to get rid of him for a few minutes. Reason wouldn't need one red cent where he was going.

Cole acted as if he were hard of hearing.

"Maybe we should get a room…." Cole spoke his thoughts out loud.

"You go on ahead if you're tired. I'll be along shortly."

Cole snorted insolently. "Yeah. Sure you will."

Reason appeared plain worn out to Cole's mind. He stood hip-shot at the bar as if trying to ease the pressure of his weight off the injured leg. Gray smudges of weariness lay trapped beneath his lower lids and the crystal blue eyes were damp with pain and suffering. Cole straightened and jerked his head towards the door.

"Come on. I could use the rest."

When Reason remained silent and steadfast, Cole turned towards him once more.

"You comin'?"

The party was over. If Cole was looking for trouble, then Reason was bound to give it to him.

"Like hell I am," he finally said as he painfully braced himself on two feet and slid his hand towards his holster.

"That's what I thought," Cole muttered to himself. With a feigned act of indifference, he glanced away, but then without warning, he swiveled at the waist and swung a powerful right hook that connected firmly with a well-known fragile spot along Reason's left jaw.

Reason's head snapped backwards and he went out like a light, even before he bounced off the bar and hit the floor with a resounding thud. Cole drew in a deep breath, then let out a long-suffering sigh.

Some men just had to do it the hard way.

CHAPTER FORTY

Reason was in a foul mood as the horses swung in the Stirrup C Bar gate and cantered easily towards the main house around noon the next day. His jaw was swollen and ached abominably. What the hell had Cole hit him with? *Felt like more than a fist,* Reason argued in his own mind. There was no call to hit him so damned hard.

Cole had never been in any danger from the start. Reason would never have shot the man just to get his own way. The idea was to scare Cole enough to get the man to back off from his single-minded, aggravating quest to protect Reason from himself. Didn't the fool realize that?

Besides Cole couldn't watch him every single minute of the day. He was only prolonging the inevitable. And the multiple stab wounds gouging Reason's leg didn't feel much better, even after Peterson's less than gentle administrations. If Reason had actually intended to live longer than a few more measly hours, he might have taken better precautions with the mangled limb. But, as things stood, he was planning on riding out as soon as they reached home to finish what he'd already started in his mind. And he refused to give the throbbing injury a second thought.

Yet as they reined their mounts towards the hitching rail and drew to a halt, Cole remained annoyingly seated.

"Aren't ya getting down?" he grinned.

"You first," Reason growled, fed-up with the varied number of games Cole was playing. If Cole would only climb down off that damned horse, Reason could easily rein Satan around and head out right now. Even Cole knew no other horse on the ranch could keep up with the stallion, given a head start.

"Well, now I would. But seein' as how you're so God-awful

touchy and all, I just want to make damn sure you don't take it into your thick skull to tear off and do somethin' entirely stupid!"

Cole's easy manner turned threatening.

"What the hell does it matter to you what I do?" Reason snapped back, furious at Cole's dogged determination. "You don't mean a damn thing to me!"

An insufferable grin swept across Cole's face.

"When you're through tryin' to hurt my feelin's," he said more softly, "why don't ya get down and I'll take the horses over to the barn."

Reason had the idea that no matter what insults he threw at Cole at the moment, nothing would wipe that cursed lop-sided grin off his face short of a bullet. With a muffled curse, he tossed over the reins and swung off the black without another word of argument.

Cole turned his gelding's head and walked both horses towards the corrals. Reason swore once more in a frustrated fit of temper. Nothing in this world was going to stop him from accomplishing his mission. He'd find a way. Somehow!

Carelessly he slammed through the screen door and wandered through the parlor towards the kitchen. Only when he pushed the swinging door wide, did he come to a complete and sudden halt.

Rachel was at the sink, rinsing off some dishes in a pink bathrobe and bare feet. And Steele was lounging at the breakfast table, mouthing a small sliver of wood between his teeth with his shirt half opened at the waist as if he had just gotten out of bed not too long ago and wasn't fully awake yet. Neither one of them seemed aware of his presence, and probably mistook him for Cole if they had.

"Be careful you don't get a splinter!"

Joe froze with his hand halfway to his mouth. Then slowly he shifted his hazel eyes towards Reason.

Rachel gasped as she veered around at the sink and water splashed to the floor from her wet hands.

"What are *you* doing here?" Her voice wavered between sudden fright and outright confusion.

"Thought I lived here," Reason went on in that same icy tone. "Did I come home at a bad time?" His glance cut right to Steele, but the man wouldn't meet his eyes.

"I thought you went to town!" Rachel's dander was finally up. It never seemed to take her long.

"I did."

"You came back awful early, wouldn't you say?"

Reason shrugged. He knew what she was getting at. She thought he had gone to see Mariah. And as a result, had finally taken matters into her own hands and bedded her ranch hand. It was inevitable. But, dammit, why did the thought hurt so damn much?

"Depends on what I went to town for."

"You went to see *her*." It wasn't a question, she simply stated a fact. And Reason saw no need to answer.

"Didn't you!" she demanded in a husky voice.

"Are you looking for an excuse for your own immoral behavior?"

Rachel gasped, and Joe rose slowly to his feet.

"Now look here, Reason...."

"Shut up!"

Joe Steele jerked slightly and blinked in astonishment. No one spoke to him like that, no matter what wrong they thought he committed in their eyes.

"What'd you say to me?"

Reason moved to face Steele. "Are you hard of hearing?"

Joe couldn't believe that Reason was talking to him this way. Or that Joe was letting him.

Suddenly Reason's pistol was in his hand.

"Now sit! Before I think you're about to challenge me to a draw."

"Reason, don't," Rachel cried out in alarm.

"Protecting your lover again?" Reason's lips curled in disgust. "Couldn't you two at least have waited one more day?"

Joe Steele's gaze slid to Rachel, and then back to Reason. Slowly he resumed his seat. The first time in his entire life that he had ever backed down from another man. And hopefully the last.

Outright disappointment clearly showed in the frown lines on Reason's face. He had truly expected more of a fight.

"Why should we?" Rachel stormed. "What would twenty-four more hours prove, one way or the other!"

Reason would have loved to tell her, but then he didn't want to

227

spoil the surprise when news of his death finally broke throughout the ranch.

"Besides, no one told you to ride into town yesterday morning," she raged hotly.

"Why shouldn't he?" Cole spoke from the door. He had handed over the horses to Largo at the barn and returned at a run, wanting to make sure Reason wasn't alone in the house. But from the sounds of all the shouting, Cole was almost sorry he wasn't.

"Don't act so innocent, Cole," Rachel snapped. "You're not without blame, either."

Cole ignored the senseless accusation for the moment and glanced around the room. Then said, "What's goin' on in here? I could hear Rachel yellin' from outside. And why is your gun out, Reason?"

Reason smoothly holstered his revolver, unwilling to further the argument with Cole, yet his regard never once ventured from Steele.

And when Cole sneaked a peek at Joe, the result was the same. They were both eyeing each other like two mangy cur dogs with their hackles raised, each claiming territorial rights over a juicy bone.

"Blame for what?" he asked Rachel, when nobody else was offering any explanations.

"You went into town with him yesterday. You knew what he was up to." Her voice dripped scorn.

"Well if you knew, then why the hell did you let him go?" Cole hollered back, astonished that Rachel would just calmly let Reason walk out the door and blow his fool head off without so much as an argument."

Rachel's head lifted in a haughty manner. "His business is no concern of mine anymore."

"He's still your husband, dammit," Cole swore. "Don't you have any feelings for him anymore?"

"Not when he refuses my bed for some whore in town."

Cole saw Reason flinch. "What's she talkin' about Reason?"

Without turning his head, Reason said, "Let it go, Cole. The damage is already done."

"What damage? Would someone kindly tell me what's comin' off in here?" Then Cole glanced at Steele as if seeing him for the first time. "What are you doin' here, Joe? Shouldn't you be out with the rest of the men? And why is your shirt all unbuttoned. You get hurt, or something?"

Steele's face flushed red. His eyes drifted sheepishly to the floor, while Cole got a quick rush of insight. The accusing amber gaze shifted back to Rachel, who was nervously fiddling with the lapels of her robe as if she would draw the two closed ends even tighter around her body than they already were and thereby become invisible to the naked eye.

"Don't tell me...." Cole couldn't finish the thought. It was too disrupting to his mind.

"Son-of-a-bitch!" So he swore instead. "Damn you, Joe! What the hell's the matter with you!"

"Don't blame him," Rachel said. "I...I...was lonely last night. And my husband saw fit to go warm himself by someone else's fire."

An unpleasant sneer crossed Cole's face. "The only sparks Reason saw last night were the ones comin' from my closed fist."

"Stay out of this, Cole," Reason warned low, as Rachel's eyes widened in confusion.

"What do you mean?" she asked breathlessly.

"Nothing," Reason said firmly, even though Rachel wasn't speaking to him. And Cole ignored him as usual.

"Reason went in to Peterson's yesterday to get his leg checked out. He could barely walk, it was so swollen and all." Cole purposely dismissed Reason's growl of discontent. "I admit we had a few beers later. But that was all. Then, cranky as all hell, he started an argument right out of the blue. So I decked him. See there?" He pointed to the swollen black and blue bruise spreading across the left side of Reason's jaw, as Reason shrugged instinctively away. "Turn around and show her, Reason."

But Reason didn't move. "I told you to stay out of this."

But Cole was oblivious to Reason's threats.

"And you thought he had gone in to see Mariah?" Cole chuckled out loud as Rachel's freckles paled and her eyes grew large with regret. "Maybe he should have, the way things are shapin' up around here. If you'd been the wife that he needed, you would have gone with him to the Doc's, instead of stayin' home makin' up flimsy excuses for what you've been wantin' to do all along, shackin' up with….." Cole didn't know what hit him, but suddenly he was lying on the floor near the stove, and his head was spinning from a blow that he never saw coming.

"I warned you twice to keep out of this." Reason's gun was in his hand, aiming dead center at Cole's chest. And Cole swallowed hard.

"Easy, Reason." Cole held up a hand in surrender, as if that futile action by itself had the power to stop a lead bullet. "I didn't mean nothin' by it. And you know more than anyone, I sometimes talk more than I should."

Damn his runaway tongue, Cole thought two seconds too late. When was he going to learn not to slander Rachel's name in front of Reason? His jaw was already aching and worse would be coming, if you could read the determined look on Reason's face correctly, unless….

There was a scraping of wood on bare floor and then Joe was standing with his revolver aimed straight at Reason's side.

"I'd put that gun away if I was you," Steele drawled slowly, yet with deadly intent. "You wouldn't want me to cripple your right hand with a bullet now, would you?"

Reason turned his head and squinted at Joe as if he were a stranger. Then, at his own sweet pace, he holstered his mahogany-handled revolver. Joe Steele was finally riled. Or, at the very least, motivated into action. This might work out to his benefit after all.

"Where's Jocelyn, Rachel?" he asked in a wooden voice, without once turning around.

"Down at the creek behind the yard, with Sally and Nick."

"Meet me out front," he said to Steele in the deadliest voice imaginable. Then he stepped over Cole's sprawled legs and headed towards the front door.

CHAPTER FORTY-ONE

Reason paced out front for a good ten minutes before Steele made an appearance. And when he did, Reason was in for a shock. He could almost swear that this was the first time in his life he had ever seen the man standing upright without his gun belt on.

"I think you forgot something," Reason sneered as Steele stepped out the front door, sauntered casually across the porch, and came down the stairs.

"No I didn't." He moved out into the yard and halted about twenty paces from Reason. "Wearing a heavy belt can get in the way of ranch work at times."

Reason ground his teeth together in silent rage. Steele was stalling, wasting precious time. Dying was never easy, and Reason wanted to get the deed over and done with before he had a chance to chicken out and change his mind.

"It didn't seem to bother you much at the breakfast table," he snapped impatiently. "Go back in and get it!"

But Steele shook his head.

"Don't think so."

"You're refusing to draw on me?" Reason wondered whether he was hallucinating again.

"That's right."

"Why, dammit!"

"Because you have a death wish. And I'm not going to be the man to grant your last request."

Reason froze. His secret was out. And every last resort was slowly being taken from him.

"Cole's got a big mouth."

"Yeah. You get no argument from me. But it comes in handy at times like these. Besides," a small grin played about his lips. "If

I kill the boss, I could be fired."

"You're fired! Now go get your gun."

"Uh-uh. It don't work that way. Cole's gotta have the final say in matters such as this. And he ain't here right now."

Reason paused. "Then just how do you figure on settling this?"

"You want an apology? You've got it."

"Apology be damned! Just what are you sorry for? For bedding my wife? Or for loving her."

Steele's body grew taut. Reason sensed that if Joe had been wearing his gun at the moment, he just might have entertained the notion of using it.

"Don't make this harder for me than it already is," Steele said low.

"Just what do you know of trouble," Reason taunted. "I reckon I don't know you very well, but I imagine whatever mess you've fallen into in your life, you've always managed to come out on top."

Joe slowly shook his head. "Not this time."

"What do you mean by that?" Reason was truly mystified by this man. He was a fast gun. Faster than himself, if Cole could be believed. Yet he had left his gun inside when he had been called upon to use it.

"It's not me Rachel loves. It's you."

Reason felt as if he had been socked in the gut. He swallowed hard. Why was the man tormenting him like this? Joe had just come from Rachel's bed. Didn't he have an ounce of decency?

"You're lying!"

Steele flinched as if he'd been struck. Then he lowered his head and drew in a deep measured breath as if he were having a hard time keeping his temper in check. His right hand clenched in a fist at his side.

"Don't push me, Reason. I have my limits."

Reason smiled. Maybe there was a way to instigate this man to draw after all.

"You don't like being called a liar, Joe? Then how about a wife-stealing bastard and a yellow coward besides!"

Slowly Steele raised his head. His keen hazel eyes were hard as flint, yet there was the subtle hint of a smile on his face.

"I know what you're trying to do. And it won't work."

"No? Okay, I give up. You're onto me." Reason raised his hands far from his body as a gesture of immediate surrender, then dropped them back to his sides. "But what if I called your sweetheart a...."

Steele tensed. Reason knew if he continued on in this vein, the man would run right in, grab his gun, and come out shooting. He'd do exactly what Reason wanted him to, and play right into his hands.

But Reason couldn't, for the life of him, speak ill of his wife out here in the front yard before Steele. No matter what she'd done behind his back or anytime in the near future.

"Go on," Steele prompted coldly. "What was it you were about to say?"

It was no use. Reason's throat closed up and he couldn't utter one more word to save his life.

He had lost the fight to Joe Steele, just like Cole once warned, without either man so much as lifting a finger. And he realized with stunning clarity, that Joe was going to be of no help to him at all. This last act was one he was going to have to accomplish all on his own merit.

Slowly he withdrew his revolver from his holster. He didn't fail to note Steele's quick indrawn breath of fear. But Reason wasn't aiming the revolver in his direction. He was centering the bore of his pistol just beneath his own jaw at the base of his throat. Then his thumb drew back the hammer. Nothing was going to stop him this time!

"Reason! Don't be a fool!" Steele made an instinctive move towards his direction, then halted in his tracks, knowing no matter what he did, he'd be too late. Reason's finger was already tightening on the trigger. In one more second....

"Don't...! For Christ sakes, man...!" he shouted across the distance, just as a childish high-pitched voice screamed "Da...dee...!"

Reason jerked in surprise, stunned at hearing his daughter's baby voice so close. His face paled. In one fluid motion, his thumb gently released the trigger, and the revolver dropped downward to disappear within the confines of the leather holster at his side as Reason's gaze flew to the porch.

Rachel was standing at the head of the steps, fully dressed in tight jeans and bare feet, with a look of pure horror on her face. Holding Jocelyn tightly in her arms, she stared at him. He had thought the child was far away, down by the creek, distracted by distance from all danger and sound.

Then, ever so slowly, Rachel lowered her daughter to the porch floor. Jocelyn ran down the steps, with a hopping little baby stride, and on up to her father. She paused inches from him and peered up at him with a disappointed frown.

"What are you doing, Daddy?" she said sternly, with her little hands on her hips, just like her mother when she was angry at him for some imagined wrong. "Mommy said you were going to do a bad thing. She ran all the way to the creek and called me away from playing hide and seek with Nick, just so I could stop you. What were you doing that was so bad, Daddy?"

Her pale blue eyes keenly glanced at the pistol now snug in the holster at Reason's hip. "Were you playing with guns so close to the house again? You know Mommy hates that!"

Reason swallowed down the sudden tightness in his throat. Slowly his eyes slid to the porch where Rachel was standing. Both her hands were pressed tightly over her mouth as if she would prevent herself from screaming, but he could plainly see the sea green eyes overflowing with tears running down her freckled face.

Finally, he had his wife's undivided attention. Not once did she glance in Joe Steele's direction.

"If you do a bad thing, Daddy, then you should be punished," she berated her father, sounding more like the parent than the child.

"Your father's been punished enough, Jocelyn," Joe said with his slow Texas drawl. "Maybe now it's time for him to start healing."

Slowly Reason's eyes shifted to Steele. Was this the man who had practically stolen his wife out from beneath his arms? Who had only hours before just left her warm bed? He didn't seem like a foe, more like a friend. But Reason didn't have any friends. Did he?

Then a subtle movement on the porch drew his attention. Cole had just stepped outside, yet his boots never ventured farther than the edge of the porch. And Rachel's gaze was still glued to him.

Reason drew a deep tortured breath. He knew, but for Jocelyn's timely intervention, he'd been a hair's breath away from blowing his head clear off his shoulders. And dammit, he couldn't even do that right. His hand went to shield his suddenly stinging eyes from view and he ducked his head low.

"Mommy, he's crying again," he heard his daughter's innocent little voice say. Then, mortified beyond belief at his disgusting lack of self-control, he swiftly turned on his heel and headed for the corral. He was going to saddle Satan and go somewhere quiet to finish the job he had already started.

He could have sworn he heard Cole's voice whisper something low, but he must have been mistaken. Then suddenly Rachel's voice cried out his name.

"Reason!"

He halted in his tracks. And he didn't know why. The sound of running footsteps caught his ears, then suddenly she was standing there before him, slightly out of breath. Her hair was disheveled and tied back with a blue ribbon, her blouse was askew over one shoulder as if she hadn't buttoned it up correctly in her haste to get dressed. Tears of remorse and love streamed unashamedly down her face.

"Reason, I'm sorry. So damn sorry. Please forgive me. I didn't know...."

Reason ducked his head to stare at the ground. It was too late for regrets.

Rachel didn't once touch him, yet she continued to stand in his path.

"Cole told me everything in a nutshell," she went on in a rush. "I had no idea what was going on. Please believe me. I never would have hurt you for anything in this world. Give me another chance, I'm begging you. Reason, please look at me." She stamped her bare foot in the dust of the yard when he refused to glance her way.

"I love you, dammit!"

Four simple words. But not so simple to a lonely man trapped in a dark abyss, riding the fence somewhere between an empty, unbearable life...and a quick, merciful death. To him they were significant words. Words that could spell a brand new start.

Slowly Reason lifted the familiar pale blue eyes that Rachel so dearly cherished above all else in this world, and peered down at her from beneath the low brim of his dark Stetson hat. His moist gaze glistened with mixed emotions of confusion, shame, hope, and love.

Without waiting for him to respond and throwing caution to the wind, she threw her arms around his neck and kissed him full on the lips. Her joy was boundless when she felt his arms hesitantly wrap themselves around her as if he were unsure of his welcome, then gradually tighten with need and desire to subtly squeeze the life out of her.

She smiled as his lips pressed down hard against her own and the simple kiss deepened into the purest form of love imaginable.

Jocelyn's little pixie face screwed up in a frown. What on earth were her parents doing tangling with each other out in the middle of the yard? They didn't appear to be fighting anymore. She wondered if she could leave now and run back to the creek. Nick was probably waiting for her.

Even in her child's mind she sensed the threat of danger was over.

No emotion showed on Joe Steele's face. He didn't so much as blink an eye. If anything, he was more resigned to his fate than ever before. He should have known, right from the start, he'd never stood a chance in hell with Rachel.

As long as Reason was alive, Rachel would always love him. And probably long after that.

And if Joe couldn't have her...then he figured Reason was the next best man for the job.

Steele's gaze slid towards the man still on the porch. Cole hadn't once moved from his position at the head of the stairs.

The only difference in his bearing was the smug sardonic grin that swept across his lean, chiseled jaw.

CHAPTER FORTY-TWO

Reason still had a long way to go. His memory hadn't returned one hundred percent, but he was starting to remember brief snatches of lost time. Cole would sit on the porch for hours with him, and reminisce about the many harrowing experiences they had shared together through the years, hoping something would click in his brain. Sometimes Rachel would join them and chime in with her own thoughts. Once in a while, even Joe Steele would grab a vacant spot on the top porch step.

Cole would always start off with, "Remember the time when you and I...."

Sometimes he'd jog Reason's memory and other times he failed to get a response. But he always tried his damnedest.

There was one important thing Reason did recall though.

Cole had resumed his tiresome duties of taking over the bills and endless paperwork of the ranch, when one day Reason strode casually into the office and tossed a flat, weathered brown paper package on top of the desk.

To Cole, the misshapen, pancake-flattened package appeared oddly familiar, yet he couldn't for the life of him place where it came from.

"What's this?" Cole peered up at Reason. "Are you givin' me a present?" he joked, with a grin spreading across his face. "Aw, you shouldn't have."

"It's more for Randall, than for us," Reason said with a smile. "But I guess we can all profit from it. Go on. Open it."

With a look of distrust on his face, Cole picked hesitantly at the string-tied bundle.

"It's not going to detonate or anything when I do. Is it?"

Reason chuckled. "Hope not. If it's what I think it is."

Cole finally tore off the string, ripped open a corner of the package and peeked inside. Then his face lit up in a wide, beaming smile.

"Unless I miss my guess, there's five grand in there." He glanced up at Reason. "Am I right?"

Reason nodded.

"Where the hell…?"

"My saddle." Reason broke in, without waiting for him to finish. "I had cut a seam beneath the seat, stuffed the money in there when I knew I was riding home alone, then sewed it back up with a strip of rawhide for safekeeping."

"You mean you had this cash on you all along? And just now remembered it?"

Reason nodded once more.

Cole's grin stretched from ear to ear.

"Reason, you just made my day. Wait until Randall hears about this. First thing tomorrow we'll both ride it over. What do you say?"

Reason's answering grin was infectious.

"Sounds good to me. Only this time I'm not riding alone."

THE END

Watch for Book Five in the Gunslinger's Destiny series
FOR RIDER'S SAKE
Coming in the fall of 2015
Reason saves the life of a younger brother he never knew existed,
and as a result falls prey to a ruthless rancher
who is hell-bent on destroying him and making him crawl.

ABOUT THE AUTHOR

I've always loved the western genre since I was a small child. Each Christmas I would beg Santa for my favorite plastic cowboy and his appropriate horse. And I amassed quite a collection.

I started writing western stories when I was thirteen years old, seated at an old Royal typewriter in front of a window overlooking my backyard. From there I would envision my favorite western heroes getting into all sorts of trouble and I was thrilled to put their stories to paper throughout my summer vacations.

The library became my favorite haunt. I brought scores of westerns home and read them far into the night, escaping to a simpler time when life was more exciting to my eyes.

Zane Grey became my favorite western author and I read every book that he had published. And loved every single one of them.

I hope that I have captured a small essence of his spirit in my Gunslinger's Destiny series. And I hope you enjoy reading my stories as much as I have enjoyed writing them.

— E. K. Knef

CPSIA information can be obtained
at www.ICGtesting.com
Printed in the USA
LVHW110747271122
734103LV00025B/467